JANET MORRIS
&
CHRIS MORRIS

STORM SEED

This is a work of fiction. All the characters and events portrayed in this book are fictional, and any resemblance to real people or incidents is purely coincidental.

A Baen Books Original

Baen Publishing Enterprises
P.O. Box 1403
Riverdale, N.Y. 10471

ISBN: 0-671-72023-6

Cover art by Gary Ruddell

First printing, November 1990

Distributed by
SIMON & SCHUSTER
1230 Avenue of the Americas
New York, N.Y. 10020

Printed in the United States of America

He pushed the door inward.

Something white blew through the open door. Something huge wrapped Tempus in a tentacle of fire and brightness, and sucked him inside. The door slammed shut.

He hit a wall, hard. The impact knocked the wind from his lungs. And in his head, the god was roaring so that his ears rang and he could hear nothing else.

White fire was all around him. Enlil was up in his skin, meeting that fire with His own supernal might.

Never had Tempus felt such pain. He was seared and roasted. His flesh melted from his bones. His eyes boiled and popped. The liquid danced on his fleshless cheekbones like drops of water on a hot iron skillet.

His whole body seemed about to collapse in a clatter of white, burned bone.

But the god wouldn't let him fall. Enlil manifested new sinew, new muscle, new blood and new skin upon his skeleton. Enlil put new eyes in his head and a new tongue in his mouth. His god clothed him anew in power and made him terrible in fury.

His god-given sword was somehow in his hand when he again had eyelids to blink and hair to shake from his eyes.

The smell in the room was the first thing that hit him: it was the stomach-turning smell of burned human being, laced with the choking odor of carbonized hair and bone.

Yet he stood. Stood, sword in his hand, facing a dragon so big that its ruff scraped the ceiling of the room and its tail lashed against the walls around them.

Book 1:

WITCH TIDES

Chapter 1:

TALE OF THREE WOMEN

Deep under the sea, where a volcano grew slowly and warmed the water, they kept the child.

In a dark submarine cavern, where phosphorescent sea life gave the only light, Jihan would visit her son at feeding time. Here the warm water was full of salty nutrients and tiny fish schooled like rainbow garlands among starfish-encrusted columns.

Here, mermaids were his nannies and squid rocked him in their arms.

Such a childhood should have satisfied any son of a Froth Daughter. Jihan called her boy Cyrus, partly after his father. She found him giant seahorses to ride. He had catfish and dogfish and electric eels to play with, and manta rays to race through the cavern's sweep. But he never felt a father's love, so Jihan told him stories meant to explain who and what he was.

And he never had a grandfather's love, for Jihan's father was Stormbringer himself, lord of the wind and the wave, who'd never approved his daughter's marriage.

The fruit of his daughter's union was a freak and an affront against nature, to Stormbringer's way of thinking. So the boy grew up in the cave under the sea, kept away from society.

Never a happy child, Cyrus's temper grew worse

3

as he grew older. One day his mother came down to
see her son and found three mermaids dead: eviscer-
ated, floating near the cavern's ceiling in eddies of
their blood.

"Cyrus," she'd called for the wild-eyed child, hoping to find him hunched in shadows, his white hair
flowing around him like seaweed. "Why did you do
such a thing?"

"Let me out of here, Mother!" an errant current
burbled.

How many times had Cyrus begged her to do just
that? She hunted and hunted for the boy in the cave,
then all along the seafloor. She called on whales and
porpoises to search to the very surface of the sea.
She enlisted nymphs and mermen to ask far and
wide for news of Cyrus.

Eventually, Jihan realized that the voice she'd
thought she'd heard was just an echo of her son's
voice, ringing in her own guilty mind. She had to
find him.

But she couldn't. Cyrus had escaped and now the
trail was cold. The boy was gone.

Jihan summoned her bodyguard of sharks and
mermen to gather up the murdered mermaids. The
sharks feasted upon the corpses with all due ceremony, until nothing was left but the mermen's tears,
mixing with the currents that still whispered, "Let
me out of here, Mother!"

But Jihan had promised her father, Stormbringer,
she never would do that. And now the boy was gone.

So Jihan went to see her father, who ruled the
tempests and the waves.

When he heard her tale, Stormbringer shook his
massive, seaweedy head. "You brought this upon
yourself," he thundered, so that the whole seafloor
quaked. "I told you not to have the child of a human!"

But she had borne the child of a man named
Tempus. And she had brought that child, Cyrus, into

a world where he was different from all other creatures.

"Nevertheless, Father," Jihan said, looking Stormbringer in one red, brooding eye, "I have to find him. He has his father's temper and your blood in his veins. He's angry and too powerful to be abroad in the world of men."

"You're sure that's where he is?" As her father spoke, the sea around them began to roil and boil up. Currents caught her and spun her around in her father's midst.

"I'm sure," she called to the rising waterspout that was Stormbringer, "that's where he's gone. He wants to find his father."

There. She'd said it.

As if the statement was more than he could bear, Stormbringer grabbed her in his waterspout arms and whirled her about and cast her out of the depths.

Up into the sunlight she came, as if the sea itself was spitting her out.

Light blinded Jihan for an instant; waves slapped at her, and she was afraid.

But then the sun on her scales reminded her body how to change itself, and the surface of the sea buoyed her until her limbs shone bronze and supple in the light of day as she began to swim for shore.

The witch called Roxane brooded in her hut near the end of everything, watching sunlight sparkle on the watery wheels surrounding the city at the edge of time.

It had cost her greatly to come so far. Now she was resting. She sat every day in the woods and watched the gleaming city, with its electrum spires and its privileged folk. Watched and waited.

Sometimes caravans came to the city. Sometimes, the city-dwellers ventured out.

Not often, that was true. And not on any regular

schedule. But Roxane was content to bide her time. Once she'd been a mighty witch of power, a great enchantress. Now she was a refugee. If not for her burning need to find the man who'd caused her downfall, she might have died of her misery.

But she had not died. She had been trapped in Hell itself, and survived. Roxane had worked her way here, feeding on the souls of rats and rabbits, and the occasional snippet of rumor that leant strength to her heart.

She would find Nikodemos, her beloved who had deserted her. Then she would begin anew.

So she had promised herself, at every sunrise when she woke, and this morning was no exception. Today, like every day since she'd escaped her prison in Hell, she pulled her battered body out into the sunlight and revealed it to the heavens.

Naked, she would raise a fist to heaven and renew her vow: revenge was Roxane's wellspring, her one true love. To wreak vengeance, one needed strength. And for strength, one needed inspiration. The man called Nikodemos, a ghost from her past, was Roxane's inspiration.

This morning, having found not only two rabbits but an unwary wanderer to feast upon the night before, Roxane was feeling very much stronger.

The wanderer with whom she'd slept soon became the corpse upon whom she slept. The poor fool gave her all his strength as he died. This morning, when she'd pulled herself out of her poor bower of fir into the light, her legs almost held her. They were no longer twisted; nor were they weak and lame. The hands she spread now in the sunlight boasted smooth, white skin—not the chicken skin of old age.

A few more days, a few more fools, and she'd be ready to approach the city's gates and bespell the guards to admit her.

But not yet. Not until she was as beautiful as she'd

ever been. When she saw her Nikodemos again, she'd find no pity on his handsome face. She'd not look into his eyes and see only memories of her reflected glory.

She must become the old Roxane, queen of magic, once again. And it was just a question of time, now. She'd known that being so close to him would inspire her.

That knowledge had dragged her across the world when any lesser witch would have died. Eating scraps, she'd remembered power. Bathing in lust, she'd remembered love. And she'd promised herself that she'd reclaim everything she'd almost had—starting with Nikodemos.

This was the only fitting thanks to the powers that had fooled fate and old enemies to set her free. Free she was, and abroad on the land once more.

Soon the very sky would shudder under her influence and she'd fly high in the clouds once more—take wing whenever she chose.

Sitting in the sunlight, she made a fist and closed her eyes. Gathering her legs under her, she sat cross-legged and naked in the light. Below the crest of her hill was a meadow; in that meadow would she make her beloved appear to her.

She willed it so. She envisioned him there. She called his name. She conjured a gem of power to manifest inside her closed fist.

The gem, she knew, still existed—somewhere. The shard of eternal strength, like Roxane, hadn't been destroyed, only chipped away from its accustomed place. So it would come to her, because she willed it.

She called the shard. She called the man. She called her power. And above her head, clouds scudded across the morning sun.

In her mind's eye, she saw the meadow, where

the last moat that ringed the city gave way to unhal-
lowed ground.

And there she swore she heard a cry of delight, a
laugh, and then another. But still she kept her eyes
closed. Still she willed the shard of power to come to
her. Still she held her outstretched fist before her.

And then she felt it. First came a sensation of
spinning, as if the clouds and the sun were whirling
above her head. Then came a prickling, a burning in
her groin that welled up and out, into her extremi-
ties and into her head.

At last there came a coldness in her fist.

Only then did Roxane open her eyes. Above her
head, the sky was bright but white, completely over-
cast, giving the land a surreal quality and stealing
every shadow from the meadow.

Her fist seemed white as snow. She opened it.

There, in her palm, glittered a cold and tiny stone.
Not more than a pebble, really. A blue pebble too
small to make a decent ring, barely enough for an
earring.

But in her palm it was. A smidgin of the jewel of
power, a fragment of the shard which had belonged
to the greatest archmage of them all. Dominion over
all the beasts of the field and the laws which they
obeyed had been the prize of any who possessed it,
once.

Now, in her diminished state, even a crumb of
power was enough.

She nearly cried out in delight. She shook her
head back and raised her face to the sky, as if to a
mirror. And she smiled with all the beauty she'd
once possessed.

Full of triumph, about to go back into her bower
to rest, she heard the laugh again.

This time, Roxane looked down into the meadow.
And there she saw, not her beloved, but a child and
a woman playing in the clover.

A child and a woman. Well, what an opportunity. Mustn't worry who they might be. Mustn't be disapointed if they were just travelers, or common folk from the city.

But her heart knew that these were more than vulgar folk, as she scurried into her bower, looking for her rags.

Rags weren't really suitable to meetings such as this, but Roxane wouldn't waste her power on vanity.

She paused only long enough to find a rabbit-fur pouch she'd made for amulets and drop the pebble into it, before she tied the pouch around her neck.

Surely, whomever her passion had summoned to the meadow would not care if she didn't look her best.

She still limped a bit, favoring her right side. There was a white streak, yet, in her raven hair. But down she hobbled, not trying to stand up straight or switch her hips. Let these see what time had done to her. She'd been the last sight of too many mortal fools to let that stop her.

Vanity had been purged from her flesh by the fires of hell, and her own determination.

When all is lost, one merely begins again. With her eyes fixed firmly on her prey, Roxane hitched her way painfully down into the meadow.

The curly-headed boy saw her first and said, "Look, Nanny, a witch!" The brat must have been four or five. Children always saw the truth. They were more dangerous than adults. And more nutritious to a soul like hers.

"Hush, don't say such things, dear," said the nanny, who had golden hair and a comely form and a dress that soon would replace Roxane's rags. "It's just an unfortunate beggar woman. It's good luck to give alms to the poor, dear."

The woman raised a hand and waved. And smiled.

And then, bending down over a wicker basket, the nanny said, "Here, Prince, take the unfortunate woman one of these rolls and a bit of this cheese. It's important for royalty such as yourself, Highness, to learn charity and compassion. Run along, now."

Roxane was sure she'd never had a better day. Didn't these foolish folk of the city realize that, beyond their walls, evil reigned? Hadn't they learned not to trust in mankind? Didn't they know enough to fear strangers, and all who had less than they?

"Here's a treat for you, Madame," called the nanny, as the child came scampering Roxane's way, dressed in blue-eyed innocence and silk.

Roxane nearly hesitated. Might this be a trick? It seemed too easy. She cast a glance at the city. Was some archmage in there, trying to trap her while she still was weak? But no, this was *the* city, the city of knowledge and wonder at the edge of time, which had cleansed itself of all evil long before Roxane came.

And the boy, upon reaching Roxane, held out a perfect hand to her, smiling. "Madam Beggar, here's your alms." Baby teeth gleamed.

Roxane took the crusty bread and the creamy wedge of cheese, then let them fall, holding on to the child's hand.

"What's your name, little one?" she asked.

The boy said, "Prince Nino, son of Queen Tabet and her consort, Nikodemos—"

A cry of joy tore itself from Roxane's throat. Forgetting all about the nanny and the nanny's fine dress, she fell upon the child and swept up the boy in her arms.

The child screamed. The nanny screamed. But Roxane was already feeding, feasting, on the choicest morsel that fate could provide.

The nanny rushed at them, but Roxane was stronger, already. Her feet didn't touch the ground.

She lifted herself, and the boy. She swooped into the air, her grip on the child becoming the grip of an eagle. The eagle wore a rabbit's fur pouch around its neck and its wingspread was twice that of a man's height.

The prince who dangled from its talons hardly struggled any longer; there was too little life left in him for that.

And the bower of fir that had been Roxane's home for so long was right beneath her as she dropped the child, and swooped down in its wake.

Then up, to see if the nanny had followed.

But the woman was weeping in the meadow, a splotch among the clover. Roxane's eagle eyes saw every crenel on the ramparts of the electrum-towered city.

Before she returned to her fir bower to finish her feast, she winged high over the city and hovered there, watching from her perch on columns of air.

So she witnessed the commotion below, when the nanny reached the city gates crying that the queen's son had been taken by a witch. She saw the queen come out into the courtyard.

And she saw her beloved, Nikodemos, come running to take Queen Tabet in his arms as she fainted.

All the emotion coming out of that place was a further delight, and Roxane's wings grew stronger.

But best of all was when, circling low in delicious danger to catch a glimpse of her lover's face, Niko looked up as the shadow of her wings fell over him.

Then it was time to be away. The nanny was yelling and Niko was pointing. On the ramparts, guards were aiming crossbows and spears.

She called out once to her beloved in her eagle's voice before she beat the air and soared out of reach.

Of course, he couldn't know what she said. But Roxane knew that, in his heart, Niko would realize she was back.

In the meantime, there was a feast waiting for her, a warm body with fresh-cracked bones and salty blood. Niko would thank her, one day, for all that Roxane was doing—and would do—to free him from some scheming woman's trap.

With every bite her beak tore from her prize, she felt better. She no longer worried about returning to human form. She had enough sustenance, in this one catch, to bring her nearly back to health.

After she'd eaten her fill, she'd fly off with her prey, north a bit, where no hunters would find them until she'd consumed every bit.

And then she'd be ready to unite with her lover once again. Beautiful and full of power. All she'd ever been.

Even Niko would see the truth of that. She'd make sure of it.

Kama was fighting her heart out, but the odds didn't look good. The Shaga caravan was a shambles: half of it burning; the rest of the wagons overturned, wheels spinning under the pale Moriland sun.

The bandits outnumbered the defenders four to one. Kama's unit had been understaffed to begin with, because the caravanner was too cheap to pay for twelve guards. The fool had thought that his gods would stand double shifts to make up the shortfall.

She'd never wanted to live past her prime, anyway, she told herself as, from her position under an overturned wagon, she shot one of her three remaining quarrels.

At her rear was a burning wagon, so no one was coming at her that way. Of course, the wagon she was huddled under was burning too. Eventually, if she wasn't killed here or dragged out of here and killed elsewhere, the wagon would fall on her and crush her.

She liked that death the best, considering her

alternatives. The five remaining bandits were bound to be miffed, having lost seven companions to three defenders, one of whom was a woman.

The problem with being a woman was, at times like these, you resented it more than you'd like. If she'd been a man, she wouldn't have to worry about repeated rape, and that was why she resented it, she told herself.

But she knew it wasn't true. The gods had made of her a woman, and women were . . . weaker; smaller; inconsequential. . . .

Consequences were something Kama understood all too well. She fitted another quarrel into her crossbow and squinted at the available killing field. Maybe if she were a man, she could have convinced herself to leap out there, in full view, yelling and screaming, so that she could take two of her enemies with her as a man would—face to face, shooting them honorably in the head or the heart.

But she wasn't a man, so she was huddled under this wagon, intent on shooting whomever she might in the bladder or the balls or the ass.

You did the best you could. She'd never been able to do any more. The smoke was thickening and the sounds of horses and men around her were hard to pick out over the roar of the flames above and behind her.

Maybe she was dead already, and she'd spend eternity thinking she was still under a wagon waiting for one of the bandits to present a suitable target.

But heaven was supposed to be cool and pleasant, and the ghost of her father's priest was supposed to meet her with a smile and a glass of pure water.

At least, that was how, all the legends said, a Sacred Band fighter died. And Kama was still a Sacred Bander. Maybe only a Sacred Bander, nothing more.

You lost everything, in life, it seemed. She'd lost

lovers, friends, a baby, her father . . . her whole
world, thanks to evil men and evil magic.

You lost everything but your self. And, if you were
very lucky, your self-respect.

The caravanner had said that only women worried
about integrity. She'd been angered enough by his
taunt to take the job anyway, despite the fact that
you couldn't guarantee the caravan's safety with an
insufficient force. Three people, she'd warned him,
were not enough.

Well, Kama hoped that the caravanner was happy
now, in whatever heaven or hell he'd earned. She'd
warned him. But she'd learned that men didn't like
to take a woman's advice or be reminded that they
should have taken it.

Since the caravanner had been the second to die
this morning, she was almost willing to forgive him
for being such an ass.

Feet moved out there, in the black smoke. She
hunkered down in the dirt, the crossbow's butt against
her shoulder, her cheek pressed to the receiver,
trying to blink the soot out of her eyes.

Big feet. Feet in boots. Nothing new about that.

She thought she heard a hoarse shout, then another.

If they were massing to attack her, she'd better
find a way to make sure they killed her. If she'd been
their leader, she wouldn't have been so intent on
finishing off one defender.

That was the trouble. She didn't think like a man.
She never had. And she didn't think like a woman,
either. Her father's blood in her veins had made sure
of that.

She'd always known she'd die like this, some day. . . .

A hand grabbed her ankle, coming from her left,
where slain oxen had crumpled in their traces.

"What the—"

The hand was inexorably pulling her out. She tried

to grab for a wheel with one hand. She couldn't use two, or she'd lose hold on her crossbow.

Her fingers grazed a wheel's rim, but couldn't hold on.

She wouldn't scream.

Everything was happening so slowly: she could feel her jerkin ride up. The stony ground scraped her back as she struggled and kicked.

Then both of her ankles were caught. Caught by two different men, from the way her legs were being pulled apart.

She stopped trying to catch hold of the wagon and cradled the crossbow to her. Maybe she couldn't get off both her remaining quarrels; she surely could kill the first man she saw, once her head was out from under the—

"Kama, don't shoot!"

Out from under the wagon, a man's swordbelt was swimming in her sights just as the shout came.

She was squeezing the trigger, taking up the trigger slack . . . The significance of the words penetrated only as her tormentors let her ankles go and they hit the dirt.

She almost shot that swordbelt anyway. She didn't care if a bandit knew her name.

But her legs were free. She got them under her, still squinting through her sights and tearing eyes, blinking through the smoke.

The two men hulking over her were great, blackened figures, backlit by fire.

Only one was a little greater than the other. She remembered the hoarseness of the cry she'd heard.

"Don't shoot, Kama," one of the bandits said. "It's me, Crit. You're safe."

"Safe?" Then: "Crit?"

Crit, a bandit? Crit, the Sacred Band's first officer? The best soldier among all those calling themselves Stepsons? The power that had scattered Kama's unit over the land was truly evil, and still at work.

The other bandit said, "Put the crossbow down and come with us. Run. We haven't much time before the portal closes."

"Portal?" She didn't understand. But since it was her father's voice—Tempus's voice—the same hoarse voice that she'd heard when she'd been waiting for death under the wagon—she followed.

If Crit was with Tempus, then it was she, not Critias, who'd been fighting on the wrong side. She kept her eyes on her father's shape, ahead in the smoke, her crossbow ready.

She was too well trained to yell questions at the moving men ahead. But when she caught up with Crit, she said, "Where'd you come from, soldier?"

"You won't believe it until you see it," said her once-lover, and took her elbow: "Now watch where Tempus disappears, and follow exactly."

That was Crit's way: to warn you just enough that you'd keep going. And so she did keep going, even after her father's form disappeared entirely before her eyes, as if he'd stepped through a curtain—or into an abyss.

"Up. Step up," Crit, beside her, ordered.

She did as he did, and saw her own booted foot disappear before her eyes.

Then a tingly feeling overswept her, accompanied by vertigo. Abruptly, she stumbled onto a marble floor in an entirely different place.

The first thing she saw there were her boots reappearing, black with soot and muddy, on that floor. Then Crit's boots were right alongside hers.

Crit's voice said critically, "I *told* you: 'Step up.'"

She looked behind her. There was no burning Shaga caravan under a pale Moriland sun. There was only a sunset framed in a doorway, as if they were in a high tower with no land in sight. And there was

Crit, pulling shut a heavy door on tracks like the door of a stable, but plated with metal.

She looked in front of her. There was Tempus, covered with soot, heading off down a hallway as if this were an everyday occurrence. She looked beside her. Crit came up to her, a broad grin on his blackened face.

He expected her to ask questions. To crumple against him in teary gratitude. To gawk at this amazing place, like nowhere she'd ever seen.

Well, she wasn't going to give Crit the satisfaction of being predictable. "Critias," she told him, "when I want your help, I'll ask for it."

She might still be alive, still be a woman, but she'd be damned if she'd play the grateful damsel rescued from distress. Not for the benefit of one of her father's soldiers. Especially not this soldier.

Crit, with a wry shake of his head, said, "Some things never change," and started down the hallway after Tempus.

Kama had no choice but to stand around gawking, or follow Crit.

So tag along behind Critias she did, like some bedraggled camp follower. When she did get to heaven, she was going to complain to all and sundry gods about having made her a woman who had to live in a world of men and live life by men's rules.

It just wasn't fair. The least her father could have done, if Tempus was bound and determined to rescue her from ignominious defeat, was choose a partner other than Crit, someone who wouldn't take such obvious pleasure in her embarrassment.

But then, she told herself, following Crit's lead through the wonderous palace, Tempus never thought about anyone else's feelings.

That was the problem with having an immortal for a father.

Chapter 2:

MAN'S WORK

Lounging on the highest balcony of Pinnacle House, the big immortal and his daughter looked as if they owned the livid sky against which they seemed to lean. Critias, on the other hand, owned nothing here but his honor, the horse he'd ridden in on, and the battle dress he wore.

Kama's presence reminded him resoundingly of that. Whatever belonged to Tempus, Kama assumed was hers without a second thought. Somehow, that included Crit once again. He could feel it in the way her eyes ran over him as she took stock, with all the emotion of an accountant, of the Lemurian kingdom her father now ruled.

Her father had brought him here. Crit had . ɔe out of habit—because Tempus asked it; becausɔ ..ɔ was needed, so his commander said, to put their old unit back together again. Come out of loyalty. Out of loneliness.

So here he was, habit's slave, focusing on his purpose—the meeting Tempus had called—because he understood meetings. And he understood his commander, as well as any man could. Kama, Pinnacle House, the nowhere land of Lemuria: these, Crit didn't understand. Couldn't hope to understand. Critias was no immortal, no demigod, no child of power. But Crit was a good soldier. He knew that understanding was not necessarily part of his job.

When Tempus held a staff meeting, the very air came to attention.

Up here, where the sea wind should be beating salt into your skin and the gulls decrying the coming of night, it was eerily quiet. Quiet enough that Critias, the operations officer of the Sacred Band mercenaries called Stepsons, wondered momentarily if he'd gone stone deaf.

Stranger things happened, in the wake of battle. Especially the sort of battles Tempus fought—against unearthly powers, using god-given means such as the portals at Pinnacle House that opened into everywhere and anytime.

Abruptly, Crit felt with full force the afteraffects of using the portal to rescue Kama. He nearly staggered back. He grabbed the balcony rail for support, leaning his hips against it. He was so tired he was seeing double; he wanted nothing more than to crawl under his bed, curl into a fetal position and sleep for a week. A month. A year. Until Kama got tired of waiting for him to wake, and left Lemuria.

But that wasn't going to happen.

"What's the target?" Crit asked Tempus.

The commander, who was never hesitant about anything, looked at him through long, slitted eyes and hesitated.

Perhaps Kama's presence in Pinnacle House—at this meeting where only the commander and his first officer should have been—was what made Tempus slow to respond to a simple query. Crit was about to rephrase his question when he got an answer.

"Sandia," said Tempus.

"Never heard of it," said Kama.

"Be quiet and you will," Crit advised. Still the wind was silent. So high above the sea and land, its reluctance to blow bothered Crit like witchsign. The Storm God, Enlil, was Tempus's tutelary, and thus the Stepsons' patron. Always, their missions were sanctified by heavy weather. But not now. Beyond Tempus and Kama, the sunset was a brilliant red and gold; the sea flat; the wind so calm that not a one of Kama's black hairs blew around her face, here a hundred feet above the ground.

"Sandia," Tempus said, so softly you might mistake his voice for settling rocks or the missing wind, "is a thousand years from here. I want the Stepsons reunited for this mission. And I want the horses from the farm."

Crit had thought it might be something like that. Yet his heart leapt, beat fast twice, and then skipped a painful beat. The horses from the valley wouldn't be hard to find, or difficult to greet after so long. But the Stepsons would be. His partner, Straton, would be. And if Kama was worth finding for this sortie, Strat certainly was. Strat was still a barb in Crit's heart.

"Everyone?" Crit needed a clarification. "We were scattered far and wide by hell's own maelstrom. . . ."

"Strat, yes. That's what you want to know."

Crit groaned inwardly.

"And Niko, if he wishes: we owe him at least an invitation." Tempus ducked his head.

Kama turned hers and stared at her father. "Niko?" The one word was an indictment. Niko had been Tempus's favorite; the commander had treated him as a son. Of them all, Niko was the most accursed soul. And the best, Crit had often thought.

"Niko, Kama. If I brought you here to live forever if you dare, can I fail to offer him as much?" Tempus shifted against the balustrade and crossed his massive arms.

"Is he your blood? Can you have failed, all these years, to offer me as much as him?" said Tempus's daughter, and crossed her arms as well.

She was always the most beautiful when she was

angry. She looked almost the same as the day Crit had first seen her, despite what they'd all been through. But then, she was her father's daughter, half-immortal.

Crit had aged rapidly these last few years, fighting where Tempus did, though his commander showed no scar, no line, no strain. If this kept up much longer, Crit would soon seem the veteran, and Tempus the recruit.

When Tempus had showed up in a barracks full of shadows and clapped Crit against him in reunion, the commander had said, "Come and fight with me, Critias, in the river. Time will be yours, and death will come only when you're ready. Or stay behind and marry dust. Your choice."

The band hadn't called Tempus "the Riddler" for nothing.

Crit looked at his hand, trying to see past the ruddy cast thrown over it by the setting sun, to the age of the skin and bone. Could he really live here, out of time, and fight wherever Tempus willed—forever?

Did he want to, if he could?

Still, the members of the Sacred Band, scattered throughout the world, suffered loneliness that no man who'd never risked his life for a brother could know.

Together, they'd be whole again. It was worth even dealing with Kama on a daily basis.

If Tempus would keep her viper's tongue in check, as he did now with a glower.

Or Crit thought it was, until he asked, "Who's first?" and Tempus said, "Niko. But we'll need Randal to find him. And Straton. On one foray. Are you ready, Stepson?"

Kama pushed away from her father's side and strode between them. "This is madness. It's too soon. Look at him, Tempus: he's not like you. He's exhausted, barely staying on his feet. How can you push your fighters so? Didn't you learn, the last time—"

"Kama."

Tempus could quiet her just by speaking her name. Maybe Crit could learn that trick. In the honey light, she was all long eyes and limbs, tight breasts and iron purpose. Seeing her try to protect him from Tempus's uncompromising need made Crit want to kiss her.

No, no, no. Not that again. *Never* that again. He was too tired.

He vaguely heard Tempus say, "Kama, this is man's work. Go find your Aunt Cime. She'll want to greet you and tell you tales suitable for a woman's ears. When we're ready, we'll call you."

Tempus could not have hurt his daughter more if he'd struck her. And they all knew it.

Crit held his breath. Kama fought to catch hers, gulped and stomped stiffly for the great glass doors, which slid aside when she threatened them.

Such a place. Such a task. Go to the future? Sandia? But it didn't matter that Crit had never heard of Sandia, or where or when it was.

First, they had to find Niko, Randal—and Straton.

"You're sure, Commander?" Crit asked when Kama was gone.

"About the reunion of the band? It's the only thing I am sure of, Stepson. Come with me. I have a window to show you."

Tempus meant the magical windows of Lemuria, which showed places nowhere in the vicinity.

Crit had only been here three days. He still had much to learn. But he had faith in Tempus as a teacher. He just wasn't certain, as he gave up the balustrade's support, if he had the strength in his body to keep up with his commander. Or if he had the strength in his heart to confront Strat again.

One thing Critias had learned, following Tempus,

was that, in so doing, you always tried what you weren't sure you could manage. Most of the time, you surprised yourself.

But never Tempus. The Riddler always asked you for everything you had. Crit trusted Tempus implicitly. Otherwise, he couldn't have followed him this one more time, into the strange halls of Pinnacle House, where everyplace was just beyond your bedroom door and dogs Crit never saw howled all night long.

In the city at the edge of time, Queen Tabet's consort, Nikodemos, gave up trying to comfort his wife and went down to the stables to comfort himself among the horses.

His son was dead. Niko could feel it in his bones. *Wanted* to feel it in his bones. If not dead, Nino was undead—far worse a fate—in the hands of a witch.

All the wise citizens and counsellors of the City were casting their dice and reading their omens, trying to decide whether a rescue party should be sent.

Niko could have told them, wanted to tell them, should have told them: time for a funerary pyre. Funerals were few in the city. They'd have to look up the ritual in their books. Once there'd been great magicians here, sorcerers of real power. Somewhere, there must be a rite to save the soul of a child eaten by a witch.

Finally safe inside the stable, Niko closed his eyes and leaned against the tackroom door. *Please let the witch have eaten him all. Please let Nino not be a minion of evil. Please let vengeance not eat me alive.*

The prayer came out him addressed not to the Storm God, Enlil, lord of vengeance, but to the universal balance, *maat*. Vengeance belonged to the god, not to men. Niko served maat—the principal of balance—in the world. He was a servant of men, not gods. Maat wanted only right action in the world.

Nino's death was not right. Nikodemos's heart felt as if only revenge would free it to beat as a man's heart should. His soul was rocking on a precipice of passion. If it tumbled over the edge, the balance he'd striven lifelong to attain would be lost.

Vengeance is the god's. He wasn't one, just a man who labored in the service of maat. Just an adept who'd forgotten his vows long enough to pretend he could have a wife, a child, a life like others had.

Niko smelled salt hay, sweet feed, harness oil, manure and the amoniac tang of horse urine.

And he smelled horse. The smell of horse, musky and clean, honorable and warm, rushed into his greedy lungs to sustain him. Nowhere out there, among the alien people of the city, could Niko even mourn in peace. If he wanted to grieve, he couldn't.

Here, he could at least be free to feel, to let his maat—his balance, his special gift of knowing—well up and heal him.

His heart ached for the boy, Nino. Yet Nino had been Tabet's son, more than his—a child of the city, with the cityfolk's peculiar hubris. The folk of the city were caretakers of knowledge. They thought that grace was hereditarily theirs, even when they fell from it. For five years, Niko had found no evil here, in the temples or the streets.

Before that, Tempus and he had cleansed that evil, with the god's help and Jihan's help, and it had never returned. But there was no good here, either. Tabet wanted perfection. Perfection of the external world was not inherently good, so far as Niko was concerned.

He was an adept of an ancient school, and the perfection he sought was the perfection of maat—a perfection of the inner self. Of the spirit. Of the soul. And the soul must be be tested in the world. The soul must be fired by strife, quenched by love, tempered by adversity.

He'd always known it. He'd always accepted his trials stolidly, with a clear eye and his head high. But then the ghost of his son had not been staring him in the face.

Good, by itself, was not the point at all. Good in the face of evil was. Without this distinction, a man was not a man, but only a creature among creatures.

Niko had come to this same conclusion whenever he had retired to meditate on his maat in the islands of his schooling. Maat brought him to his own truth, always. Where there was no temptation, there could be no exaltation. Where there was no challenge, there could be no success.

So now he could not fall into madness, cry vengeance from a hoarse throat, or even blink away the sight of his son's murdered, beautiful, blue-eyed face. He must wait for the ghost to leave upon its own, let it stay with him until it did.

Discipline untested was nothing. Only against the undisciplined forces of greed, lust, and self-absorption that combined to make evil—only in the world did Niko find the balance he sought.

And now the ghost of his son, Nino, was leading him back to the world. Nino had been of his mother's people, born to be content with knowledge—as if knowledge were an inert thing, like gold or corn, to be hoarded. Knowledge was not wisdom without a test of the soul.

Niko hoped his son had been given time, by the gods, to test his soul and find it, before the witch had changed to an eagle and eaten him. The wraith hovering before him looked too placid to be the spirit of an undead.

Niko's maat had no doubt that a great witch, not merely a great eagle, had taken the boy. And his maat had no doubt that his son was dead: the ghost-face of Nino faded, faded, and then was gone.

Niko could feel the world's light just one soul darker now, with the boy dead.

He opened his eyes to the velvet shadows of the stable. Its smells were rich, fecund. His palms were sweating. They would not make a funeral for the boy, these folk of the city, for they were afraid of death.

Death was a stranger to them. They kept death beyond their walls with all their wisdom. Thus death, when it came here, was a terror, not a natural thing. The folk of the city, who knew so much, feared the unknown with a panic that Niko could never share.

Panic resulted from being confronted with an event you were untrained to handle. In the misty isles, Niko had trained for confronting all the world's wickedness, absorbing it, transmuting it, and tempering his soul in its depths.

Transmuting the murder of his son was a test beyond any he'd thought to face. But then, adepts of maat didn't marry and bear sons. He'd asked for this, turning his back on the world. He'd let his soul get stuck in the city at the edge of time like a frog in amber. The whole time he'd been here, he'd been imprisoned in the rock-hard sap of the material life, which had hardened around him without him even feeling it.

He could leave now, if he wanted. His face was on every fresco in the Storm God's temple here. Tabet could talk to the walls for company. They would not argue with her the way he often did—about what was fit and what was meet when a society had everything and shared nothing, only hoarded.

But he had wed the city's queen, and his word was something Niko took seriously. And yet, how seriously could he take a woman who could not, would not, so much as admit that her son was dead? Though his word bound him to a wife, it did not tie him to this place unendingly, never to venture out again.

He walked aimlessly through the stable, loving the thickness of the air and the animal company of the softly snorting beasts in their stalls. He wandered through the tackroom, touching the smooth leather. No one went anywhere, from here. Not really. Everyone was always in by sunset. Or, at the longest, back by the full of the moon.

The horses were not great horses, by his standards. Not so great as his Tros mare, which Jihan had bequeathed him. But they were good horses, real and subject to life and death, on the outside. Here they lived a quiet life with death held in abeyance.

It was the city's power of abeyance that made Niko feel a traitor, a coward, a fool in the face of his son's death. He was worse off than the dead: he'd been living a dream, a waking dream—not living at all, but only thinking that he lived.

Life is nothing without death at the end of it. Maat is nothing if not at work in the world. Niko was nothing but a rusting instrument in the corner of fate's barn if he stayed here now. Vengeance had no part in his decision, he told himself. Only the balance must be served.

Tabet wouldn't credit Nino's death until she had a cold body to crush to her breast. Niko's own heart couldn't credit the death of the soul with the body. This difference between them was irreconcilable. He needed to get out of the city, where he could breathe free and hold his head up as a man should. He needed to face his destiny, his enemies, his mortality.

He needed to perform a rite for his son that would clear a father's heart of the ice than now surrounded it.

Grief was inappropriate to such a moment of decision, yet he felt it like lead weights on his feet. He had made no mistake by coming here, or by siring Nino and holding his tiny hand, he told the dark-muzzled mare who stuck a head over her stall door to see him.

Without Nino's life and Nino's death, Nikodemos would have stayed forever in the city at the edge of time, forgetful of his maat and his duty in the world.

The horse snorted softly and rolled one sable eye at him. Jihan's parting gift to him was this Tros mare with a black muzzle and lips, whose nostrils had pink velvet lightning bolts piercing them.

He opened her mouth and looked at her square, yellow teeth. Seven, perhaps eight, chronological years old. A good height at the shoulders for long journeying.

He'd never really looked at the Tros before—not with an eye toward endurance and trekking. He hadn't been anywhere since Jihan, leaving here, bequeathed him the mare.

The city had let him taste what he was protecting, in the world: home and hearth, youth and folly, love and laughter. Maat had not meant him to join the flock, but to become a better shepherd.

He opened the stall and, clucking softly, led the horse out and crosstied her. Black stockings, a black mane and tail; a huge, dappled rump; fine breadth of barrel. A big heart was beating in that wide chest.

Beautiful ears. This mare had tiny ears that were always twitching. She watched him with her ears.

"Want to go for a ride, horse?" he asked her softly. "Out of here, where something may actually happen?"

The horse snorted and shook her head as if an errant fly had flown into one ear.

"Now, you could get hurt out there, horse. I could take another."

The Tros mare pawed the ground with a forefoot, as if reminding him of the Tros horses' fabled endurance.

Niko's maat reached into the mare and his eyes saw her surrounded with a blue nimbus. The mare and he would go into the world together, he decided.

He saddled her up.

When he was done, he checked every strap and tied a bedroll on the back of his saddle. Then he led the mare into the early evening.

One of the guards came up to him. "Sir Consort, you can't . . . that is . . . I—"

"I'm going to look for my son. Tell Tabet I'm not coming back until I find him."

The guard looked at his feet, assuming all sorts of things that were untrue, but saying only, "As the consort wills."

They all knew his face: Niko's was the face of the god in the temple, a face that had been there for thousands of years before Niko had come this way. He frightened them and awed them. So he had no friends among them, only covert worshippers.

Biding here had taught him how lonely Tempus must be, in the world.

He swung up on the horse and said, "And don't tell Tabet until I'm safely gone. No need to bother her."

No, there'd be no funeral here for Nino. He wouldn't insist that they make one. In return, they wouldn't curse him for leaving: he was off to find the prince of the city.

Niko saw renewed hope, and admiration, in the guard's eyes: "Safe journey, Consort. May you and our young prince be soon returned to us."

What could Niko say to that? No better message could he sent to Tabet. She'd interpret it in the way of the city: she would have hope.

She always had hope. All folk of the city did. Trying to tell her that her son was dead was . . . unnecessary.

And worrying her about undeads and witches was worse—it was foully spiteful and mean.

Niko squeezed the mare with his knees and they headed for the gates, which opened slowly, just enough to let them through.

He'd come here without even so much as a horse, he reminded himself. Come in a whirlwind. Come in a maelstrom. Come in a storm and a rain of fish. Yet this night was clear, as he loped the able mare through the gates—clear and full of stars.

The moon was rising, huge because it was so low between two hills. It spilled light over the waterways surrounding the city and, as they crossed the first one, the Tros mare whickered in pleasure and joy.

Good. The mare's haunches seemed made of moonlight as Niko reined her north, the way the eagle had gone.

Looking up at the moon, he thought he saw wings before it.

He blinked. The wings were gone. Wings he might have seen, though. Real wings, or ghost wings to match Nino's ghost-face from the stable. His son had been taken by a witch who turned into an eagle. From the instant he'd heard the tale, Niko suspected what witch it might be.

And when he'd seen the eagle circle over the city's ramparts, hunting him, he'd been certain.

Now, outside the gates, he could admit he'd left the city partly to draw the evil one away. But only partly. Maat must be served, balance restored—inside Niko and in the world.

His son was dead. Tabet could have another, with a city dweller. One thing even a retired Sacred Band fighter knew was when to pack up and leave.

He had not lied, back there: if he found the boy alive, he'd bring Nino back. But if the ghost of Abarsis, the Slaughter Priest, had the boy's soul, then the priest of Niko's heart would make all things right in heaven.

And if the witch had the boy's soul, keeping it from its destined rest, then Niko's maat would make that matter right.

Out here, where the wind was clean and the land was growing wilder by the mile, he had more hope that young Nino was dead. To be alive and in the clutches of a witch was a terrible thing. Niko knew this better than most men. He'd suffered more at the hands of witches than any mortal could have survived without the help of maat and his commander, Tempus.

He pushed memories away. His responsibility to the city was ended, if ever he'd truly had one. His greater responsibility was to lead the witch away from the city, where no evil magic had a right to dwell.

The city folk were not evil, but they were not good enough to withstand evil, since they knew so little of it.

Niko knew a great deal about evil. He knew witches and sorcerers by their first names. And the name of the witch who'd soared over the ramparts, holding his son's limp body in eagle talons, was Roxane.

Niko would have bet his life on it—was betting his life on it.

But he wasn't angry. He was only sad. And that, now, just a little. Anger might come later; if it did, his maat would see him through all the stages of grief. First came sadness, then came doubt, then ripe confusion; next was helplessness in the face of fate; and thereafter, the killing fever: fury, venegance, and cold murder.

The ice around his heart would protect him, until there was no more work to be done, until the rites for Nino were said, until this matter between him and Roxane was settled. Through it all, maat would help him keep his hold on his soul and his eye on his honor.

He'd been a fool to think he could just walk away from the world. He'd tried before, and failed. The world always came after you, one way or another, and thrust you back into it.

Niko had learned that truth long ago. Only for a while, in the city at the edge of time, with Tempus's blessing, he had forgotten.

Roxane had not forgotten Niko, though. And on Niko's account, his son Nino had died.

So there was much for Niko to do in the world, right now, to restore the balance.

Witch or no witch, wife or no wife, the death of a man's son by violence was not something that a man could ignore. If the world wanted him back so badly, Niko could not fail to go back into it.

Cyrus wandered along the shore, picking up shells and learning what he could from those he met and things he saw. He had much to learn. His new body was strange to him, and ungainly at first. But it was obviously a good and serviceable body, perhaps even an enviable body, from the way men and women reacted to his appearance.

Men of the shore would throw things at him and yell, whenever he came into view. So he began collecting these sharp gifts aimed at him, and learning to yell the same words. Then whenever he saw a man, he would throw sharp gifts and yell the words that everyone yelled at him.

Often, the men would not yell back and throw shiny, sharp gifts in return, but simply run away. But enough responded that Cyrus decided he was greeting the men correctly. Some were greeters and throwers, and some were runners, who served a different function.

So it was in Stormbringer's kingdom. So it must be here.

The women he saw were very different from mermaids; they had split tails, the way his mother often did. And, of course, these split tails were exactly right for his new body to enjoy. Whenever he found a woman strolling upon the shore or washing things in the water, he would stride up to her, throwing his shiniest sharp gifts and yelling as loudly as he could. Often these women were so flattered that they offered themselves to him immediately. Sometimes they cried with joy. Sometimes they ran but these were, clearly, the runners—the servants of this place.

He didn't see nearly the number of folk he'd expected, until, suddenly, a whole group came out to meet him at once. These folk threw so many sharp gifts and yelled so loudly from so many throats that Cyrus became confused.

He couldn't catch all those sharp gifts or answer so many greetings from one throat.

So he split himself into a dozen parts and let the parts do the catching of the gifts and the yelling from twelve throats and the throwing of sharp gifts in return.

Somehow, this didn't turn out as he'd hoped. Some of the men failed to catch their gifts. These bled. Three fell down. The rest turned and ran. Looking down at his twelve selves, Cyrus saw that three of those were bleeding as well.

Then it occurred to him that he might have misunderstood the intentions of the men who greeted him with shouts and thrown gifts.

So he reconstituted himself as one unwounded being and sat upon the sand, watching the single survivor: a wounded man, obviously dying. Cyrus knew all about death. He had lived in the ocean. He had killed to escape his prison.

Everything killed something to survive. Usually

one ate one's kill. He was hesitant to eat this man.
But he knew he must salvage something from this
mistake. In his grandfather's ocean, everything was
used, nothing was wasted. Waste was an affront to
nature, Cyrus knew.

The man who lay before him on the sand, bleeding
from the mouth and from the stomach, knew many
things that Cyrus did not yet know.

So Cyrus sat, watching and waiting. When the
man's chest began heaving in death rattles, Cyrus
put his lips to the lips of the dying man. If he could
catch the soul coming out of the man's mouth, he
could learn something.

He sucked up the soul from the dying man. Now
Cyrus knew more things than he had before. He
knew enough to put his hands on the dying man's
skull and crack it open. In the sea, one wasted nothing.

He ate the brain of the dying man, learning what
the man knew in his brain as if they were both in the
ocean, and not on the land.

Then Cyrus knew he must cover his body before
he met more human folk. And he knew he should
not yell and throw sharp gifts, because these were
not friendly acts.

He also knew, now, that the women whom he met
on the shore were not always glad to see him. He
thanked the body of the slain man for its wisdom.
Then, because the land-dwellers' custom of setting
fire to the dead made no sense to him, he lifted the
body and gave it to the sea—where nothing would
be wasted.

He was disappointed that this man knew nothing
of his father, the great Lord Tempus, of whom Jihan
so often spoke. But now he knew how to talk to men
and women, and how to move among them without
too much problem.

Of course, he would have to change his skin from
sharkbelly white and his eyes from fish eyes; he

would make his hair brown instead of greenish white. He would make his stature smaller, like that of a man. And he would grow hair on his body, instead of scales, wherever men had hair.

Then he would find his father. He would elude any pursuit mounted by Stormbringer or his mother.

When he killed to escape, Cyrus had known he was going into exile. At least until he found his father. Then Cyrus would learn what the man had to say for himself.

Tempus had breathed life into Cyrus and let that life become a misery. When Cyrus found his father, he would demand a full accounting, and all that a son should have from a father. If Cyrus didn't like what transpired, he would have revenge for all the misery his father had heaped upon him and his mother by deserting them.

Life in Stormbringer's realm had not been easy. For the first time, Cyrus was glad of that. As he manifested the hair of a man and the shape of a man upon his person, he cried in agony. But it was nothing compared to the agony of living life in a cave that was a cage beneath the sea, where neither his curiosity nor his energy had any outlet.

Now he was out. He had let himself out. And he had met human men and human women, and had congress with both, as suited the sexes.

Since he was not afraid of death or life, but only of Stormbringer's wrath in eternity, Cyrus was very happy as he put on the clothes of the man he had killed and headed up the beach, toward the setting sun.

Chapter 3:

PERCHANCE TO DREAM

In the land of Shaga, magic wasn't against the law. Enchantment wasn't immoral. The practice of sorcery wasn't an affront to man or nature.

Randal, the warrior mage, was thankful for small favors. He was alive. He was free. And if an inimical maelstrom had set him down in a land where adepts were inept, where magicians were maladroit, where enchanters were anemic, where sorcerers were more larcenous than lethal . . . well, you paid your money, as the saying went, and you took your choice.

Tonight in Shaga City, Randal's choices were seeming slimmer than he liked. But he stumbled into the stinking hut behind the Fifth Army's barracks, to wait for some customer to duck under the rug tacked over the door and name his pleasure. A journeyman enchanter's life was not an easy one.

While fighting for his very existance in the heart of the maelstrom, Randal had made an ill-considered wish. That wish had brought him here, to Shaga, a country so deeply embroiled in war with its neighbor, Moriland, that even a prestidigitator could get a job counseling minor barons about the future or selling soldiers' charms to keep their heads on their bodies.

He'd wished to be somewhere he could ply his trade and not be persecuted for it. He'd wished for precisely this—he'd bespelled this fate upon himself.

After years of fighting archmages and fiends, shoulder-to-shoulder with magic-shy soldiers under orders from a war-god's avatar, Randal had spelled himself right out of hell into Shaga.

Hereabouts, exactly as he'd wished, everything was much simpler. But he'd come to rue the universal ear's propensity for taking his whispers literally.

The citizens of Shaga were simple folk. They killed simply, bestially. They believed, simplistically enough, that anyone who looked or behaved differently was soulless and simply must be obliterated.

If the people of Shaga even began to wonder whether you might be short a soul, as they reckoned one, you were in for a slow and simple death at the hands of the local circus folk. Dismemberment of the soulless was Shaga's most popular weekend entertainment.

Because sorcerers usually were called upon to mediate any argument between the accused (those reputedly soulless) and the accusers (those with a bone to pick or a profit to make), hanging out a sorcerer's shingle in Shaga hadn't been the wisest course for Randal to take.

But he'd realized too late what sorcery meant in these parts. By the time he'd learned, all he could do was specialize in something that would keep him out of the circus ring. So he was specializing in what he knew best: the needs of armies.

Counseling soldiers meant dealing with all manner of things to which Randal was, in varying degree, allergic: animals, plants, dust, and the like.

So he was hard at working maintaining an unstuffed nose and an ache-free head in Shaga. And, of course, plotting to get out, once he managed to pick up the trail of his fellows.

If curses were not so volatile, these days, he'd have cursed the power that scattered the Stepsons

over the land. The maelstrom had orphaned him.
He'd lost all his friends from the armies. . . .

No use evoking memories, or invoking hungry
forces that still might be searching for him through
the planeworlds.

Sniffling, he wiped his nose with the back of his
hand. He blinked, saw ghost-fingers doubling his
own, and blinked again. Then finally he sneezed.
That brought him to his senses.

There must be a cat in here, hiding somewhere in
this filthy hut, or a rat or a chicken. Or the wind had
blown in the hair of horses, or camels, or dogs.
"Blast," he sniffed, careful not to specify what he
wanted to blast.

But a little puff of smoke came up from the dirt in
front of him, as if a miniature explosion had deto-
nated before his eyes.

And another, to his left. A third, to his right.
"Stop!" he said, but it came out "Stob!" so stuffy was
his nose.

Randal had never been a poor adept, a minor
wizard. Ever since the maelstrom, he'd become even
stronger. But these strengths were a plague, slipping
their bonds at the odd moment.

He'd be asleep and he'd have a dream. The dream
would shake the house he'd rented, open all the
cupboards, and send pottery flying around the room
until the clatter and the shatter woke him.

Woe was a lonely, powerful wizard in a land where
almost no one did real magic. He was terrified that
someone might find out how talented (by local standards) he was, and hustle him off to serve the local
ruler, who was losing badly and desperate for help.

Randal had been on the losing side in one long
war. He didn't have any interest in serving the na-
tional interests of Shaga. He was only waiting for a
rumor of Stepsons to come his way and he'd be

off—in whatsoever direction rumor pointed, even if that meant Moriland.

Moriland, he'd heard, was even shorter on real wizardry than Shaga, but—

The soldier who'd left a coin and taken a number from Randal's box shoved his way past the old, natty rug into the little shaman's hut.

"Siddowd" said Randal, whose nose was still stuffy, "Make yourselv ad hobe." Blinking through watery eyes at the hulking soldier, he tried mightily to clear his head.

The burly man in nondescript helmet and leather was full-bearded, armed to the teeth, and filthy.

The smell made Randal's sinuses twitch as if he had a tic under his eye.

"You're the enchanter?" growled the man.

"I ab," Randal sniffled, and swiped at his nose again. "Stade your bidnis. Ad be quick aboud id." He snorted, and spat over his shoulder in disgust. Clear the nose; that was what counted.

This man probably wanted some rival of higher rank to contract a withering social disease to make his organ drop off before he touched a contested female again. This Fifth Army was as poor a bunch of fighters as Randal had ever seen.

The soldier peered out of his helmet at Randal. Its nosepiece shadowed his eyes and came down nearly over his lips. "Don't you recognize me, Randal?"

"I—Strad! *Strat!* Whad are you doing—"

"Same as you, I expect," said the mercenary, and held out a hamlike hand.

Randal's vision blurred again. This time, taking the big man's hand, he didn't try to dispel the blurriness. Strat and he had both been rightmen—partners, each sworn to a man who likewise swore to fight always on their left side. . . .

Strat pulled him close and hugged him, "You little rat. How have you been keeping?"

"*Achoo!* Well enough. I see you're in the cavalry again." The smell of horse was all over Straton. Randal wriggled out of the soldier's bear hug.

"And you've got another cold. Watch those drafts, Hazard."

No one had called Randal 'Hazard' in far too long. He was certainly a hazardously powerful wizard here, where power was in such short supply, but the term belonged to those other times and places Randal had sworn to forget.

"Strat," Randal said, "was it you who took a number from my box, on Duck Street? If it wasn't, we're about to be interrupt—"

"It was me, little brother. I need some kind of help."

That sobered Randal. Of course, Strat would. Strat had been sucked nearly dry by a vampirish creature whose power was far beyond Randal's. If *she'd* followed him here . . .

"Not troubles like . . . before?" Randal asked, his nose clearing entirely as fear sped his heart.

"No, not like before. I don't think." Strat took off his helmet and Randal could see the haunted eyes of the Stepson, three sets of circles under them like concentric bruises.

"What *do* you think, then?"

"Am I . . . accursed?"

"*What?*"

"Can you find out? If I'm cursed, presently? If something's . . . following me?"

Randal's hackles rose. He'd thought he was safe. He'd been sure of it. He sniffed deeply. About Straton hung no smell of witchery, not the faintest wisp.

"What kind of curse do you mean?"

"I'm having dreams with . . . Crit . . . the commander . . . you know—everything in them."

"No, I don't know, Strat. Tell me." Everything: witches, vampires, fiends, demons, devils?

"Here?" The tortured officer looked around. "Not here."

"Then where?"

"Your place?" The hope in Strat's voice made Randal want to comfort the other man somehow. But how, with Straton? Strat was partnerless in this place, this culture. So was he. They were veterans of the same holocaust. Better be careful. Emotion could blind him to something that Randal must try to see.

Strat hated magic. If Straton had come to a wizard, even Randal, then Straton was in deep trouble.

"Let's go, Stepson," Randal said, forgetful of how many memories the title evoked—for them both.

Strat put on his helmet. His face, within it, was unreadable. "In the dreams, they're looking for us. In the dreams, there's trouble. Woman trouble."

"Not—"

"Niko's sorceress. And Jihan . . . just like before." Critias's rightman headed for the rug-covered door.

"Nothing," Randal told Straton, "could be as bad as that was, before."

Randal wasn't sure he believed that, especially after he followed Strat outside and saw the horse.

Somehow, Straton still had the damned thing. The ghost horse. A gift from an inhuman lover. On the horse's withers was a patch that wasn't horseflesh. A patch like a tiny window into hell. Strat had loved that horse beyond measure. When it died, a creature who snacked on men's souls took pity on the soldier and brought his horse back to life—back from the grave.

But how did he have it here? Strat's bay was probably the most potent piece of witchcraft in all of Shaga. The big soldier swung up on the bay, who snorted and pricked its ears in Randal's direction. "Your place. Right away."

"I'll meet you there." Randal waved to the cavalry officer and went off on foot through Shaga's back streets. The mage who'd been the staff wizard of a cavalry unit still wasn't comfortable around horses. But he'd have swung up behind Strat on any other horse, just to prove he could.

When he got to his rented house, small and white-washed, Strat was waiting. The ghost horse was tied out front, as in days gone by. And, as in bygone days, the cavalryman waited in shadows, a crossbow under his arm.

"Strat, put that down." Randal used his wards to open the house, making a pass and muttering a key word. The peepers stopped peeping; the frogs fell silent. The shadows around the house changed from blue to black. Then all creatures resumed their nightsong, as if nothing had changed.

The bay snorted at the familiar smell of magic done and Randal preceded Strat inside, lighting lamps with a touch as he went.

Strat didn't remark at Randal's trick with fire and oil lamps. He threw himself on a blanket-covered couch and said, "We've got to find out if I'm cursed. And quick. Before my dreams start coming true."

"Dreams of women, Strat?" Strat would dream of women for a long time, perhaps forever. A woman soul-sucker had nearly made him into her undead lover. Only some shard of infernal compassion or unfathomable luck had saved Strat from a fate worse than his horse's.

"Dreams of—nothing." The big man shot to his feet. "I shouldn't have come. Just wanted to see an old friend. So I forgot: among Stepsons, I don't have any friends left."

"We all still love you, Strat. What's done's past and—hopefully—forgotten. If you're having dreams, then you've come to the right place." A sleeping potion ought to do it.

"No friends at all," the soldier muttered as if he hadn't heard a word Randal said, swaying uncertainly before him, a looming portent of destruction. If Strat came loose from his reason and decided that Randal's magic was at the root of his troubles, no wizardly spell would be quick enough, in these close confines, to keep Randal's head on his shoulders. The big mercenary's right hand was white on his sword hilt.

Battle fatigue wasn't something Randal usually treated with enchantment. But his usual client wasn't someone like Strat, who'd been waist-deep in maddeningly murderous sorcery and barely survived.

"Strat, I'm glad you're here. Good to see a fellow veteran. I didn't think I had any old friends left. I can't talk to any of these petty prestidigitators about what really matters. They don't know—"

"Don't know squat," Strat muttered. "Don't know which end is up . . ."

"They think they've got troubles. . . ." Randal talked as fast as he could, saying whatever came into his mind to soothe the distraught mercenary.

And slowly Strat sat back down, resting his head on his big fists and his elbows on his knees.

"I know what you mean," growled the bearded man finally, taking off his helmet. "There's nobody but us, who understands . . . what it was like. . . . Maybe we don't even understand."

"But we know what we need," Randal said softly. "Let's drink to found comrades." He'd give Strat a potion to assure one decent night's sleep. "You'll stay here, where my wards can protect you tonight. Tomorrow we can talk of other places we might—"

"Get out of here, yes. Before they find us."

"Who?" Randal had his hands on the blown-glass decanter full of multicolored quaff. It would put Strat out like a light. Better get him to a bed, first . . .

"The women. Those accursed women. I tell you, Randal, we need to talk, not sleep."

Randal poured out two portions of the potion. He could hold himself above the effect of the draught:

he'd made it a multipurpose potion, amenable to various spells; it created suggestibility in the client.

"Drink this," he told the Stepsons' officer.

Straton took it, watching Randal with narrowed eyes.

"And you, wizard?" Old suspicions died hard, even between veterans. Tempus's Stepsons had never been easy about having a sorcerer on staff. . . .

"Right here." Randal held up a glass, just like Strat's, and put it to his lips.

"Swap with me," said Straton.

Randal did, but said severely, between gulps, "Remember: *you* came to *me*, Stepson."

"I did. Because Niko's witch is in my damned dreams. You know: Roxane."

And Randal almost dropped his glass. Too late to close his ears. He said, "She's nothing. She's not a problem. She's penned up for eternity," because he himself needed to hear it: he hadn't yet tuned the potion.

Had drinking the untuned potion made him more vulnerable to Roxane than he was before he heard her name from Strat's lips? *Was* she free? And if she wasn't free, was this some trick from beyond the graves of hell to use Randal's wizardly powers to free her?

He sat down, hard. The potion could make you dizzy.

Strat said, "You look as though you've seen a ghost."

"Neither of us," he said severely, "will see any ghosts. No mage or witch, wizard or adept, fiend or demon will have any power over us. No necromant can call us to hell. No netherworld minions can reach up through the mud and drag us down. Nothing evil can touch us. Do you hear?" Having tuned the potion, Randal should feel relieved. He didn't. "Strat, say you hear."

"I hear," said Strat, smacking his lips. "And I like the sound of it. But I dreamed what I dreamed."

"What, exactly, did you dream?" With the invocation made, Randal could only follow the path of the conversation and hope that Strat would soon fall asleep. While the mercenary slept, Randal must conjure a ward for Strat—one strong enough to make truth out of all Randal's boasts.

In a state between waking and sleeping, Strat started telling Randal his dream: a dream of towers, fiery sunsets, and a sea where a monster lurked and Jihan swam. The dream had Tempus and his sister in it, plus all the Stepsons, even Niko. And Roxane, on the wing.

Somewhere during the telling, Strat and Randal both must have fallen fast asleep.

Because the dream was Randal's dream, and Roxane was in it. The Stepsons' mage would never forget those eyes rushing up straight from hell to stare at him.

The next thing Randal knew, a hand was shaking him. A familiar voice was saying, "You're right, commander. Both of them. Stoned, dead to the world."

Randal fought to open his eyes. "What now?" he heard.

Obviously, this was part of the dream, for it was Crit's voice. Critias was Straton's better half, Strat's leftside leader.

A voice (one Randal would know when his soul was old) answered, "Bring Randal. I'll carry Strat. And be careful with the mageling. Who knows what ties he has to this place."

Tempus!

Even in his dream, Randal was filled with joy. And with trepidation. Crit's voice said, "Anything you need, Randal? Talk to me, man. You can manage that."

"Strat's horse," Randal croaked in his dreamvoice. "You can't leave Strat's horse."

And a dream-Crit swore to raise the dead, saying, "I'd like to kill that horse. But it wouldn't stay dead, would it? You hear that, Commander?"

In his dream, Randal was leading them outside, through the wards again, because Tempus himself came to him, lifted Randal's eyelids, and asked it.

Outside, the dream-bay snorted and stamped as first Straton, then Randal, was boosted onto its back.

Then a dream-Tempus led the horse, with Crit on its far side steadying Randal's rump, right into nothingness.

Randal saw the figure of his commander disappearing; then Crit and the horse's forequarters disappearing; then lastly, Straton, right ahead of him on the horse, disappearing—before Randal himself disappeared.

And since he had disappeared, it was clear to Randal that the dream was ending. He could go back to sleep, begin another dream.

If this dream had continued, it might have had Tempus's women in it. Randal wanted to dream a dream free of accursed women.

But before he could embark upon a different dream, Randal heard himself sneeze and a woman's voice say, "Wouldn't you know they'd both be drunk as the dead?"

The voice belonged to Cime, Tempus's mage-killing sister! This dream was too silly to be an omen. Relieved, he drifted into a blessedly dreamless sleep where there was a soft bed under him and silken covers over him and fine walls around him, just the way there should be in a dream.

Not since he'd left the mageguild had Randal slept in so fine a dream, or so fine a bed, or so fine a palace. Randal decided that—even if Strat had somehow managed to incapacitate them both and, while they were senseless, the witch Roxane had ensorceled them—he'd stay right here, in this dream, where the beds were comfy and the pillows didn't make his nose itch.

He was wizard enough to do that much, at least, even if he hadn't been able to save Straton from whatever fate had in store.

Chapter 4:

BIRDS OF A FEATHER

Cyrus was fighting alone against a maddened horde of humans when he felt the touch of something . . . hungry above his head.

A shadow flitted over his face. Despite the men who cast sharp javelins at him and shook their fists, Cyrus looked up.

A bird, wings spread wide, circled overhead. This bird reminded him of a manta. Abruptly the world in which he was wandering was not so strange: a bird upon the air made the air like the ocean.

The ocean had depths, many currents, many ways to travel and live—not just the bottom. These men who were harassing him had backed him onto a precipice, and there Cyrus was making his stand, in the way of a man.

At his back was a rock, and beyond that rock was nothingness—a drop to more rocks, below.

All he had done was eat a bull in a field. The bull had been garlanded with white flowers on its neck. It had sported colored streamers on its horns. Its cloven hooves were gilded. Why shouldn't he have eaten it? It was obviously prepared for feasting—let loose as a sacrifice to the gods.

Was he not, in terms these humans understood, such a god? Was his grandfather not Stormbringer? Was his mother not the Froth Daughter, Jihan?

Yet they had come chasing him, and he had run from them, confused and frightened.

This eagle above Cyrus's head was not frightened. The eagle was hungrily enjoying everything. Cyrus could feel her pleasure. As if she was sucking up the energy of the dying men in the horde.

Too many men in that horde were not dying to suit Cyrus. And all were pelting him with stones and throwing sharp javelins. If he weren't so frightened, perhaps he would have realized what to do earlier.

But he had been frightened. He had run from the men, when they wouldn't listen to reason. He had said that the bull was his, a due and lawful sacrifice, and tried to thank them for it. But they were angry. They didn't want the bull to be dead. And when he restablished it with life in it, they were angrier still.

He couldn't very well put back the real life he had eaten, or the bites he had taken from its haunches, or its stomach or its entrails. All he could do was make it get up and walk. And he had done that, to give the people a miracle, so that they would acknowledge him as a good and honorable lord for their accursed town.

Instead of bowing down before him, they had screamed. Cyrus thought perhaps it was because of the woman that they were angry with him—the priestess of the bull, who had been part of the sacrifice.

Too late now to worry about that. Before him were wide eyes filled with bloodlust and wide mouths filled with curses. Javelins pricked him like thistles on the wind. And above were the wings, circling.

Cyrus pushed back against the rock and closed his eyes, arms over his face. His brow furrowed and a horrible wailing began to come from him.

The wails of pain were impossible to quell. All over him, he was pricked from javelins, but that was not what hurt: changing his body hurt.

Sprouting wings from his shoulder blades and ribs

hurt. Sprouting feathers for the wings hurt like a thousand javelins.

He was screaming so loudly that he couldn't hear the mob any longer, only the noise from his own throat. He would soar on the air as if he were swimming in the sea. Up, around, back and forth. The world of vicious men would be far below. The precipice would be a launching point.

And he would have a friend to play with in the currents of the air.

When he opened his eyes, he realized that the men had stopped yelling at him. They were not as close as they had been before, either. They were all down upon their knees and only some few were looking at him.

Good. He should have done this before.

He staggered upright, stumbling as he sought his balance on two legs with a pair of huge wings sprouting from him as well as arms.

He pinwheeled his arms and his wings beat as if they knew how to fly already.

One wingtip hit the ground and he screeched.

This screech was high-pitched and an answering screech came down from heaven. Good: the bird was still up there, making eagle's circles in the heavens.

One of the men screamed hoarsely, "Look! Look!" and raised a hand.

Cyrus didn't flinch from an expected javelin. He was running toward the precipice, full-out. His wings were stretched wide on either side, catching the air.

He felt the down draft on his back and wings; he felt the lift currents catch his wings' forward edge. His legs pushed against the ground as hard and fast as he could run. His run soon turned into a bounding stride that synchronized with the beat of his wings.

Beat. Run. Left. Right. Up. Down. Beat. Push. Beat. Push. Beat. Beat. Push. Beat. Beat. Beat. . . .

His feet didn't touch the ground. His lungs labored, as the new muscles twisted his ribs. His arms hugged his sides, and his hands worked strangely.

But he was aloft. He was aloft and he cried in joy. He could see the crowd below and he had an inarguable need to swoop down over them. As he did, his bladder prompted him, and he sprayed them from above.

The bloody cuts all over him were drying in the high, cold wind of his flight.

He heard a cry, and another. Then he remembered the eagle. She was waiting for him. He angled his arms and legs and arched his forepinions. Cyrus soared upward, feeling each beat of his mighty wings like beats of his huge heart.

Up he went, and up—not straight, but spiraling toward the eagle in the sky.

The eagle, too, was spiraling heavenward. And then she seemed to hover, right before the sun, a dot of taunt and welcome.

He sped toward her, his throat making hoarse calls that belonged to the air. He loved this flying. He loved the air currents, so like sea currents. He loved having up and down at his disposal.

And he loved seeing the frightened folk below scatter as his shadow would pass over them.

He should have realized before how foolish it was to appear to humans as a human—they detested and disrespected each other, and had no regard for strangers. He climbed through white clouds as cold and wet as his grandfather's heart.

If Mother could see him now! Just as he burst out of the clouds and saw the eagle's great golden eye staring at him, she dove.

She tucked her wings about her and plummeted toward earth so fast that Cyrus nearly tumbled as he tried to hover and watch.

Was she falling? Had the she-eagle been hit by

some flying missile? But no, the humans couldn't throw their javelins so high in the air.

Her screech came back to him, thin and reedy.

A game, was this? He furled his own pinions, his arms clutching his thighs, and dove after her. The sound of the wind rushing past was a roar louder than anything he'd ever heard. Then it was silent. He fell through a silent space so great it seemed as though he wasn't falling at all, just floating. If his eyes were not whipped nearly dry by the wind, he'd have believed he was floating.

The dot below him raced ahead.

As the ground sped up to meet them, the dot suddenly sprouted wings again. The eagle stopped in midair and screeched, then shot off toward the setting sun.

Cyrus spread his wings wide, too fast. Pain wracked him. His ribs nearly cracked. His wings nearly tore the skin from his chest. He tumbled. He fell straight down, spinning, trying to control his wings and his descent.

One wing half out, the other closer to his body, he stopped his spin. He did a full overhead loop, and at the top of it, he straightened. He could just see the dot of the eagle, racing away.

Level, with lift under his wings and fury in his heart, Cyrus began chasing the eagle as fast as he could.

When he caught her, he was going to teach her what it meant to flout a living god.

Chapter 5:

SANDIA BOUND

"We go now. Tomorrow," Tempus said implacably to his sister, who sat among the gathered fighters as if she were one of them. He pointed to the Lemurian windows in the great hall, each set in a pillar with dials beneath to focus them on where and when he willed.

Almost anywhere and anywhen. He hadn't been able to find Niko's locus with the Lemurian windows. Something was keeping the magic of Lemuria's portals from reuniting Tempus with his lost fighter. And Cime knew it.

"What about dear, sweet Niko, brother?" she said, in front of all his Stepsons, as if they were alone. 'You know you can't leave without your pet soldier." Cime was as aware as he of what she was doing.

"You'll stay behind, sister, till Niko comes, and direct him to us when he arrives."

That shut her mouth, if only briefly. But silencing Cime was the least of Tempus's problems. His sister was as much the owner of Pinnacle House and its temporal portals as he. And as much to blame for the sorry state of all these rescued fighters.

"Me and who else, Tempus? Surely you don't expect Niko to make it here on his own, when none of these could." Cime shook her dark hair and waved a hand at the assembled fifty fighters as if they were her courtiers—or her audience.

"You, and Kama will stay here. Randal and Straton will find Niko, with your inimitable help—" He grinned nastily. "And then you'll send them on. As we agreed."

They hadn't, but no one knew that. Cime didn't want any of these Stepsons in her wondrous palace. They reminded her of who and what Tempus was. And she didn't like that. Her nesting instinct was out of control in Lemuria. She thought, for some reason he couldn't understand, that he was going to stay here and hold wool for her while she knitted.

There was only one cure for such fantasies of luxurious indolence: a mission. Sandia, where he'd long wanted to go anyway, was drawing him like a magnet.

The band was nearly reconstituted. Once they'd sortied to Sandia on his behalf, Cime could no longer argue that they had no rights in Lemuria. Lemuria had servants, guards, citizens, dogs; it needed a fighting force such as the Stepsons' Sacred Band. He'd said all this to Cime, but she wouldn't listen.

Nothing new about that. He'd told her to work some magic on Kama that would turn his daughter into a woman, from a frustrated camp follower trying to become a man, but she hadn't done that either. Living with the woman of your dreams can become a nightmare. He'd always known that. It was why he'd waited so long to try it.

And now, Cime was purposely trying to spook his men. She knew very well that among the Stepsons, there was still great uneasiness. A fool could see it. Gayle, swarthy and solid, drank concertedly, not saying a word, near the fireplace, a dog he'd found outside nuzzling his knee. Straton, much the worse for wear and so big that none could fail to notice, kept staring around at the walls of glass, at the fabulous hearth and the balls of unflickering, heatless light, rubbing his arms as if he were cold.

Strat's partner, Critias, was alone on the other side of the room, his arms crossed, eyes downcast.

Eyes averted from Kama, rather. Kama had dressed like a man for this meeting, never content to be what she was, bristling with combative possessiveness of the Lemurian kingdom and all its power.

And Randal, the flop-eared, freckled mage who'd fought wizard wars with this band, was sitting by himself in the room's one empty corner, curled in a chair, pale as a ghost and biting his lip.

Not one of the Stepsons said a word to Tempus about who would go and who would stay, not even Kama. Not a good temper for the beginning of a sortie. But then, Cime had set the tone. In her eyes, if you were not slaying sorcerers, you were playing war games. All that mattered to her were the great battles. She cared not one whit to see how the Shepherd of Sandia was faring, having gone home from Lemuria with a boon secured last season.

In fact, keeping Cime out of Sandia was probably the only good thing to come out of this evening's meeting. Tempus said, "Dismissed. We leave at sunup. Crit knows what you'll need for provisioning. Any special requests, come to me before morning."

They were feting the newly reunited band in the big dining room. It bothered Tempus still that, whenever they needed many servants, as they did tonight, those servants appeared but the dogs were fewer. Cime said the servants came up from the town. He'd never seen anyone in the town who resembled half of these servants.

But there was one dog, a big bitch, he'd come to like, even though dogs were unclean by his custom. This bitch had taken to sleeping in the stable near his horse's stall, as if she were guarding the herd brought here from Hidden Valley.

As the men dispersed, Tempus went to the great window, thrice his height, and stared down at the drop to the sea. Any who needed to talk to him would find him, as the night wore on.

He was content to have them here. All of his true obligations were now discharged . . . except for Niko. And all he'd found out about Niko was that Niko no longer resided in the city at the edge of time.

Finding out even that much had taught him something else: the Lemurian windows were not infallible. This disturbed him as much as his missing fighter did. You could say that Niko, of all men, was not Tempus's responsibility. But Lemuria undoubtedly was. He had received the stewardship of this place from the former Evening Star, whom Cime had succeeded. From Lemuria, the fates of all the civilizations of time could be changed. A man and woman here, he'd come to understand, undertook the most proper stewardship: a couple was more than any single man or woman could be.

What a man knows and what woman knows both were necessary to administering the magical technology that made Lemuria the place where errors of time itself could be erased, and grievances redressed. No man or woman alone could bring to bear the special wisdom needed; half had been given to men, and the other to women, by the knowledgable gods. Only the merging of both could steer Lemuria's course, and thus eternity's.

He wished it were not so, but the truth was clear to him. So, if he did not have a wife, he had a partner. And if he did not have a lover, he had a mate. He and Cime had always been two halves of a certain coin.

Since it was the coin of conflict, he hoped that, together, they could become more: the coin of tolerance, of survival, or progress. For a god-ridden soldier and a sorcerer-killing harlot, this was rather a lot to ask of heaven.

But he would try. He had begun this undertaking,

and he would finish it, if it took his whole extended lifetime—even though he'd had no idea, at the outset, what caretaking Lemuria could come to mean.

"An unmentionable for your thoughts, Riddler," said his sister's husky voice, behind him. Forever would she tease him, and forever would he rise to her bait. The responsibility of Lemuria had not changed that.

"I was thinking that we're not doing very well with our first venture," he said, to irritate her. "I'd hoped you'd learned enough about Lemurian secrets to bring the whole band back together, not just part."

"*Part*?" she flared. She was the most beautiful woman, to his eyes, that creation had ever fashioned. Her eyes were full of storm, her skin was pale, her limbs more shapely than any he'd ever beheld. For years they'd thought they were blood relations, and suffered wizards' curses and their own because of it. Now, knowing they were not, only the god in Tempus's head and the mage-killer in hers kept them at arm's length. "Part? I brought your band, all but one, plus the mageling, Randal—and your obnoxious daughter, to boot. I'd say that's mastering the secrets."

Behind her, the men were filing into the dining hall. Only Randal hadn't risen. The little mage looked as if someone had taken all the stuffing out of him and sewed him back together carelessly, leaving something undone.

Then Tempus, looking over Cime's head, saw Straton, who looked little better. "What about those two? Can you do anything for them?"

She followed his gaze: "The mageling and Straton are both lovesick, Riddler. You should know the signs by now: Randal's pining for his Niko, fearing all sorts of wizardly intervention."

"Which might be real enough. Even you can't say there is no magic at work, blocking the windows."

"More likely," Cime sniffed, "your god Enlil's jealousy: your god doesn't want your favorite boy here any more than most of the rest of us do. And as for Straton: talk to your daughter, before you go, leaving me with your lame and halt. If she'd stop torturing Critias, who can't please someone who wants the impossible, then Straton and Crit could make a pair again."

"You think that's it?" Sacred Band fighters paired; it was tradition. Randal's pairbond was to Nikodemos; Straton's was to Critias. Kama was unbound to any man, because she was so determined to be one she couldn't find a friend under heaven.

"Take Kama with you, Riddler. We'll fare better looking for Niko without her. She hates him almost as much as she hates Strat, because of you."

"We will do it as I decreed it."

"Why? Because you *said* it? Your word is law, now? Aren't we taking ourselves a bit seriously, this season? These are people you have here, Riddler, not horses."

"I'm taking Crit. Kama needs your tutelage."

"Kama needs yours. She doesn't see any value in womanhood." Cime's tack changed, and with it the look in her eyes. "Come upstairs with me before dinner and I'll remind you where some of that value lies." She touched his face.

The union of their bodies, so long denied them, was Cime's answer to every dispute between them. And sometimes it solved things—for a while. Always, it was an indisputable ecstasy. "A man can die of indolence and pleasure."

"Not as easily as he can die of stubborness and arrogance," she said, and thumped him on the chest. "Come to your mercenary table then. Enflame your fighters with tales of derring-do and sorcery met, of battles won and comrades lost. I think I'll take a tray up to my room."

But in the end, she came to his table and hosted

the feast, as the Evening Star was meant to do.

And he was proud of her, casting covert glances upon her willowy form, and thinking there was nothing the Shepherd of Sandia could do for him—really— that Cime could not . . . except idolize him, respect him unwontedly, and make him feel like a child's vision of a man.

Sometimes Cime could see the future, he knew, without the help of Lemurian windows. Tonight, did she see it? She was subdued whenever she looked Randal's way, or Straton's, or Kama's. Did she want him to change his mind to protect those he'd so recently gathered to him?

Cime wouldn't tell him if he asked, so he didn't ask. He presided over his table, and the roasts of lamb and pork, and goose. And he offered libations to the gods, starting with Enlil, the Storm God, patron of the armies.

When that was done, they ate and drank until the moon was high, and everyone found something to laugh about but Kama, who was glowering at him the whole time.

So he took his daughter away from the table and said, "What is it, Kama? This is a night for celebrating."

"I . . . keep trying to be perfect," she said, and he realized she was drunk. "For you. So you'll notice me. Value me. I'm as good as Niko. I'm as much a fighter as any of your men."

"But you're one of my women. I want woman's wisdom from—"

And she slapped him, hard, across the face, and stomped away.

She was simply aching for what could not be had, unless Enlil would grant her a set of late-growing organs. And that would be a shame.

He shook his head and started back into the dining hall when he saw Cime, with her hand on Kama's

arm, leading her off toward their rooms. Just then
Crit came up to him: "Sir?"

"Critias?" Crit had been the most competent first
officer ever to serve under Tempus's command. If he
wasn't embroiled with Kama too deeply, he might
still be.

"Kama—she really thinks she'd be more use, with
us, in Sandia, than here—"

"And what do you think, Critias?"

"I think . . ." Crit sighed and squinted at Tempus,
rubbing his dark jaw. His features were fine and
regular, his gaze usually as clear as water. But not
tonight. "I need some time with Straton, if I need
any of them. But . . ." He sighed. "I guess you're
right. We'll do better—I will—without internal problems, at least until we get our bearings."

"And when will that be?"

"Commander, what do you think we're facing
there?"

"In Sandia? A good time, fighter. Only that. A
little policing, perhaps, but it's primarily a diplo-
matic mission: we're going visiting."

"We're all ready for that. If that's really all, we can
leave within the hour."

"At sunup will do. It's the way of it here. Go into
your room, have a night's sleep. In the morning,
when you wake, take all your men and gear to the
stables. When you bring your horses out at sunup,
you'll ride into Sandia. Don't take anything—or
anyone—you don't want with you."

They'd done it before. But Tempus didn't blame
Crit for being leery of the process: you stepped out
of your room or your barn in the morning, into
exactly wherever you'd determined to go. So far, it
had worked every time. But Tempus and Cime were
still learning the ways of Lemuria, and they were
alone here with no guide but what Cime guessed and

Tempus remembered from his tutelage under the previous Evening Star.

"That's clear, sir. I'll make sure everybody's on time. Can I tell them, then, we're going visiting, and that's all?"

"Tell them what you will, Critias. We're going visiting."

"Yes sir—visiting."

Crit, as he left, looked back askance over one shoulder. Tempus had never led Critias into anything less than a life-threatening situation in all their years together.

Nor would Tempus say for certain that this would be any different. He could hope. But all he could know for sure was that, in Sandia, he'd be away from Cime and Kama and the everpresent dogs.

So Tempus didn't blame Crit for assuming that there was something he wasn't telling, something the band didn't need to know.

Perhaps the fact that this visiting party was uninvited qualified as such a something. Perhaps it didn't. When they got to Sandia, they'd know for sure. Learning to control the Lemurian windows was the most important part of this journey: successfully going and coming, on a schedule, without incident.

To do that, you had to get up before dawn, saddle your horse, and ride into the sunrise. There just wasn't any other way.

Chapter 6:

TRAIL OF TEARS

Cyrus's trail wasn't hard to follow: he had left a track of destruction and tears across the land.

Up the coast Jihan went, ever faster, always more disturbed when she left a place than when she'd entered it. Each time she'd come upon a town, the Froth Daughter would think: *Here I'll find him. Here he'll be. I'll spank him until he's blue and he'll cry remorseful tears. Then I'll forgive him, and his tears will change to tears of joy and repentance. He'll hang his head and take my hand and we'll wade together back into the sea. All will be well, once I have him in my arms. And Stormbringer will be chastened, after so long without us both.*

Thus cheered, she would ride into this town or that on a sea horse she'd cajoled into the image of a real horse, dressed in her scale armor, with her burnished shield over one arm and her heart in her mouth.

But Cyrus never would be where she ventured. He'd always just departed, or be well gone. All that she'd see was the destruction in his wake. All she'd hear in the taverns and the inns were awful stories of his depredations.

If she'd been a human mother, she might have blushed, or wept, or put her head on her arms and confessed to having spawned him.

But she was no human woman. She was the Froth Daughter, a power in her own right with dominion over cold and water. She held her head high in the midst of her son's carnage, and listened, one hand on her armored hip, to the red-eyed townsfolk spew their tales of woe.

If her son was as bad as they made him out, then death and destruction would surely be his lot. But these folk had sullen months and filthy bodies and worse minds. They grew lies in their heads as profuse as the lice in their hair: these were the people of the shoals, and they worshipped anything that brought them comfort.

Some tried to worship Jihan, riding out of the surf in her armor, auburn hair streaming behind her and the sun glinting off her copper skin. Others tried to hire her, to protect them from the "horrid, white-skinned demon": her son.

Money talked in these parts, and what it said reminded Jihan of the days when she'd lived among men.

Every town she visited, she quit within the day. Some man would try to make her a talisman of his power, or hire her, or—when all else failed—get her drunk and bed her, just to show he could.

She'd craved that very thing, when she was younger, above all else. She'd come to walk the earth on special dispensation for a year, to start. All she'd wanted then was to be a human woman—feel love, and connection with the earth; understand the impenetrable ways of men, who ruled it, and rule them in her turn with her beauty and her wiles.

She'd wanted her belly filled up and her life made real, as men knew life. Because they fought so to keep it. Because they feared so to lose it. Because, she'd once thought, anything worth so much misery must be better than all the powers of the gods: to be human, to know tears, to know transporting joy and even sickening fear.

She still loved the feel of human skin against her almost-human skin, the feel of a horse between her knees, the wind on her cheeks, and her hair blowing free about her head.

So, if life as humans led it still enthralled her, how could she blame her son for wanting to live it? After all, he was half man, and she was not. The earth and dominion over it was in his blood, a gift from his father's side; the love of it and longing for it was in his heart, from her side.

So the fault in Cyrus's actions was half hers, and half his father's. Wasn't it?

She hadn't seen Tempus for far too long. But she couldn't go to him saying, "Your son has escaped his prison under the sea and gone raiding among men, killing them like cattle." How could she?

Tempus had never wanted to give her a child. She had tricked and wheedled and nagged and, finally, bargained the seed out of him. Had he known it would come to this? He was not like other humans; a god resided in him.

If not for Tempus's meddling god, Enlil, she'd never have borne Cyrus in the first place. Enlil had taken her side in the matter of her child. For all she knew, the child was Enlil's, not Tempus's.

The thought eased her, as she rode a lonely trek up the wild coast, looking for her errant boy. Telling Tempus he'd been right and she'd been wrong was something Jihan couldn't bring herself to do. At least Cyrus was nowhere near his father's stomping grounds. She must find him and stop his raiding before word sped across the land to Tempus's ear, and Cyrus's father came hunting him with the whole Sacred Band behind.

On she urged her seahorse, who hated his new legs and his hairy mane and his long, soft tail, and wanted to go back to the sea. On she urged herself, having remembered enough of what it was like to be a woman to carry on.

Womanhood had a magic to it, and this drew her onward as it had drawn her out of the sea once before, so long ago. The natural woman knew a oneness with the universe that nothing else shared. She was creative and ontologically complete, as nothing else was. Jihan had seen this in the eyes of human women when they cavorted in bright pools with their sisters. She'd felt it in the sea when a woman coupled with a man there and the ecstasy traveled through the depths like whalesong.

This day, she would find her son. She could feel it in her human bones. She went into the town and tied her horse at the local inn, to ask of him.

Inside, she heard tales of a god come to earth, demanding sacrifices, killing bulls and men, and then turning into a great winged bird and flying away, toward the west.

It could be none other than Cyrus. But, a bird? Flying, was he? Jihan couldn't have done such a thing. But then, who knew what special skills his father's blood had given his hybrid flesh? Or Enlil's favor? The Storm God was certainly whispering in the boy's ear, judging from his bloodlust and his kills so far.

She was careful, in the tavern, to appear only modestly curious. Softly, she asked her questions: "What was he like? How tall? How wide? What did he say? Was his face beautiful? How old was he? Are you sure he turned into a bird? How big? Where did it go, exactly? Was he hurt on the precipice? Was a wounded bird what you saw in the sky?"

A hand fell on her shoulder. She didn't flinch. She prepared to defend herself. Sometimes drunken men ignored all the warrior accouterments upon her person and took her for a traveling whore. Ready to gut the intruder, or freeze his blood in his veins if she must, she turned.

"Randal!" Jihan gasped, and then wasn't sure the freckled face belonged to an old friend, after all.

"Jihan," said the wizard. "A piece of luck, finding you here. Come sit with us." The wizard was haggard and drawn; his cloak was dusty, yet his eyes and voice were clear. Every lineament of his modest person screamed urgency, controlled, and power, fielded.

Jihan took her drink and left the bar, following the wizard to a corner, thinking that Randal wasn't as scrawny or as funny as she remembered him, from the old days when she'd ridden with the Stepsons' leader.

In the corner, she knew she'd fallen in with fate: there was Straton, huge and solid as mankind's hold on the very earth.

Then Strat looked up and his eyes were as tortured as Jihan's soul. The big, wide face was set in stolid planes. It was the face of one enduring the unendurable.

She sat. "Straton," said the Froth Daughter tenderly, and took his rough, callused hand. "Seeing you is a joy that warms me." Her voice said more; she couldn't help it. She was a woman in form, and woman's love for man came with woman's flesh.

"Too soon for a party, Jihan. We're looking for Niko. Not having much luck. Want to help?"

Randal would have taken all night to ask the question. The mage sat heavily beside the soldier, blushing. "Jihan, for old times' sake—we need your counsel."

"I, too," said the Froth Daughter, "seek someone." What would Tempus say, when he heard? For now he surely would. No chance of finding Cyrus and keeping his story quiet, not with Tempus's men right here.

Yet instinct had drawn her here like a suicidal moth. And she trusted this body of hers, attuned to its place. They wanted her power. She would bargain it: "Help me, without a word to anyone, and my aid is yours in finding Niko."

Nikodemos was a curse to these fighters, one who asked too much of himself and everyone around him. But finding Niko was simple: all she had to do was send these two to the city at the edge of time, which moved about the earth and was sometimes inaccessible to mere mortals. But never to Jihan. So she smiled, and added: "Bargain?"

Both the Stepsons smiled, clasping hands with her in the way of the armies, and repeated: "Bargain."

So it was agreed. And so, now, it would be done.

But on the way outside, Straton said, "We've tried everything. The commander's lost track of Niko since he quit the city."

And Randal added: "Even the Lady Cime, with all her skills, can't find him."

"Not at the city at the edge of time?" This would be more complex than Jihan had expected. "Then seek him in a dream. He has a dream place, Niko does. And the dream lord will help us. Tempus wouldn't try that."

No, her beloved Tempus wouldn't try the dream lord, or seek anything in sleep. He didn't sleep. Couldn't sleep. His enemies still roamed the land of dreams.

Coming out onto the street, Strat said, "I'll get my horse." And left them.

"Where are we going, in the middle of the night?" Jihan wanted to know.

"We've no time to spare," Randal said. "Up the coast, I think. I've asked around, here and there. I think Niko's wherever this disruption is."

Disruption: her son. "Disruption?" she remarked casually. "You mean the young god hereabouts?"

"Whatever it is, yes. But I think it's a witch, playing games."

"Not *that* witch," Jihan said, and her skin grew cold under her armor.

"So I fear. What else could have brought a bull to life and paraded it about the fields, entrails dragging? Or disemboweled a priestess?"

Jihan knew what else could have done those things, but she didn't argue. Fate and instinct had led her to human helpers. She would explain, when the time came, that no witch was at the heart of this. If thinking there was one made these men ride night and day, then fine.

Jihan needed to find Cyrus before he was found by witch-hunters she didn't know and couldn't influence. Even Cyrus could die here, while in human form, if fate took a hand.

Only his father was deathless among men. But neither Tempus nor she could do what these folk said they'd seen: change shape on the spot and fly off upon the air.

What was her son, that she had spawned? And what evil fate brought Niko into this? The secular adepts of the misty isles thrived where nature was out of balance.

There was nothing imbalanced about Cyrus. He was just young. Just a boy. Just lonely for his father. Just . . . trying his wings?

When Strat brought the horses around, Jihan recognized his and hissed involuntarily. Witchcraft on the hoof. The gods hated witchcraft. Jihan's folk were no exception.

Men were not meant to wield such power; they usurped the gods' places, and only evil came of it.

Jihan's seahorse looked at the undead horse and whickered loudly, in the way of a land horse. Sea spume frothed at its mouth.

The undead horse looked at the seahorse as if

recognizing something quite as unnatural as itself, and pawed the ground.

Jihan swung into her saddle. "Well, Randal, you're the one who scents magic best. Lead on."

And Randal, with a sniff and sneeze, mounted his unmagical horse and trotted ahead. So they were three, riding north and west out of that sorry little town, single file: Jihan, in the middle, with enchantment before her and enchantment behind—toward Cyrus, wherever he might be, on the wings of eagles; and toward Niko, the best and worst of the Stepsons.

Chapter 7:

SET FOOT IN SANDIA

Crit's horse was wheezing. All around, the sand-storm raged.

"Commander!" Through its vicious gale, he yelled to the big shadow he could barely see, though Tempus's horse was so close to his that the Riddler's right knee brushed his left whenever one of the horses slid in the sand.

"Riddler, we've got to stop! Rest the horses. Water them."

"Not yet, Crit. Ride a little longer," came the commander's hoarse voice on the moaning wind.

A little longer. How long had it been? Crit had lost track. Tempus didn't tire like the Stepsons. Even his horse, a Tros, was unnatural in stamina and endurance. The rest of them were . . .

Men and horses, lost in a sandstorm in a feature-less land. Parched and abraded, tasting blood and blister serum from blackened lips. Hawking sand and more blood from their lungs.

For his horse's sake, if not his own, Crit tried again: "You call this a good time, Riddler? You call this 'visiting'?" Crit's voice, cracked, nearly gave out. His throat was so sore that talking hurt. Sand seemed to be sliding around inside him, choking him.

Holding his ribs, Crit coughed until little lights danced before his eyes, bent low over his saddle.

The horse stumbled, but recovered on its own before Crit had wit enough to help it with his reins. Visiting *what*, here? Their deaths? Eternity?

Tempus might be tired of living. The band had no home any longer, just Lemuria, wherever that was, lost in the sandstorm behind. Maybe Tempus was leading them out into the desert to die, rather than desert them. A man got strange in a single lifetime as harsh and bloody as theirs had been. How much worse could an immortal's mind be twisted, century after century, watching his comrades die?

Again, Crit's horse stumbled.

This time, he had the presence of mind to pull up on his reins and use his weight to help the horse. But it went to its knees anyway.

Crit's left foot hit the ground. His right slid out from under the horse reflexively. He stood, for a moment, straddling his horse who lay in the sand, its legs half folded under it.

He could see the dark shadow of Tempus's Tros, moving off through the sandstorm.

Decided, he yelled, "Riddler! I'm stopping here."

Behind Crit, he could make out Gayle's horse's ears, twitching in the murk.

The Riddler didn't answer, or make any sign that he'd heard, just kept moving.

Scrambling to his horse's off side, Crit got out his water skin and the horse's nosebag. You didn't let your mount die, or ride it till it dropped.

Let Tempus go on without him. He took a strip of his jerkin and wet it, wiping the sand and mucus from his horse's eyes, its nostrils. If they'd had cloth to spare, he would have made the horse a hood. It might have helped. He sponged the beast's wrinkly lips, and a tongue coated with sand poked out, questing for the moisture.

Good. His horse was going to be all right. It must be.

Gayle said, "Taking a little rest, Critias? A frogging fool place to do it, if you ask me."

"Go around me, Gayle," Crit suggested raspingly. "When my horse is rested, we'll catch up."

Sand showered him. He looked around.

The Tros towered above him, its eyes seeming to glow where nothing mortal shined.

From its back, Tempus said, "We'll wait, Gayle."

So Tempus wouldn't leave him, after all.

At least, not yet. Not to die alone where all could see.

Still on his knees, Crit looked up at the mounted shadow of his commander in the storm. "Why are you doing this?"

"To visit Sandia, I told you." The deep voice rustled like shifting sand.

Then something came flying through the air and Crit lunged reflexively to catch it.

A full waterskin, after so long trekking. It was impossible.

"Camp, if you must. Water all the horses. But get that one up, and keep the others on their feet. If they lie down, they might be buried alive."

And the shape receded.

Gayle slid off his horse and came to the rump of Crit's: "Ready?"

"Let me give him the water first."

Once the horse had had a little water, Crit roped its rump and slid the rope through his saddle rings, then took its head. With Gayle pushing from behind as if he were pushing a mired wagon, they tried to right the horse.

Crit pulled on his head. Gayle pushed on his rump. They had him halfway up and he fell back.

And then the commander was there again, on foot.

"I'll take his head, Crit," said Tempus.

And somehow, with Tempus at his muzzle, the horse lunged upward in an explosion of limbs and sand and then stood, legs spread wide, snorting and heaving. The awful growl a horse's belly makes when it's riled echoed in Crit's ears.

"We can . . . go on now, I guess," said Critias.

"Take your rest, Stepson," said Tempus as he disappeared into the sand, toward the darker shadow of the Tros horse who needed no water.

Gayle's horse put its head in the shelter of Crit's mount's rump, and switched its tail angrily. The two men, head to head, nearly leaned on one another.

"Do you think he's lost?" Gayle wanted to know.

"I don't know," Crit admitted. And almost said he'd rather be lost than engaged in ritual mass suicide. But then loyalty reasserted itself: "You've seen too much to be short on faith. Whatever this is, he knows what he's doing."

It sounded quavery, but it was the right thing to say.

This place was a hellish expanse where nothing grew and no sky was ever seen. What was here, that Tempus wanted? Nothing lived here, it seemed. Nothing at all.

The Tros snorted, up ahead. And then rumbled. But no, it wasn't a horse rumbling. It was the earth's.

Or the sky's. Or both.

The sky, which Crit assumed on faith was there, somewhere above the curtains of sand, turned dark. The sand blowing in it scudded like snow against the darkness.

Gayle's horse screamed a belly-shaking neigh, head up, nostrils flared.

Then Crit's horse raised its weary head and trumpeted to heaven.

"Earthquake?" Gayle muttered under his breath.

And then the world cracked open. Thunder roared down the desert, shaking it. Everything shocked white, then blacker than before.

"Lightning!" Crit yelled over the thunder. The Storm God Enlil had not forsaken them.

Up ahead, in a second bolt's bright light, Crit saw the Riddler, on his Tros horse, who was walking hind-legged, pawing at the sky.

Rain came soon after, on a cold wet wind. Despite the chill and the driving rain that was half mud at first, the horses stretched out their necks and closed their eyes and opened their mouths.

Crit's fairly licked its lips with its tongue.

And then, as quickly as it had come, the storm abated.

In its wake, before Crit's astonished eyes, green grass started to sprout. And flowers. Growth came up out of the sand as he watched. Cactus bloomed. Wildflowers unfurled lavender petals.

And tiny frogs began to hop around his feet.

Critias was so enthralled by what he saw, and the task of keeping his horse from gobbling too much of the quick-sprouting grass that sprung up at their feet, he forgot about the commander altogether.

Forgot until he heard, "Mount up!"

The order had him in his saddle before he thought about it.

Gathering his reins, Crit finally looked beyond his horse's feet.

And saw a sight that took his breath away: the whole desert floor was green and gold and pink with hungry desert flora, reaching for moisture.

Crit licked his own lips, scrubbed his face with his hand, and sneezed. Blinked. And stared.

Tempus was waving them on, toward a portal that had opened in the very earth.

The Tros horse was standing before a descent down into a hillock in the ground, an oblong that had opened out of what Crit could swear had been featureless desert.

Great sand-encrusted doors were swung wide and

a tunnel downward was lighted with globe upon globe, as far as Crit could see into it.

He squeezed his horse with his knees and with only a halfhearted complaint, it started forward.

When he reached Tempus at the opening, he saw a gentle slope leading down and down, to where the lights seemed to meet the floor.

"In there?" Crit said dubiously.

"For a good time in Sandia," Tempus said with a quirk of his lips. "Time to go visiting."

With that, Tempus turned the Tros down the incline. The big gray picked its way carefully, lifting each foot high as if walking on eggs. And as Crit's horse followed the Tros's swishing tail into the tunnel, something told him that Tempus had known it would be this way all along.

Following the Tros's dappled rump into an unknown subterranean world, Crit wasn't anywhere near as doubtful as he'd been in the midst of the sandstorm.

Even then, he told himself, turning in his saddle to make sure all the rest of the Stepsons were following in good order, he shouldn't have worried: the Riddler knew what he was doing. Hadn't they always come through every trial?

Hadn't each venture been worth the risk?

Now that shelter was at hand, and the sand wasn't scouring him to death, Crit could admit he was curious as to what Sandia might hold.

But not anxious. The switching tail and fine rump of the Tros was ahead of him. Tempus sat easy in his saddle. The unburning globes strung above their heads seemed to go on forever, like his commander.

After all, how many men of Crit's stature had been where he had been? Or could go where he would go? Or where any of the Stepsons would go?

Whatever Sandia was, it was more than a mercenary's burial ground. Not that Crit had ever truly doubted Tempus's intentions.

Not truly. Not ever.

With Sandia ahead, he could rest his horse, who deserved the best that Crit could provide.

He pulled the beast off to the side of the horse line to take a head count. Before he trotted slowly back to his place behind Tempus, he needed to make sure everyone was accounted for.

The Stepsons were all there. Crit took one final look back the way they'd come. The doors he'd seen were closing, very slowly, without anyone attending them.

Well, Tempus knew what he was doing. And Crit had no real interest in riding back the way he'd come. Ever.

When they quit Sandia, maybe Tempus could find them another trail, one not so sandy or so stormy.

But when you traveled with the favorite of the Storm God, you took all of nature's fury in stride. It was the way of things, in Tempus's service.

Chapter 8:

FOUND IN SHAGA

Niko was up to his neck in troubles here in Shaga. The Shagans were primitive and suspicious, sorcery-shy, and poor from a wartime economy.

Yes, a mercenary could make a good living in Shaga, if that mercenary wasn't being chased by a witch. The slightest hint of witchcraft could get you a long and public death in Shaga's amphitheater. And even without Roxane hot on his track, Niko's skills were enough to get him branded as a wizard and flayed alive in Shaga on the weekend.

To complicate matters, Niko's horse and gear branded him as a successful soldier of fortune. "Soldier of fate, more's the truth," he'd told the local baron, but the man used his ears to hang jeweled rings from, and not to hear.

We'll have none of that false modesty, fighter," the baron had said, and hustled him off to meet the Shagan chief of staff.

You couldn't tell these people that they didn't want you because you came with a witch at no extra charge.

So he was serving Shaga, rather than end up in jail because he wouldn't, or accused of spying for Moriland. Either of these accusations would get him in nearly as much trouble as being deemed soulless.

And if not for the way his neck itched whenever

he thought he felt Roxane's breath upon it, he'd have been content enough, slogging through the Shagan army's mire while he awaited the witch.

He knew Roxane would find him here. A place like this would draw her like a magnet, especially with him in it. The Shagans feared sorcery above all things. Roxane fed on fear. Shagan murdered Shagan on any pretext, greedily absorbing one another's wealth. Roxane fed on greed and murder. The Shagans hired magicians and self-proclaimed wizards to tell them who had a soul and who did not, then executed those found wanting. Roxane fed on souls, the finest feast of all.

So she would come. Rumors of a terrible enemy, a slaughtering, ravening thing—a god of destruction come to earth—were already blowing up the coast like a summer tempest. The Shagans knew evil was on its way here. Niko would do what he could to help Shaga ride out the storm of violence to come.

Getting up from his desk in the Shagan army barracks, he blew out the three candles and found the window by the shine of moonlight it let into the dark of his room.

His son had always loved the moon. Tabet had proclaimed it "Nino's joy in the sky." Every time the moon disappeared for a while, Niko would be called to comfort Nino and promise him that the moon would come back.

In Tabet's city, no one believed that the moon was eaten up by hostile gods, or that a demon must be fought to return the moon to the sky, or that the moon was a chariot wheel of the god of night. The moon, in the city at the edge of time, was just the moon.

Out here, among the superstitious Shagans, the moon's disappearance made the natives even more suspicious and dangerous than they were when they could see it in the sky.

The Shagans fought in gangs in the streets at the dark of the moon. They fought between households; they fought in clans, over imagined slights and real ones, as if by shedding blood they could bring back the moon.

These Shagans seemed barely better than animals, hardly worth struggling to save. Niko saw no friends, only enemies, in just-met faces. Yet Niko's maat knew his heart would soften unto himself and others. Sometime soon. When all this was over.

When the witch was dead. Or he was. When maat was satisfied.

Waiting for the witch to make her move, he could feel her, almost see her in the moon's half-face. By the time the moon was dark, she'd be upon him. His gut knew it the way he knew that the Shagan baron wanted to see Niko romance his daughter and fall into Shaga's tar pit inextricably.

The last thing Niko needed was a woman. The thing he needed most was a clean battle. Yet the battle with Roxane would not be clean. She was, after all, the witch who had seduced him more than once, who'd tortured him and nearly killed him, who'd said she loved him, and protected him from other netherworld powers.

Steeling for contact with the witch, he forced himself to recall her madness, her death's touch, her irredeemable lust and greed.

In Shaga, there were so many despicable folk who'd trade their souls for baubles that Roxane could raise a local army in a weekend—an army with supernatural powers and carnal tastes.

"As maat will have it," he muttered to himself, and turned away from the window just as two dots came racing across the moon.

Thus he didn't see the winged silhouettes, battling each other in the moonlight. Closing and breaking apart, diving and dodging, spinning and tumbling.

Back and forth the black wings fought, while Niko, on his cot, saw nothing.

But when an eagle screamed in the still night air and something answered with a deeper, almost human, screech, Niko's hackles rose and he sat bolt upright.

By the time he reached the window, the shadows before the moon were gone, swooping low over Shaga city, as if looking for something.

And Niko, after peering out, up and down, to the right and to the left, pulled in his shutters and bolted them tight with a stout bar before he returned to bed.

On his cot, he pulled his blanket up over his neck and curled on his side, one arm over his face to protect it.

He knew what he'd heard. Roxane's eagle call was scratched into his very soul. As for the other sound: he willed with all his might that the screech he'd heard didn't come from the tortured soul of his son.

Shivering, though the night was mild, he lay there waiting for the thud against the shutters, the splinter of the bar, the dark and smoky whirlwind of a witch materializing in your room.

Well into the night, when nothing had happened, he threw off his covers and got out his weapons to sharpen their blades.

All his weapons: the ancient cuirass given him by the dream lord; the sword with its scabbard on which Enlil's bulls and lions strode; his shield from the wizard wars, embossed with the faces of forgotten gods.

For this battle, his leather jerkin and beltknife would hardly be enough. From his belt he took his throwing stars, poisoned and sharp, and laid them on the table, in the bowl of his shield. Then, in the way of the misty isles, he prayed over his equipment:

He envisioned the battle, as he would have it: he

and Roxane, alone, face to face. He envisioned the tactics he'd use against each of her onslaughts. He envisioned himself winning through at each confrontation. And, lastly, he envisioned himself, as clearly as he could, with the battle won and his son's funerary games in progress. He saw tears of relief and happiness on his own face.

But he couldn't see the way the witch would die, or the moment that he triumphed over her. Try as he might, he couldn't wrest that foresight from the vault of heaven.

Shaken, but determined, he put his throwing stars carefully in his belt, donned all his weapons but his shield and helmet. And there he sat, motionless, meditating until the witch should come.

When a knock came upon his door in tentative short bursts, his stomach flipped and he took three deep breaths before he said, "Come."

By then, the candles in his room were burning low. He hadn't expected Roxane to come knocking on his door like a servant. . . .

But it was a corporal who opened the door—or Roxane in corporal's guise.

"Sir," said the corporal, a pinch-faced youth with a crop of pocks, "three er . . . travellers to see you, who asked for you by name and claim you'll vouch for them. They got into trouble at the gates, and so . . . I know it's late."

"Three?" Niko was up, ignoring the boy's puzzlement at the foreign fighter who sat around all night in his dress uniform with his weapons out.

"Three. Two soldiers and a woman in scale armor."

A woman in— "Right. Be right down."

This could be a trick of Roxane's, but . . . Trouble at the gates?

With a suspicion in his heart that warmed it for the first time since he'd heard his son was dead, Niko left his room, locked it, and hurried down the stairs, pulling his cloak around him as he went.

If it was who it sounded like . . .

At the front door, the three stood patiently with guards who had no idea what their fates might have been if any of the three detainees had lost patience.

Niko's heart beat fast, then steadied. So it was not his commander, as he'd hoped. Dreamed. A big man, yes: Strat.

Niko embraced Jihan first, nearly pulling her off her feet with welcoming fervor.

"Lady," he whispered in her ear, "I have your mare, safe and sound, if that's what you've come for."

"For you, Nikodemos, on our commander's orders," she whispered back, and Niko's whole body started to shake.

Tempus *had* sent for him.

He hugged Randal next, then pushed back. "So rightman, it's been too long." The bond must be acknowledged.

Randal straightened. "My left side leader's been hard to find."

"With good reason." Niko turned to Strat: "And Crit, the band? All must be well, if you three are here together."

"You're the last we had to find," Strat growled. "Tempus is waiting. Let's go. This place is a pit. Randal and I both quit it once before."

Detained at the gates for deserting the army? That would explain the fuss. Behind, Niko heard the muttering of the barracks officers.

"Easy, Strat," Niko cautioned. "I have something to finish here that can use your help. And yours, Randal, Jihan. I swear we'll make you welcome." He turned on his heel: "Won't we, gentlemen? These are comrades of mine from hard fighting in many lands. Skilled and always victorious, they'll be welcome advisors to your battle planners. And they'll share my quarters, if we've nothing better."

Someone said, "The baron must hear of this."

Another, older, added, "Not tonight. Post a guard."

And the captain in charge of quarters said, "A woman? It's highly irregular."

"A better fighter that I am," Niko said pointedly, "is the Lady Jihan. Treat her like you treat a woman and you'll have your manhood in your helmet. Now, can we quarter these esteemed guests tonight and work out the details in the morning?"

Of course, that worked. It always did. Then there was the stabling of the horses to be attended to, and billeting.

All the commotion and the unexpected reunion made Niko want to forget the scream of an eagle and the screech of something not quite human.

And he almost succeeded, until Jihan, alone with him in his room, put her elbows on his desk, pushed away the clay tablets of a moronic war, and told him why the three of them had come.

And then he said: "The commander's son? Sprouting wings? And you haven't told the others. Why, Jihan?"

"Randal thinks magic kept Tempus's boys from finding you for so long. There's something in this place—Lemuria—where Tempus is that I don't understand, but it should have brought you home to them long since. I—"

The door opened. In came Randal and Strat. Jihan shrugged.

Niko was already sitting back in his chair and now his heart was icebound once again.

He should have known that Randal wouldn't be here if there wasn't magic involved: all his presentiments of sorcery were precisely right.

And Tempus thought the situation grave enough to have sent him these prodigious reinforcements.

"Sit down, Randal, Strat. We have much to talk over before sunrise," Niko said, and couldn't help glancing at the stoutly barred shutters behind Jihan's back.

A son who took wing, a changling creature: what did it mean? Niko had heard Roxane scream through an eagle's throat—and something screech a challenge—this very night.

Chapter 9:

CLASH OF THE TITANS

Roxane wheeled in the air, heart thumping, pinions beating with majestic power. A scream tore from her throat, filled with rage and frustration.

She dived.

Behind her, the thing followed, close on her tail.

Far below, Shaga lay spread out before her, vile and ripe for the plucking. In its midst was Nikodemos, prize of prizes.

If only she could elude the unnatural thing that plagued her, she could have her Niko, here and now.

Shaga expanded with terrifying speed as Roxane's eagle-form plummeted. Trying to kill this creature, she had nearly killed herself three times already. And always, it managed somehow to survive.

This was no great hawk or eagle or any natural thing, behind her. This was something terrifying and implacable.

She braced herself and spread her wings, nearly tumbled. Then steadied, swooped right.

Just once, the thing would overestimate itself. It was heavier than she, bigger.

Let it fall to earth and smash upon the city streets. Let it crush itself and its arrogance. Let it be gone.

But the thing was not gone. It screeched and pummeled the air with mighty wings, yet behind her.

Eagle's eyes see clearly. She caught too many glimpses of it as she winged her way over the city, and off again.

Dawn was almost nigh. Time was fleeting. She must get to Niko before his accursed friends alerted him.

She could feel the presence of the mage in the city as someone human might smell mildew, or a leaking, noxious gas.

The Riddler had sent his troops to protect her Nikodemos. Fool that he was. Fools they all were. Enemies Roxane hadn't faced for ages walked those streets.

She itched for battle, the taste of warm wizardly blood, an adept's heart, a Froth Daughter's throat in her beak.

But she had this thing upon her track.

And the thing was indefatigable.

But so was she.

Climbing the air with the alien thing trailing behind like a kite's tail, she tried to steady herself. To think.

The trouble with eagles was that their brains were small. All predator, hunger and speed, carnal knowledge, yes—but no stealth or guile such as Roxane must use now.

Finally it occured to her to shed the eagle form, at least long enough to make a plan. Her mind crowded the skull of the eagle; its brain was not big enough to think the thoughts she needed to think.

To change shape, she must find a safe place, if only briefly. Land somewhere. Land without the thing falling upon her and making good its every inarticulate threat to shred her limb from limb and leave her features blowing willy-nilly along the ground.

Roxane feinted right, dove left, and headed for a grove near the city's edge. Let's see the thing follow her through close-growing branches.

She was barely agile enough and small enough to make it through that grove without breaking herself upon the trees.

What could it do, then?

Into the grove she swept, her eyes half closed against the lash of leaves and twigs. The sound she made, crashing through there, was horrendous.

Behind her she heard only a screech of rage, then nothing.

Good. In the dark grove, she'd won a respite. As she would win the day, Niko's soul, and triumph over all her ageless enemies.

She found a high branch, thick and strong, a fork in a sturdy trunk. And there she huddled, baiting her wings until she calmed enough to change her shape.

Above, something rustled high, then crashed about in the uppermost branches.

She screamed and nearly took wing. But fleeing this adversary had gotten her nowhere. She was exhausted.

She needed to become something the thing couldn't threaten.

Roxane wanted to be a woman again. She wanted to see her Niko. She wanted to hold him in her human arms and soothe him. After all, he'd given his only living son to her regeneration. She owed him much.

But the thing wouldn't let her be.

The whole tree shook, as something tried to batter down to her from above.

More frightened than she'd admit, she forsook her branch and glided to the ground.

An eagle on the ground was easy prey to wolves and ferrets. But she wouldn't be one long.

The fury in her was mounting so fast and hard that womanliness eluded her. Combat was uppermost in her eagle's mind.

She hopped on the ground, wings spread, dancing from scaly foot to scaly foot. She stared at those feet and formed the proper invocation as best she could with an eagle's tongue.

Oh, blast and damn this impromptu shape-changing, this exhaustion in her shoulders that made her wings ache so and caused her whole body to tremble. As she danced there, wings out, beak open, she wanted only to defeat this enemy who was crashing above her head.

Branches fell upon her, showering her with leaves and twigs and fear.

In the middle of her shape-changing ritual, this final burst of terror at being vulnerable, plus the ache across her shoulders and her tired wings and her unwieldy tongue, changed her ritual, her mind, and her needs.

Thus her shape, too, changed from that she'd previously envisioned.

On the ground beneath the tree, Roxane grew. Her wings grew greater, not smaller. They widened and lengthened. Her feathers fell out. Clawed hands sprouted from her wingtips, from her mid-wings. Her neck lengthened, and thickened with scales. Her jaw and beak both grew long, more scaled, ruffed and protected.

Her tongue, now, became long and forked at its end, sinuous and facile, as agile as her mind. The skull encasing her brain grew, too. So did her hind legs, and the claws on them.

And her haunches, scalier by the minute, thrust her up off the ground, so that her head, with its scaled ruff, nearly touched the lowest branches of the great tree.

Her tail feathers were gone. A lashing tail with spines replaced it: a long tail for grabbing enemies around the neck and strangling them, for batting them off their feet and crushing them.

And her eyes grew huge and luminous. Her little slit nostrils, those upon her once-beak, were now big and wide. From them, as she snorted in delight, smoke issued.

Let the thing face a true dragon, breathing the fires of hell, and screech its challenge.

Let the thing match *this!*

With a bay of triumph and a howl of joy, Roxane thrust her dragon's head up through the trees, exploring with her long tongue, singing leaves out of her way with puffs of her malevolent, fiery breath.

She gnashed great sharp fangs and licked her lips with that tongue of hers, which could choke the life from man or beast.

Her eyes, with their protective fireproof membranes, sought the thing in the treetops.

She bellowed a challenge to it, one more time, and burst upward, fast and hard, as the tree around her started to burn.

She heard a scrambling, a crashing sound. She felt a frantic flapping of wings. Nothing more.

Then she saw it, issuing from the treetops like smoke, its wingtips scorched.

It was running away! It feared her now. It was in full rout, ungainly flight!

Roxane laughed a dragon's laugh and poked her head up through the highest branches of the tree whose flaming leaves merely warmed her scales.

Ah, to bask in fire as a dragon does. A dragon's laugh split the night.

She tried with her long tongue to catch the thing, but it was too fast for her. Tiny thing, what did it matter, anyway?

It was like a gnat to her now, like a flea or a pesky starling.

She didn't care about it one bit, not anymore. She cared about Niko, though.

The dragon who was Roxane still cared about

Niko like she cared about the hunger in her belly.

Setting things aflame eased that hunger. So as she headed toward the city, she burned whatever she might be pleased to set afire.

She breathed the smoke and the smoke made her stronger.

She stomped through the flaming copse and out into the lower city, so tall she towered over its tenements, flailing with her wings at rooftops, toppling statues of impotent gods.

She stepped on folk now and again, because it pleased her, as they fled their burning houses. A woman raised a fist at her. She picked up the tiny woman in her jaws and cracked her open like a beetle.

The woman's blood ran out of her mouth and down her scales as she chewed on the warm, twitching flesh.

This was very salutory, this eating of warm humans. She caught another with the clawed hands on her wings, and this time roasted it with her breath before she bit it in two.

The thighs of men, she soon found, were particularly tasty; breast of woman, and heart of child, gave great strength.

Impervious to the screaming folk who hardly reached her knees, she strode through them, upon them, burning down their city as she went. She thundered straight ahead, her tail lashing, charging through masonry like cobwebs.

As yet, she hadn't taken wing. Her wings were shopping bags for snacks of man and woman. Each time she ate, she grew more powerful.

Her sight grew clearer. Her voice grew louder. The fire that she could spew from her nostrils and her throat grew brighter.

And thus she bore down on the palace, with its army barracks, free of care and inebriated with delight and the taste of bright blood, looking for Niko.

She saw the army coming out to meet her, and laughed a fiery laugh.

The palace would soon be rubble beneath her great, clawed feet.

And in it, she would carefully search until she found her Nikodemos. Him alone would she spare from her revenge upon humankind, here and now.

Those who had once despoiled her rest, like the Sacred Band fighters come to snatch her beloved from her very jaws—*arms*, she corrected herself: these she would disembowel at her leisure, catching them alive and torturing them exquisitely before she let them die.

A little man ran up, casting a tiny spear she could use for a toothpick.

She snapped the spear in her claws, and roared.

Roxane was just about to stomp this small, ridiculous defender of the palace when she heard a roar like thunder and looked up.

There, on the palace's far side, was a mirror-image of herself.

No. Not quite. This was a dragon white as snow, with fishcolored scales. It had little arms with human fists, sticking out from its barrel chest.

These fists it beat against its chest as it strode forward, climbing over the palace walls with exaggerated steps that crushed olympian stonework underfoot.

The thing was back!

Worse, it had matched her grandeur and power. Worse, still, it was spewing fire her way.

Roxane's every scale stood on end. Her huge, leathery wings began to beat. Self-preservation took over: before she knew it, she was aloft, spewing humans from her wings and fire from her nostrils and beating the air desperately to lift herself up and up, into the clouds.

Would the thing follow?

She dared not wait to see. She lunged, neck out, breathing as much fire as she could, down toward it.

She showered its head with flames. She quested for it with her murderous long tongue.

The thing spat smoke, It jumped high, standing nearly on its tail, to meet her.

Her questing tongue wrapped itself around one of its ugly little arms. She pulled.

Something gave.

It screamed. She tugged and lifted, spitting all the fire she could from her gut, hoping to char it dead.

It weighed as much as she. She churned the air, trying to lift if off the ground. Her tongue stretched. The thing's weight seemed about to pull her tongue's roots right out of her mouth.

Something cried an awful, bone-breaking cry: herself? It?

Roxane didn't know. Only the high clouds promised relief. She could see nothing in the smoke and fire of their battle.

Then she was abruptly free, aloft: weightless. Her tongue snapped back against her mouth, and the arm wrapped in it struck her snout, making her eyes tear.

So suddenly released, her body shot upwards, borne on dragon wings still trying to lift twice her weight to heaven.

She soared, too exhausted to even scream her war cry. She nearly ate the arm she'd pulled from the chest of the thing, but something stopped her.

This was not flesh like any she'd ever encountered. Who knew what it was? Where from? What it could do?

She looked down, far below, and the distance to earth dizzied her. No pursuit, as yet.

But all of Shaga was a jumble of destroyed and burning toys, with insect-sized folk dragging themselves through the rubble, and others scurrying into the surrounding woods.

Niko was down there, somewhere!

Had she killed her beloved in mindless battle? She blared a wordless clarion of distress, and started circling down.

The shape you take twists your thinking. She'd nearly forgotten all about her beloved. If the thing had killed him, she would hunt it to the ends of the earth.

Lower and lower, her leathery wings took her. And then *it* burst from the burning city, all white wings and horrid purpose, speeding up to meet her!

The thing was back! With a scream of frustration, Roxane veered off. Flew high. Flew as fast and hard as she could, away from the thing, toward heaven.

Even as she did, her sharp eyes and her magic found what she had been seeking: Nikodemos, alive, fleeing the city with his companions.

At least he wasn't dead. Shaga surely was, or would be soon.

The thing was wounded. She'd pulled an arm from it. Roxane could tell it was ailing by the way it flew—unsteadily. It was clumsy as it came.

So be it! Let the thing follow her. She would exhaust it with her stamina. Cavort in the air until it dropped of exhaustion to the ground so far below.

And all that time, she would keep her beloved in sight, where he scurried in his little body toward safety, wherever Niko thought safety might be found.

Whither he went, she would follow, paying only slight attention to the thing that flapped unsteadily in her wake.

Was she not Roxane? Did she not owe her beloved a debt of gratitude?

Anything that threatened Niko on his way, she would destroy utterly. And once the thing was dead of its hubris, she would sweep down, change her shape back to one that Nikodemos could love, and take him away with her, where he'd be safe.

Forever.

Chapter 10:

TO LIVE AND DIE IN LEMURIA

"Kama, what is it you think men are, that you might want to be?" asked her Aunt Cime, sitting by the fire, petting a great brindle dog who had its head on her knee. "These men's rules you speak of are just games that women are too clever to play."

The Lemurian sunset came in the high wall of windows, gilding the room and the two women in it with rose and royal purple. Kama sipped tea from a cup so thin she could see her fingers through the porcelain as she lifted it.

"Aunt Cime, you know that isn't true. Everything that anyone respects is what men naturally excel at: fighting, accruing wealth, playing at power. . . ."

"You think men hold power? Then you've been taken in by the game." Her aunt sat forward, and nuzzled the dog playfully before she said: "Look, child, a woman bears a child and she's sure of immortality. A man can never, ever, know that any child is truly his, therefore he's combative, vicious and mean, trying always to write his name in history, for otherwise no whit of him will surely survive."

"You say all this, because you're—"

"A sorcerer-slayer? I'm barren of offspring, dear. I made a choice to be so. I play men's games by their rules."

"And you're telling me to get pregnant and I won't

care about everything that's important to me now?"
Kama wanted to shout. Instead, she carefully set her
cup down in its saucer. "What if I want to be like
you: respected in my own right?"

"I told you, the real respect is woman's: it's the
respect of nature. Only a woman can give immortality to a man, and that's all they really want."

"But it's not what I want. I want honor, glory—"

"I know," Cime said with a sigh. "Would that I did
not. You're your father's daughter. What else should
we have expected?"

"He's never once said he's proud of me."

"Tempus? Tempus isn't proud of anything or anyone, dear, including himself. His world is one of
continual battling. Even offspring to him are nothing, because his lustful god uses him so badly. If you
were got out of some ritual coupling, and Tempus
tolerates you, it's because he values you as a person."

"Women aren't persons to him—"

Cime got up abruptly and the dog growled, then
settled down grumbling before the hearth, putting
his huge head on his paws.

"Look, you spoiled brat. All women aren't whores.
All men aren't marauders. All women aren't wives.
All men aren't heros. People are, you little fool,
people—each seeking value as seen by a unique set
of eyes. There's no way you can have what you want
if all you know is what you don't want, what you fear,
and what you can't be."

Cime's words hit Kama like rhythmic slaps across
the face. "And what should I want?"

"To be the best you can. To do the most you can.
To live fully, every moment. And, in the end, not to
regret all of life precisely because you've chosen to
be unhappy for every moment of it. Child, all that
counts is how you spend your time. If we die tonight, you'll die bitter, cynical, unhappy and unful-
filled—because you chose to view everything that's

happened to you as an affliction rather than a blessing."

Kama nearly stuck out her tongue at the self-satisfied creature who now shared her father's life. Whenever Cime shook her hair free, she drove sorcerers to their grave. When she entered a hall of evil, the powers of darkness trembled. And she was saying that none of this mattered, except that she'd happened to enjoy it?

"Accomplishment is a real thing."

"Then accomplish something, besides making everyone around you miserable."

"Like what? I keep trying to make Tempus see that I'm—"

"By Enlil's prong, girl, forget your father. This obsession of yours will get you nowhere. Accomplish everything: make a life. Get out from under Tempus's pantaloons. Comport yourself as a comrade to those soldiers you work with. Make a friendship with Critias, at least. Honor your band oath. Be useful to yourself and others. Give life a chance, before—"

"Crit? What does finding a bed with a man in it have to do with it? That's what I mean: a woman's nothing if some man doesn't validate her by—"

"You're hopeless, you know."

"I know," said Kama with dark satisfaction, and picked up her tea once again.

Cime sighed a deep sigh and came over to her side. Kama thought the ageless whore was going to touch her, but Cime's hand stopped midway.

"Now what, do you think, is this?" Cime asked in a soft and emotionless voice that Kama had heard before: it was Cime's cat-and-mouse voice, with which she announced the coming of real trouble.

Kama turned to look at what Cime saw.

One of the small, magical Lemurian windows set in black pillars had come alight, by itself.

"Is it supposed to do that?"

"Does the god defecate? How do I know what it's

supposed to do? Tempus and I are learning as we go, as everyone but you is content to do, proceeding through life."

"Well, shouldn't we do something?" Kama ventured, setting her tea aside and getting up.

Cime was already at the lit window, twiddling the strange controls there. "Something, probably. What would you suggest? Perhaps you'd like to talk this window into telling us what this means."

"I—" Kama bit off the comment. Cime was telling her to keep shut. Her eyes filled unaccountably with tears.

Banished by her father into Cime's tutelage, all she was learning was to hate women more than men. Men, at least, were honest, not at pains to show you what a fool you were.

In the little Lemurian window, inset into its black column, figures were moving, before a pall of smoke. As Cime's long, beautiful fingers cajoled the magical studs and nipples, the image cleared.

"It's just Randal, bringing Niko," Cime said with a dry laugh. "Aren't they a sight?"

In the window, Kama saw the fire behind the Stepsons, the confusion. "Something's wrong there."

"Something's always wrong everywhere but here, dear. Don't fret. Let's make sure we're ready to give them a proper welcome. Go to the kitchens and tell them we'll have four more—perhaps five, for dinner."

"Five?"

"Just go, Kama. When it's time for you to inherit the care of Lemuria—if it ever is—Tempus or I will teach you what you need to know. Before then, life must find a way to teach you simpler lessons."

"You're an arrogant witch, you know that?"

"So I've been told. Scat," said Cime.

Banished from Lemuria's heart, Kama went to the kitchens, where a servant fussed over pots. You never saw more than a few servants around here. The place was spooky. But you always found one when you needed one. Or ten if you needed ten. No one seemed to know where they slept or waited, but no one cared, either.

For Cime, a woman who'd spent her career slaying sorcerers, to end up in this domain of magic was as strange as for Kama to be shut up with such a woman here, learning nothing whatsoever, because her father had decreed it.

Kama didn't have to obey Tempus. She could quit the band any time. They all could. But no man would leave because Tempus, as Crit would say, was "about a little ball-busting." Men were vile to each other all the time, and made jokes of it, contests.

She did have much to learn.

Wandering the corridors of Pinnacle House, Kama's footsteps asked, "Who am I?" For that, she had no answer. Her father's daughter, perhaps: once even that degree of identity had been enough to strive for. Now she was clearly that, and had found no dignity conferred on her therewith. No special status came with lineage in Tempus's eyes—or anyone else's.

She'd better find out what she wanted, she supposed. Or she'd spend eternity sharpening weapons and guarding caravans, with no other purpose than to be as lethal as possible.

Like the men and the gods she knew. Perhaps Enlil would come to her, if she asked, and make things clear for her as He had for her father.

But she was hesitant to enter the service of a god. She'd seen Tempus, Niko, and Cime in extremis. She wasn't sure she wanted such misery as that.

But miserable she was, and usually proud to be so.

Although tonight it seemed that not just Cime, but the very walls of Lemuria, were watching her, and misery was not an appropriate emotion in these ancient halls.

So she went upstairs and changed her clothes—

three times. She changed her hair four times; then took it down and came out, at last, dressed exactly as she'd been when she started, if a little cleaner.

She wouldn't give Aunt Cime the satisfaction of seeing Kama alter her custom as the result of some snide lecture.

She couldn't.

Her father had no business living in with Cime, anyhow. They were—

"Niko! Randal!" Kama gasped in surprise. "Strat . . ."

"And Jihan," said Niko, with his slow smile that melted women's hearts. "You remember Jihan, surely."

Cime had said, "four more—or perhaps five."

"What happened to you? You're filthy. Are you hurt, Stepson?" Kama strode into the great hall, glancing only once at the little window that had lit itself. It was dark now.

"We're fine, Kama," Randal said, wiping his grimy face with a cloth. "Fine enough, and grateful to be sheltered in Lemuria." The wizard was clearly relieved and embarrassed; his ears flared red.

"Where's Cime?"

"Gone to see to something," Jihan answered her, stretching out in Cime's chair before the fire. "Ah, it's good to sit where danger isn't."

Jihan was one of her father's playthings, decidedly more than human, a creature of such beauty that she made Kama glad to be plain.

To be pretty, like Cime, would make you despondent in Jihan's shadow. What would happen when Tempus heard Jihan was . . . "Does my father know you're here?"

"Strat's going to take me to him. Aren't you, Stepson?" said Jihan, brushing smudge from muscled arms that reflected the firelight's glow.

"If the god allows, we'll all go in the morning,"

Strat growled, upending a bottle from the bar and chugging it where he stood, before the fire.

"Of course. We're leaving first thing," said Kama. She was going, too. Cime couldn't make her tarry longer, now that Niko was found.

She strode over to Niko and kissed him firmly on the lips. "I can't tell you how glad I am to see you, Nikodemos. Now we can all join my father and quit this place."

"What is this place?" Niko wanted to know, looking around with shadows in his narrowed eyes.

"It's Lemuria—"

"It's dinner," Cime interrupted from the doorway. "During it, we'll hear of your adventures. Then we'll provision you for morning. Sandia's a rough trek."

"Not too rough for my father," Kama said, and gestured toward Jihan, by the hearth. "And surely not too rough for any who have Jihan's power with them. And Randal's."

"Perhaps not. You'll do as you wish, I'm sure. Now can we eat, children?"

Cime was such a bitch, here on her own turf. What every man worth having—from Askelon, the dream lord, to Kama's father—saw in her aunt, Kama still didn't understand.

Maybe it was the way she switched her hips as she led them in to dinner. Or perhaps it was her acid tongue, that could kill a person's heart in an instant. But whatever it was, Cime's like was that last thing Kama wanted to become.

Jihan, on the other hand . . . "Jihan, I've long been wanting to talk to you of life," said Kama, taking a seat next to the Froth Daughter in the dining hall.

"Of life?" said the magnificent Froth Daughter, and frowned. "What do I know of life? I visit it, when I can. Right now, I wish I'd never come."

"What—?"

"Hush, Kama, and you'll learn what you need to know," Cime decreed. And: "Now, Randal, perhaps you'll be so kind as to explain the whole thing, from the beginning, up to and including why you think Roxane and—ahem, Jihan's . . . son . . . may be chasing you. And what we can do about it, if they are."

"What we can do," Randal said in his reedy voice, "is get out of here as fast as we can, so as not to visit them upon you."

"Not until morning. Jihan, are you sure about your . . . son?"

"Cyrus." Jihan bowed her head. "I saw him, in the city of Shaga. In hideous change-form. I called to him, but his mind was in its dragon form, and his soul is already bound up with the witch's." Jihan shook her head. "I am so sorry and ashamed to have brought this upon you all."

Kama couldn't believe her eyes. The proud and impervious Froth Daughter seemed about to weep.

Niko reached over and patted Jihan's wrist. "It's all right, Jihan. Not your fault. Probably mine." Then he looked at Cime: "Say the word, Evening Star, and Jihan and I will go another way—out of here, on foot or horse, to anyplace this matter can be settled with as little harm to others as possible. . . ."

"Don't be ridiculous, Niko," Cime said. "My brother sent for you. Left strict orders: send Niko on to Sandia. So to Sandia you'll go."

"You didn't see what we saw, Cime," said Randal, so rattled he was nearly impolite.

"Whatever you saw, I'm sure I'll see. You think I can't keep this place secure? I've kept your beloved Riddler safe from sorcerers and demons none of you could have faced without wet pants. Now do as you're told, children. Eat your dinners. Pick your horses. Get a good night's sleep, and ride to Sandia in the morning. After we've had dessert, I'll see if I can let my brother know you're coming, so someone will be there to meet you."

"But, Evening Star—" Strat began.

"Straton, eat your food or I'll feed you."

Jihan giggled softly.

Randal said, "Our lot is cast, travelers."

And Kama said, "As soon as we're done, I'll show you the horses." At least the trip was still on. For a moment, she'd been worried that she'd end up staying here, the last place she wanted to be.

And once the horses were chosen, the trip seemed assured. Once she got Straton alone, she used the Sacred Band oath to pry the whole story, such as Straton knew it, from his lips.

It came out in short sentences, single words, and impossible descriptions: "Big as seige engines. Fire-spouting dragons. A white and a black: claws, scales, the whole wagon-load. Destroyed the Shagan city, just about. Almost us with it."

"And?" Kama prompted, as she was saddling the last horse who stood, haltered and crosstied, in the barn.

"And, we escaped." Straton shrugged. "Probably Randal's doing. Who knows? You get the mages involved, and Jihan, you always have trouble."

"Trouble?" She tied the horse's reins around its neck and hung the bridle's headstall from its saddle: no use bridling them until just before dawn; otherwise, every horse was now ready. "This seems a little more than homegrown trouble. What's this about Jihan's son?"

"Tempus's son, the way I heard it."

"Oh, no."

"That's right. So who knows where that will lead? The commander and Jihan spawned some changeling that was locked up under the sea until now."

"How'd it get here?"

"Escaped."

"Locked up for good reason, if I understand."

"Don't ask me. I just want to get back to Crit—that is, back to the Step—"

"I know what you mean," said Kama coldly. "Look, Straton. You and your leftside leader have a bond and a relationship I want no part of. It's Crit who can't get that through his head. Help me, and we'll both be happier."

"Help you what?"

"Um—" She had no true answer. Find herself? She couldn't ask that of Straton, whose self was shattered and held together with baling twine. "Help me make everyone comfortable. I just want to be one of the band, not break up a pair or cause trouble."

"We'll ride together, in the morning," said Strat, and clapped her on the shoulder so hard she nearly fell against the saddled horse.

But by predawn, it seemed they might never ride anywhere, alive.

The whole of Lemuria was shaking as if the earth itself wanted to dislodge it.

Overhead, a storm of malice raged: things in the sky dived down at Pinnacle House and battered at the huge window walls, screaming. Cime's orders were hard to hear over the din.

The dogs of Lemuria were going mad, barking and howling and baying and whining, as Cime yelled, "*Go*. Go now. Down to the stables! Get ready. I'll send you as soon as I can."

Only Strat said, "What about you? And them?"

The dragons charging the spires were spitting fire and roaring. Sometimes they'd attack one another. Sometimes they attacked the glass, throwing themselves against it. The huge glass walls overlooking the sea were scored with clawmarks.

Cime had to shout over the barking of the dogs and the thunderous attack: "I'll handle this, here.

Once you're gone, there's nothing here they want. *Go!*"

Niko came up to Cime, a baying dog jumping at his chest: "Let me stay. I'll go out on one of the balconies. It's me she wants!"

"You have your orders, Stepson," Cime flared, pointing. "Begone."

And Jihan was at the window, her face pressed to it, tears streaming down her face, when, on Cime's orders, Kama started to drag her away.

"Come on," Kama shouted as gently as she could, nearly bowled over by a dog the size of a pony who leaped at the flaming, winged apparition that was hovering eye to eye with Jihan, beyond the glass. "We've got to go."

For a long instant, Kama was sure that Jihan would refuse to leave. This thing outside, spitting fire and beating leathery, clawed wings, must be her son.

Tempus's son.

The thought made Kama want to retch or kill, she wasn't sure which.

Dragging Jihan by the hand through the melee of dogs and servants come from nowhere, Kama headed for the barn.

When she got there, she heard a terrible crash.

"The windows!" Randal screamed, his eyes wide. A terrified sorcerer is an awful sight. It shakes your faith in heaven.

"Mount up, Randal," Niko demanded, and grabbed the mage by the collar.

Kama met Niko's eyes and both of them knew that Randal was right: the crash they'd heard was the shattering of one of the towering window walls up at Pinnacle House.

But Niko was right, too: they had to go, while they still could. With Strat in the lead, they rode out into the sunrise once Kama and Randal had pulled back the stable door.

Beyond that door was an expanse of white such as Kama had never seen.

Up on her horse, Kama hadn't urged him two lengths into the morning heat and sand of a desert world when she looked back: there was no stable behind her.

There was no Lemuria, anywhere. There was only desert, behind the horses. Behind Niko's sable mare, Kama could see the place where the tracks stopped, as if they'd come out of nowhere.

Which, of course, they had.

From up ahead, Strat called back, "Now what do you make of this?"

And when she'd turned around in her saddle, Kama saw riders whose like she'd never seen before, coming across the desert toward them at breakneck speed.

Chapter 11:

KEEPER OF THE GATE

Cime stood firm in the wreckage of the Lemurian windowwall, diamond rods of power in her hands. The ravening things outside were bellowing and spouting fire—at one another, currently.

Colliding in midair, these dragons had turned upon each other briefly. Now they were breaking apart.

And hovering—if such potbellied, scaly things could be said to hover—outside the broken window, looking in at her with baleful eyes. Their necks outstretched, their wings beat gusts into the room that made the broken glass tinkle as it skittered across the floor.

Cime crossed her rods at their tips, and backed slowly toward the black pillars in which the true power of Lemuria lay.

Instinctively, she wanted to protect those windows. But she wasn't sure, this time, that her diamond rods could do the job. She raised them, questing with her mind down their targeted lengths.

The diamonds started glowing in her hands. So one dragon, at least, was pure sorcerer.

She might kill the one, then. But the other . . . It didn't register on her weapons as an enemy.

The beat of the monsters' wings was whipping her loose hair around her eyes.

If the sorcerous one, the darker one, came in first,

111

perhaps she could slay it and scare the other away. Years of killing magic wherever she found it had trained her to do just that.

The old hunger to kill an age-old enemy warmed her, making her long muscles tremble in anticipation. The universe she inhabited began to shrink, until there was only the sorcerous dragon with its scaled, questing head, its disgusting long tongue, and glowing eyes—only this enemy who snorted fire at her, in all of creation.

It arched its wings back and seemed to stand on the air. The wings were tipped with clawlike hands, and these grabbed the windowwall's frame, as if it would lever itself inside.

Cime backed a pace, nearly stepping on a dog. It yelped, and got out of her way. Then it cowered again, alternately trembling and whining, then barking with its head low, haunches up, froth decorating its chin.

Even the dogs weren't sure if they'd survive the day. Funny, she hadn't heard their cacaphony until she'd nearly tripped over one.

No matter. The dogs didn't matter. She didn't matter. Only the magical windows of Lemuria, each set in their black housings, mattered.

She thought: maybe I can use the windows, to shunt these things into another time and place.

And behind her, one by one, the windows sprang to life. Could she do this? Did she dare?

Could she not?

The first of the dragons was almost inside now, coming slowly, its hind legs flexing over the glass-strewn rug.

Upright, its dark head nearly touched the vaulted ceiling.

She had to try. It was smoking from the mouth, as if preparing to char her where she stood with a blast of fire from its nostrils. Its jaws were wide. That forked tongue was lolling, searching, as long as her whole body.

Cime took another step back, rods still crossed in her two hands, still targeted on the first dragon.

Then—as she was looking over her shoulder at the Lemurian window into Sandia—the second dragon, with a bellow, leaped onto the back of the first.

Both came tumbling into the room, grappling.

Fire exploded everywhere. Huge bodies thrashed. Tails, lethal and lashing, splintered furniture, caught a dog, and sent him flying, baying through the air to crash against a mirror.

Cime staggered back. Her elbow hit the black pillar holding the window into Sandia as she fell. Both her arms came up to protect her face, her rods out of contact with each other.

She hit the carpet hard. Above her head, a gout of flame jutted, licking the black pillar and the window there.

It exploded. Sparks showered her.

She rolled away, singed and deafened by the dragons' bellowing, trying to get to her feet before she was crushed beneath the two monsters, who'd forgotten everything else, locked in mortal combat.

For a moment she saw both dragons, as she gained her knees and focused her rods: the dark one had its jaws in the throat of the light one. The light one had its teeth in the shoulder of the dark one. One of the white one's manlike arms was ripped away. Both were leaking fire from their mouths and the stench of roasting reptile was noxious.

Then the air around them began to shimmer, as if they were smouldering.

She crawled backwards, afraid they'd explode then and there.

The air about them spun, and grew thick with white dust, fine and sandy.

The dust mixed with the smoke. Flames seemed to come from everywhere.

And then . . . nothing.

The dragons were gone. The fire was gone. All that remained were the wounded and crying dogs and the shattered furniture and broken glass—and the wind blowing inward off the Lemurian sea.

Shaking, Cime got to her feet. She looked at the diamonds in her hands, shook her head, licked her lips, and bound up her hair once again with her rods.

Only then did she think to survey the magical windows in their pillars.

An involuntary groan came from between her gritted teeth. Her favorite dog limped up to her, whining softly, and nuzzled her dangling hand, trying to make her pat his head.

She scratched his ears absently as she said, "Well, that one's done for."

The window into Sandia was entirely destroyed. The black pillar in which it was set was burned and melted. The window itself was only a hole with smoke and colored wires coming out of it.

Another window, one behind and to its right, was ruined completely also. The remainder, she soon determined, were functioning still.

She stood before the window into Sandia for a long while before she sat down on the floor with one of the wounded dogs and stroked him. He had a seared flank, hairless and blistered. She could heal the flank with her hand, no trick for one of her abilities.

But could she heal the window? She didn't know. And if she couldn't, could she make one of the other windows look out onto Sandia? Failing that, could she find a way to bring Tempus and the band home?

Were they trapped in Sandia, wherever that was, eternally?

And where had the dragons gone? Which of the Lemurian portals had the dragons used? Which gate had she, a poor gatekeeper, unwittingly opened for them?

She prayed it wasn't the most likely one—the same one that might now, with its window broken, be shut forever.

The open, empty socket of the eye into Sandia drew her like a magnet. When servants swarmed the room, chattering and sweeping up the damage, she hardly noticed. When men from the town came up to replace the broken windowwalls overlooking the sea, she forgot to ask them where they were from and how they got such glass to fix it.

She merely stared at the portal into Sandia, which was no more, and worried.

Finally, when someone brought her bread and tea, she sat on the hearth, feeding one of the dogs her bread.

"Well, dog," she told it, "we'll just have to learn enough about the inner workings of Lemurian windows to fix that one before my brother wants to come home. Won't we?"

The dog, having gobbled the last morsel of bread, cocked his head at her and whined.

She wanted to whine herself. All alone here with the weird servants of Lemuria and a clutch of dogs, she felt like a failure.

How could she have let this happen? Tempus was counting on her to keep the gate. And she'd let those dragons through, though she could have stopped at least one. *Should* have stopped at least one.

Cime wasn't accustomed to regrets. She shook them off. So she'd made a judgment call: trying to save all the windows, she'd lost one—two—and the dragons had gone through to . . . where?

She couldn't know for certain.

She'd need a Lemurian window to find out where the dragons were. When she'd done that, she swore, she'd personally go after those two travesties of nature and put their twisted souls to rest.

This she promised herself, and the dog with the braised flank, who hobbled after her as she started searching Pinnacle House for tools to fix a broken window into another time.

Not a moment to lose. She had much to learn, and out there, somewhere, Tempus was waiting.

If he tried to come home and failed, what would he think of her? And all the Stepsons, with him? What if all were lost to her, because she'd hesitated when dragons battled in Lemuria's great hall?

She thought of everything she'd said to Kama, about the worth of womankind, and snorted to herself. Without the beloved souls she cared for, she was as adrift as Kama.

No better. Just older. With sharper edges and more power. More power could make for more powerful errors.

She'd just made what might turn out to be the worst error of her life.

She kept trying to understand why she hadn't used her rods to kill the dark dragon, and could find only one reason: she'd thought if she killed the first, the second would have run even wilder. And the second was . . . Tempus's son.

Bad call. Everybody makes them. There was still time.

There was still time: this was her litany, her work chant, as she labored through the day and night and on. There was still time.

What Lemuria conferred upon its Evening Star was mastery over time itself, so Tempus had told her. She hadn't learned enough to understand her options, that was all. She'd dawdled with him here, thinking they had forever.

They did have forever, if she hadn't lost it for them. Searching for wisdom in Pinnacle House, the

Evening Star would find what she needed. And win all. Or not find it. And lose all. For everyone she loved.

As she worked, her palace guard dogs got bigger, following her from room to room, sitting around her feet when she'd stop to read or think or compare notes from one document to the next.

The dogs sensed her anguish, her self-condemnation, and her misery. Cime wouldn't cry. She'd given up tears long ago. Anyway, she had to see to work.

But the dogs cried for her, soft little whuffling moans and long, sad yodels of loneliness that echoed around the empty rooms of Pinnacle House all day long and far into the night.

Book 2:

DESERT SONG

Chapter 12:

PASTURES OF PLENTY

"But Faun," said Tempus to Sandia's beautiful Shepherd, in her underground fortress of sterile air and vibrating floors and unblinking lights, "why is it so dead above, if Lemuria brought your seas back to life as you asked at New Year's?"

"The seas are alive again, Riddler. What you've seen is not Lemuria's fault. What wastrel mankind destroyed takes time for nature to put to rights." She tossed her long hair, the color of wheat and honey, and stretched out in a padded chair, smoothing her skins of office down over her knees. "Don't be sad for us. Because of the Evening Star, and Lemuria— and you too," she smiled softly, lacing her fingers over her flat belly, "we have a second chance."

Faun was a lithe and animal beauty. Tempus and the Storm God Enlil had craved her and had her, with her blessing, on Lemuria's balcony in a storm one night last season. Her belly should have been big with child.

The god in Tempus's head prompted: *Where's our seed, mortal? She should be showing.* Enlil was rattling around in Tempus's head here like a caged tiger: looking out his eyes, roaring questions, lashing a figurative tail that made Tempus's whole body thrill with passion. The Storm God, Lord of Rape and

121

Pillage, of armies and men and murder, was both curious and distressed in Sandia.

Nor was the god the only one. Sandia's subterranean world made Tempus uneasy. When he'd first met its Shepherd, Faun, in Lemuria, she'd been asking for a New Year's boon of living seas. Then he'd seen only the dead seas of Sandia through Lemuria's magic windows.

On the trek here, he'd come to understand what years of dead seas and parched land could truly mean. Now that he was here, he couldn't understand what that flat belly before him and those come-hither eyes could signify. He and the god had never failed in raping, impregnating, or any sort of begetting known under heaven.

In Faun's private offices, where the walls were hung with pictures of waving grain fields and heather-covered mountains and waterfalls, he could finally ask the question uppermost in the mind he shared with his god.

He must, or else the god would take her again, here and now, to answer that question for them both. The pressure in him was mounting so that he could hardly hear over the god's ragged breathing in his ears, and the god's heart beating fast in his chest.

"How is it that we—that I see no signs of the child we conceived in Lemuria?" he asked bluntly, getting up as he did.

He stood over her. Faun pulled her hair off her face to peer up at him as if she looked into bright sunlight.

For a moment, her heartshaped face mirrored pure shock. Then what might have been embarrassment. Then concern. Delight. And something like amusement that raised his hackles.

"Commander," she said huskily, "I didn't realize. . . . That is . . . Please sit down."

The god didn't want to sit. Tempus found their

shared voice and it was a warning growl. "Answer me."

She blinked and stood up, too. "All right. Here you have it: we don't do . . . ah, personal conception here. Our chances are too slim. Your . . . seed, what we could salvage, and what eggs were fertilized of mine, were taken out of here," she slapped her tummy, "by our doctors, to be raised in perfect wombs, where gestation can be controlled."

"Seed? Eggs?" Even the god was taken aback. Enlil peered silently out of him with bated breath. "What are you saying, woman?"

Shepherd of Sandia or not, this woman clearly felt she'd tricked him. Perhaps she had. Uncomfortable in the face of something he didn't understand, and the god didn't understand, Tempus was left with only the Sandian Shepherd's guidance as to how he should feel.

Faun, surely, felt sheepish. And hesitant to explain. But under his glare she said: "You remember I spoke of carrying your seed back into Sandia—with the Storm God's blessing."

He snorted an assent, arms folded.

"Here, we can make many babies from one man's . . . ejaculation and the eggs in a woman's womb. Sometimes, we can take that seed and introduce it to many eggs from many women. So when I got home, we tried to salvage as much of your gift to Sandia as we could. . . ."

"You're saying there is a baby? More than one?"

"I'm saying there are . . ." Her voice grew tiny. "Six, ah, ongoing fetuses, and another seven . . . frozen embryos." She smiled weakly, nearly shrinking from him. "The god surely won't mind if we take as much of his blessing as our knowledge allows."

"Show me these thirteen offspring of a few minutes' passion in the rain," he nearly thundered.

His gaze was on his feet; his eyes seemed filled

with blood. The fury in him was inexplicable. The god, not sharing his sense of outrage, was laughing uproariously, saying, *Ha, mortal. You've finally met your match and Our dream. I like this world. It needs me. We shall stay here and spread Ourself far and wide. All the enemies of these Sandians shall be Our enemies. My blessing upon these people shall make them supreme over all other peoples. . . .*

"Silence, Pillager," Tempus muttered aloud. He couldn't hear the woman over the god's nattering in his head. She was leading him toward the door, talking over her shoulder. He followed the doeskin-clad rump, waiting for the god to subside.

At least his physical desire had subsided. This was a truly alien world. But then, he told himself, it had every right to be: this was the farthest into the future of humankind he'd ever ventured. And no place was ever like home. Now that he had a home, even if that home was Lemuria, he compared everywhere else to it.

The god was too taken with this scoured and dead world, simply because of the Shepherd's boast: lust here could go farther than even Enlil had ever dreamed.

Like a child behind its mother, Tempus followed the Shepherd through her warren beneath the desert, until they came to a series of white rooms with clear partitions. She took him inside one, where she talked to machines. Colored dots resulted from Faun's conversation, dancing on black cyclopean eyes that reminded him of Lemurian windows.

He saw only three people during that whole tour, and these were pale folk of puny stature who stared at him from behind doors opened just a crack.

"See," Faun said. "Here we are: There's one."

She gestured to one of the magic windows. In it, a thing recognizable as a black-and-white tadpole hovered.

Then he looked closer. It was more than a tadpole. It had a thumb and it was sucking that thumb. It had a human sort of head, but an ugly, warped, and deformed head, huge and ungainly.

"You say this is what?" He straightened up and crossed his arms.

"Actually, that's my own child—ours. Or will be in five more months." She looked at him now with that unmistakably proud and dazed stare of a mother.

He said, "It's deformed. You should kill it now."

Her mouth opened. Her eyes widened. She said, "No, no. It'll be fine."

She tapped a button below the window. The thing disappeared. "Here's another." A second tadpole materialized in the window. This one had writing below it.

"Another." She tapped yet again.

"Enough." He couldn't tell one from the next. He didn't like the look of them. But the god was demanding to know who the mothers were. "Who are the mothers?"

"I . . . could introduce you, but honestly, I'd rather not. It has to do with our culture's manners, sense of propriety. You're still intimately involved only with me, and that—" She blushed. "—only if and when you want to be."

The god hooted, and snarled in delight.

"We'll see." Tempus knew a proposition when he heard one. He didn't like such forwardness. And, too, the god usually was not aroused by less than raping an unwilling woman. Somehow, the idea of impregnating women whose thighs he'd never seen, merely by the power of his will, titillated Enlil.

"Of course, we'd be delighted if you and . . . ah, the god . . . would donate to our sperm bank while you're here, but . . ."

"No!"

". . . but it's not required." Clearly discomfitted,

Faun tapped the window dark, and motioned, "If you've seen enough?"

Lead us to the sperm bank, mortal cow, said the god.

When my body is cold and stiff, and You find Yourself another avatar, Your Rapaciousness, Tempus raged silently, *You can milk him as You will. Right now, I say to Thee, thirteen children in a desert warren is by far enough.*

"Enough," he said aloud to Faun. "Show me something different. How you feed your people. Show me something that will make me understand what Lemuria did for you."

In the hallway that seemed to stretch endlessly, she turned and embraced him. "Lemuria did *every*thing for us—whatever hope we have, beyond that of your gift—comes from the seas' regeneration. I heard there was a thunderstorm just before you entered the airlock."

She meant the tunnel, he knew. At its nether end had been a set of doors between which your ears popped and the horses neighed angrily.

And suddenly he was as angry and impatient as his Tros had been then. "The thunderstorm came from Enlil, woman." Seas didn't make storms; the god in his head did. "Make things clear to me, Faun: are your men impotent, like the ground above? How many are you? How do you feed your people? Who are your trading partners? Your enemies? What is the lay of the land here?"

He took her arms from his neck. "You invited me here, and I am come. So tell me the purpose. Why did you ask for us?"

"I—reciprocation. Politeness. We're not beggars. We're desperate, yes. We're the last flicker of life here, but Lemuria's boon is enough of help. I was just . . . in love, for a moment, and grateful."

Women. He would never understand them. It was

hopeless to try. "You have no enemies in need of routing?" He had brought the Sacred Band here. Her invitation, as he now realized, had been nonspecific.

"Enemies—surely. Ourselves. Other folk, in other small pockets like this: 'closed ecologies,' we call them. We produce everything we need. If someone's system fails, and they can't get what they need, they'll try to steal what you have. It's human nature."

"What do they want to steal?"

"Water. Food. Children. . . ." She looked up at him. They were still standing in the same place in the hall. Doors up and down its length were cracked open.

"Oh, Riddler, you *don't* understand and it's my fault. We're fighting to reestablish life on the surface. Life as we once lived it; as they lived it in your time. That's why people were so excited when you brought all those horses. We'd like to take samples— take eggs and seed and raise some horses. Would you mind?"

"No harm will come to them?"

"I promise." Something in him said not to let them touch the Tros. "Every horse but mine," he allowed. "If you have the grain to feed their foals."

"I'll show you." And now she moved off, obviously grasping the pretext to get them out of earshot of the doorways.

When they'd gone into a closet and out again, she walked him through a huge garden, where every sort of flower and fruit grew. And on, among a maze of water troughs where tiny fish coursed.

"I see no animals, or trees, or—"

"No, no meat or wood. . . . We harvest everything we grow. We use everything. We make gas for power from garbage; we use the urine and feces of every person. We recycle endlessly. It's all we can do."

They were at the place where the horses were stabled. Tempus smelled them before he saw them, or recognized the amphitheater, big as a town square, hewn out of solid rock and lit from above with bright strips.

"How are my men? You're not harvesting and recycling them without my permission or their knowledge, are you?"

Faun trailed her hand back to catch his. Her backward glance reproved him. "We're so honored by your visit. You're probably right: your god brought the thunderstorm. But a thunderstorm is such a blessing. All that ozone. All that rain. . . ."

He reminded himself that there was no comprehending this woman, beyond the comprehension necessary to keep hold of his fate and his life. He'd promised her a week's stay when he arrived: the Stepsons needed the rest.

She'd been keeping him so busy since he got here, he'd hardly seen his men. Crit had come by Tempus's quarters to say the horses were well and tell him how and where the men were billeted.

He'd assumed they were all still asleep. Now he wondered.

"I'll look over my horses, before we go."

It must have been his tone that hurt her feelings. "Of course," she said, subdued, and led him down the row of boxstalls.

Out of one, Crit hailed him. The Stepson hadn't bathed; he had a week's beard still. Crit said, "Riddler, look at this."

Into the stall Tempus went, and saw a bit of blood under the tail of one of the Stepson's mares.

The god knew what that signified before he did. "Faun," he called, angrily. "Look at this! Why ask permission after the fact?"

Crit looked between the beautiful, blushing woman who was biting her lip, and Tempus, who was holding up the mare's tail.

"I'm sorry. Somebody jumped the gun." This was

said in a language Crit didn't know, one Tempus had learned during his first Lemurian sojourn.

He told her harshly to speak in terms his man could understand. Clumsily, in the language of the armies, Faun said, "We want some breeding stock. We get it without live cover."

"Oh," said Crit, squinting at her. "Fine with me, Commander, if it's all right with you and okay for the horses. . . ."

"Let's go—"

A local was standing there, whitefaced, barely tall enough to see over the half door: "Shepherd," the slight man said. "I need to speak with you alone."

"Coming."

Tempus went with Faun, a viselike grip on her arm. She looked up at him once pleadingly, but didn't object.

He could feel in his gut that what the man had to say would concern him: he'd seen the man's furtive glance at him. And at Crit.

In Faun's tongue, the man said: "The rest of their party has arrived, but the Drekka have got them."

Faun slumped against Tempus. She knew he'd understood.

Then she said, "Riddler, I wish you'd have been more specific about when to expect your friends, or gone out to meet them. Now we'll have to trade for them. . . ."

"How many in the party?" Tempus asked the man in the little fellow's own language, to make things clear.

"Yours? Two women, three men."

"And theirs?" A shot in the dark, but worth it to Tempus. He'd known the Shepherd had been lying to him: every association of men has enemies.

"The Drekka? A regular raiding party of two dozen. The others, I don't know."

"Others?" Tempus echoed.

"What others?" the Shepherd demanded.

Out of the corner of his eye, Tempus saw Crit lean his arms on the stable halfdoor, listening unabashedly as best he could.

"Others: We saw two . . . somethings, for sure. Really, I can't describe them. I think we might be able to show you. . . ."

"Tell us, first, what you can," Faun told the man with a shake of her head.

"Two very rapacious, flying . . . physiologically reptilian . . . large, say two, three ton . . . flying, fire-breathing . . . *things*, came out of nowhere, just about the way the additional expected visitors did. Since it was a surveillable locus, and we were set up for it, we have a sensor record. You can do a density slice on the things if you want. But they're . . ."

"They're what?" the Shepherd almost shouted, frustrated and angry.

"Well, Madame Faun, they're . . . ah . . . dragons, ma'am. Fire-breathing, scaly dragons as big as small satellites."

"They're what?" Faun asked again.

But Tempus said, "These dragons, where are they?"

"I believe, if our sensoring packages are accurate, that they're approaching the Drekka stronghold."

"Good," said Tempus. "I would go there. Crit!" He turned to the Stepson. "Ready the band. Provision for desert warfare. Get whatever help you can from these locals. We leave in—"

The Sandian ruler's hand squeezed Tempus's arm. "Tempus! Don't you think you should consult me?"

"How long until your force is ready to leave, then, Shepherd? Our men will travel with yours, at least until we've rescued our people and slain the dragons."

" 'Slain the dragons'?" came the slight man's unbelieving voice. "I need to get some sleep."

"We'll come to get you, Tempus, when we're ready. Unless you'd rather spend the time with me, learning how we deal with the Drekka. They're not your average bandits."

"Did I say they were? If you're ready now to tell me what's going on, I'll be glad to listen." Frozen babies. Multiple breedings. A smokescreen, to enthrall the god, Tempus now realized.

"Not just now, Tempus. Bring Tempus to me, in my office, in an hour or so, Joe—when he's ready," Faun told the little man before she hurried away, toward the rows of plants.

Tempus sauntered over to the stall door on which Crit still leaned and said in their own tongue, "What do you think, Critias?"

"Two women and three men, you mean?" Crit had heard what Tempus heard, then. "Well, we were expecting Kama, Randal, Straton, and Niko. Maybe Cime came along."

"And if she did, who's guarding Lemuria?" Tempus said dismissively.

"That's true. Well, we'll know when they turn up, I guess. You know Niko: always picking up stray skirts."

Tempus hoped that was all Niko had picked up. "And the dragons?"

"Maybe they have dragons all the time here," Crit shrugged. "Once we get Randal from these Drekka, dragons won't be a problem."

"Good." Tempus always took his first officer literally. In the local language, he added: "Then you see to the band, and I'll go learn what I can about these Drekka before we find ourselves forced to slaughter them to the man in order to satisfy honor and get our people back."

The little man named Joe was looking at him through eyes wholly black with pupil. "Ah, yes, that's good. Well, if you'll come this way, Commander. We'll be briefing in the Shepherd's theater as soon as the data's tabulated. . . ."

"Tell me what you do about these Drekka, Joe," Tempus said, "when you don't have Stepsons at hand."

"We . . . coexist? We don't . . . go out there much, anyway. We keep . . . a balance."

Tempus looked again at this little man. Was he a devotee of maat, like Niko? If so, Tempus had underestimated this land.

But he thought not. It would be difficult to underestimate a race so inept as to have destroyed its fields and water and left itself with no place to live but underground and nothing to eat but its own recycled wastes.

The Drekka, he had a feeling, weren't the worst of Sandia's problems. But they might be the worst of his, if Faun wasn't willing to help get his people back.

Tempus wasn't about to trade for his fighters. He was going over to the Drekka encampment and demand his Stepsons back.

Then what would happen would happen. If he saw any dragons on the way, then the god was with him.

But he hadn't looked so long and trekked so far to reunite his band to lose any members of it in this blighted land where a thunderstorm was cause for celebration and the dung of a horse worth its weight in unborn babies.

He hoped it was Cime, with his late-arriving fighters. Only Cime could make heads or tails of a place such as Sandia had turned out to be.

And as for Faun, whose hips had invited him last season . . . now she was not nearly so inviting.

Even the god was beginning to agree with that.

Chapter 13:

DRAGONS IN THE SKY

Cyrus was maddened with pain, lust, rage, and guilt.

He'd tumbled into the parched wasteland below, just behind the eagle who'd become a dragon, in the midst of their battle.

This changeling who'd torn his very arm from his chest would be dead by now, except for Mother.

Cyrus had finally caught up with the changeling marauder, and there Mother was.

Funny, how small Jihan looked when you were as big as Cyrus had become, and she was in the shape of a human. He couldn't keep his mind on his quarry, even now.

Cyrus kept seeing Jihan's face, through the clear barrier that had separated them like stubborn water. There had been tears in her eyes.

He felt awful. She'd seen him . . . not winning. She'd seen him with a stump instead of an arm. She'd seen him in ravening bloodlust.

When he'd finally broken away from her sad, wonderful face, everything inherent in this maddened form he wore had overcome him once again.

He'd jumped right on top of that womanly mass of muscles from hell and ridden her into the humans' cave.

He still wasn't sure if he'd been hoping to ravish it

or murder it. Its huge backside was so thrilling. He'd been chasing that backside for almost the whole time he'd been on land—or in the air.

And the changeling, mean as it was, was behaving in the ways of a temptress. He would teach it a lesson before he killed it, he'd decided, grappling with it there on the floor. He would show it who was master. He would make it smoke with passion. . . .

Then the world had spat him out, and his changeling, darling enemy with him.

Now here they were, in parched air, continuing their flight and fight over a nearly featureless earth.

There were humans here, too. And, oh, woe, Mother was with them. The fire-breathing changeling, like his mother, seemed to follow certain humans. At least, she [the changeling was resoundingly a "she"] was leading Cyrus where the humans—and Mother—had gone.

He saw their little bodies, their tiny mounts, and the roaring wagons of the local folk collide, but he was too busy trying to catch and mount his tormentor to pay too much attention.

Mounting her in the sky was surely the best choice. He would come upon her from the rear, invade her hot depths, and ride her till, exhausted, she flapped beneath him all the way to earth.

Then he would finish her in the sand. And when she lay under him, breathing hard and moaning, puffing little smoky sighs, he would exact payment for his arm, ripped from its socket.

Cyrus wasn't sure what payment that would be, but it must be severe. Perhaps he would eat her alive. She certainly deserved it.

He screeched his challenge to her once again and, over her mighty wings, she looked back and hissed fire at him.

Tease. Slut. Murderous temptress. As he flew on, toward her, he started trying to regenerate his arm.

He ought to be able to do it. He could feel an itching at its stump.

He didn't know why he was sure he could do it, but he was. Somewhere he'd heard that his father, the great lord Tempus, could regenerate his own limbs. Cyrus didn't want Mother to see him again until he had an arm where his stump now gaped. It was too embarrassing.

When he found the much-vaunted Tempus, he would have a full accounting from the father who'd deserted Cyrus without teaching him anything—like how to regenerate an arm if you got one pulled from its socket. But first, he must deal with the female who fired his soul. Lovers often courted murderously.

And sometimes, in the sea, one lover ate another after the deed was done. Never mind that the eater was usually the gravid female.

Cyrus was on the land now, making his own rules. And this land, such as it was, seemed nearly devoid of other life.

He was getting hungry, in fact.

So must she be, ahead of him.

But *she* wasn't trying to regenerate a limb.

He started looking for something to eat, content to fly along behind the dark dragon ahead of him, always careful to keep her marvelous tail in sight.

There was very little below him in the way of warm meat; only the riders on horses and the humans on the roaring wagons with glowing eyes.

Somehow, he knew it would be importunate to eat one of his mother's traveling party. He wasn't at all certain, now that he came to think about it, that Mother was happy traveling with these folk who had met her when she arrived here.

Cyrus swooped down for a closer look.

Mother definitely didn't look happy, though she rode placidly with her companions. Her seahorse was very *un*happy, in the dry heat, and Mother was concentrating on making the seahorse stay in land-horse shape. And neither Mother nor seahorse liked the men with the loud wagons. Cyrus could feel that, even at his lofty altitude.

Well, then, Mother wouldn't mind if Cyrus ate one or two of the men with the wagons, since they weren't friends of hers.

He stretched out his wings wide, and circled lower over them, letting out a blast of fire to test his belly.

And his belly was good, filled with fire and smoke.

He screeched loudly, once, and tucked in his wings, head downward. And dived straight at the men on the wagons.

Openmouthed, breathing flames, he swooped down over them, catching three in his hands and feet, one in his tail, and frying a fifth dead where he sat.

Then Cyrus flapped as hard and as fast as he could, to gain altitude with so much added weight.

Ascending, he ate as fast as he could, chomping up the first man and swallowing him in three gulps; then stuffing the second into his mouth as he flew onward.

The living one in his tail was writhing too much to allow Cyrus proper rudder control. He dropped that one. He could always come back for it later.

And, wonder of wonders, with a blast of sidelong fire and a clarion roar, the dark dragon who'd been plaguing him darted down to seize Cyrus's discarded prey.

Something in his heart warmed, as he circled cloudward, eating his next man ruminatively. She might think it was a gift. He didn't really care if she did. Oftentimes, Mother would come into his cave and leave him a fresh kill.

He'd never once been less than thrilled by the gesture.

As Cyrus ate his last man, the itching at his stump grew so fierce he could barely stand it. He started scratching it, and realized he was scratching with a hand that had formed from the stump itself. With a bellow of joy, he somersaulted in the air, forgetting all about Mother, far below.

And as he somersaulted, he saw that his changeling companion was picking off more of the wagon-driving humans, but leaving the horse-riders alone.

He was glad that this was so. Otherwise, he would have to interfere.

And then something—like fire but sharper, like lightning but straighter—spat at him from one of the wagons on the ground.

It nearly holed his left wing. He sped off to the right.

He saw a flash: the wagon was attacking the dark dragon with its spear of light.

Roaring in fury, he sped to intervene. If anyone was to have the privilege of destroying the changeling dragon, it was he. Hadn't he assumed dragon form, to make the game better? Hadn't he chased her all this way? Hadn't he learned what he needed to know, in order to be fearsome in her sight?

Wrathful and trumpeting, he descended on the last wagon, and incinerated it with a mighty, blaring breath.

He thought he heard Jihan call, "Cyrus! Son! Come back," but of course he couldn't have heard that. He couldn't have heard any such thing.

His mother was going wherever she had to go, and Cyrus was going wherever he had to go.

With a full belly and a new-growing arm, his course was clear: follow the dark changeling, receding ahead of him in the white, bright sky.

Follow her to the ends of creation, until things were settled between them.

He screeched his accustomed greeting, as loudly as he could.

And, from far ahead, she screamed back.

The echo of her voice was music to his ears.

Chapter 14:

FALSE GREETING

Randal had cast a language spell. Not because
Kama had ordered it. Because Niko had insisted that
doing so was no flagrant use of sorcery, just a neces-
sity for the Stepsons in this strange and blasted
land—so that they could talk with those who'd come
out to meet them.

So, when out of the Sandian sky came fire-breathing
dragons who attacked their Drekkan hosts, everybody blamed Randal it seemed, as if the dragons'
attack was sorcery gone awry.

He could see condemnation in their faces. Jihan
wouldn't look at him. Her eyes were swimming with
unshed tears. Niko's jaw was set and his gaze fixed
on the blinding horizon where the dragons had—
thankfully—disappeared. For now. Kama glared at
Randal as if somehow he could have fended off the
dragon attack. Strat looked as though he'd tasted
something rotten, as he helped the six remaining
Drekka tend their wounded and pick up pieces of
their dead.

No one talked, now, as the party hurried toward
the Drekkan fortress. The language spell had allowed
the Stepsons to lie with impunity: when the Drekkan
men swore that the dragons weren't indigenous to
Sandia, the Stepsons had told the Drekka they knew
nothing about whence the dragons had come.

All Randal's compatriots were sure that his spell had summoned the dragons here from Lemuria. No one said to Jihan, who was so morose that her horse kept flickering into the likeness of a giant seahorse, that she should have stayed behind and dealt with her son. No one said to Niko that all these Drekka had died because of Niko's witchy lover, who would chase him to the ends of creation.

Oh, no. This was all Randal's fault. He was the Stepsons' staff enchanter. He should have been able to stop the dragons in mid air. ". . . stopped them before they got even so far as Lemuria," Kama muttered to Strat in an undertone that Randal couldn't fail to hear, as their hosts signaled a halt before a huge cave's mouth yawning in a sandstone cliff.

Randal turned in his saddle, fixed Kama with a baleful stare, and said, "There's more than enough fault to go around, here." Then turned back before she could answer, with a hot flush crawling up his already sunburned neck.

Here they were, precisely because Kama, the Riddler's daughter, couldn't turn away from any danger, no matter how daunting, if her pride was at risk—and now she was blaming it on him.

So it had always been with Randal, among the Stepsons. He was their eternal scapegoat, their reason for everything that went wrong.

Niko's horse sidled over to his and nipped at its neck. Niko said, "Randal, I'm sorry. I tried to argue that Jihan and I should stay behind. . . ."

"And I," said Jihan, joining them, her sad face worse than any indictment. "I should have destroyed them, when they attacked, but I . . . couldn't."

One was her son. "I know, Jihan. If I'd cursed the dark one, the other might have been felled by the same words."

Niko said, "We've got to do something."

Randal could feel maat working in his partner,

making Niko thirst for justice. For the first time ever, Randal thought that he, a lowly sorcerer of slight stature, was better off than all those he traveled with—better off than all the Stepsons for whom he'd risked his life so often. Straton was a mere shell of his former self, his mettle gone, his heart broken by all he'd endured and all he'd seen. Jihan was a travesty of power, nothing more than nature's beauty and nature's passion in a human guise. Niko was—a tool of principle, a servant of ideology whose whole life was dedicated to death in pursuit of the unattainable. And Kama was . . . a half-thing, the Riddler's daughter, more than a woman, less than a man, not comfortable with anything about who and what she was.

Randal, at least, had a brain unaddled and a mind that belonged wholly to himself. His soul might be sold to magic, but magic was the working of man's will in the phenomenal world, using recipe and artifact.

And, for the first time among an army that despised and hated sorcery, Randal was proud to be a warlock: proud of mankind, proud of his learning, proud of his years of study and every spell he'd cast. Weren't spells better than prayer? More dependable? Wasn't an understanding of nature superior to craven, superstitious fear of it? Weren't the horrors of hell no more than the horrors ignorant men made in their minds? As a white magician and a warrior-mage, Randal was a second-class citizen to those he served.

But not, as of this moment, to himself. Here, in the desert, he could breathe freely and see clearly. No plants itched his eyes. The horse under him was hypoallergenic, a matter of washing it in the proper potion. The two miserable souls closest to him were in need of help. And help he'd give them.

"Look, you two," he said as the Drekkans with the stinking wagons stopped fiddling with the things at the cave's mouth and came back. "The doors are opening. Inside there, somewhere, we'll find the Riddler. Then, since you don't trust my judgment, you can have his. But I swear, it will be the same: we did right, coming here together, as we were ordered. Those . . . dragons, both of them, were and are problems we'll meet together. They're nothing to be ashamed of. Stop harassing your own hearts and be the soldiers your commander expects to see."

This brought Jihan up straight immediately. You only had to tell Jihan what was expected of her. She was taking her cues from Niko's guilt, as much as from a mother's instincts, Randal was sure.

Niko slapped his horse's muzzle away from Randal's horse's ears, and said, "So you think we can solve this, Hazard?"

Hearing Niko speak to him that way made Randal sit up straighter too. "Of course. When have we not? We'll go to the Riddler and hear his wisdom. Then we'll do what we always do: prevail over evil."

"My son's not evil—" Jihan blurted.

"Roxane's influence, Jihan," Niko answered bitterly. But Randal saw Niko shiver. Somewhere in the devotee of maat lay an affection for the witch that drew her from nether hells as effectively as any spell. Niko must shake his fascination with her evil before that evil could be forever banished. Randal knew it.

And Niko knew it too. As one of the helmeted Drekka came back to their wagons, he said, "We're having a little trouble convincing our people what happened out there. Before we can go any farther, would one of you come and—Oh, no!"

The Drekka peered into the sky.

Randal said, without looking up, "Our commander will explain everything to yours. Let's just go where Tempus is waiting. You promised—"

"They're coming back!" another Drekka called.

This one was on one of the horseless wagons,

which smelled of burning oil, and had three piles of
corpse remnants in its back.

Jihan's horse leaped into a gallop, and thundered
by Randal's.

"Niko, get her," Randal called.

Strat's horse was already lunging after Jihan's.

"Carefully, Strat," Randal muttered under his
breath. Jihan could freeze the blood in any of their
veins with a gesture or a touch. If the Froth Daughter was truly griefstricken, there was no telling what
pursuit might make her do.

"Come on," called a Drekka dressed in sand-colored
clothes from the portal where the gates had paused,
half-open. "I've got it. We're clear to enter."

This strange, staccato tongue of theirs was neither
elegant nor polite. It was filled with imperatives and
declaratives.

Something told Randal that this culture was best
displayed by its language. He turned to look at the
sky and saw no dragons.

"I see no dragons," he called to the Drekka who
had.

The man said, "Well, you're just using your eyes,
ain't that so?"

Randal was about to argue when Kama put her
horse squarely in front of his and said, "Randal,
Niko, let's go. Strat will bring Jihan. My father is
waiting."

"Are you sure?" Randal asked, surprising himself.
Niko looked at him askance. Then at Kama, whose
hair was filled with sand. "Whatever the Drekka
saw, I wouldn't doubt him."

"Your maat tells you this?" Kama said scathingly.

"My gut, if you prefer."

Still Randal could see no dots flying their way on
the horizon. But the Drekka wagons were filled with
strange humming and glowing magic boxes, like
Lemurian boxes.

And behind Randal's back, the doors in the lee of the cave were winching apart with an earsplitting complaint of metal.

"Let's go, folks," called a Drekka lieutenant, who had colored bosses on his sand-splattered uniform. "No time to lose."

Randal wouldn't enter without his companions, any more than Niko or Kama would.

"Assholes," one of the Drekka opined. "Maybe I ought to go get the woman—"

His superior in the foremost cart said, "Not unless the big guy can't get her," in a strange tone with a tinge of cunning in it.

Niko urged his sable horse closer to Kama's. "See the dragons?"

"No, I said," the Riddler's daughter told him. "To hell with the dragons."

"I tried that," Randal reminded her. But he thought now, far down the featureless sky, beyond the two horses racing, he did see them.

"Strat's got her," Kama exulted.

And this was true: the big man's horse had cut off the Froth Daughter's. Hers reared. The two horses started back at a good clip.

"Cant' they hurry?" said a Drekka in one of the closer wagons. He was fumbling with something in his wagon, a metal thing like a crossbow, which sat on a flat bed heaped with bits of dragon meal that once had been men.

All these Drekka wore unfamiliar helmets. These were nothing remarkable, until you looked closely, as Randal now did, at one of them. This helmet had eye-shields of shiny glass, with colored lights that ran across it.

Similar colored lights were running across the plinth of the great crossbow as the Drekka aimed it at the sky.

Randal could hear tiny voices. Since those voices

didn't come from the dead, but were definitely emanating from the wagon, he assumed they were magic voices.

His hackles were rising as if they were. All his hairs were beginning to stand on end. The closest wagon, which had always been loud and stinky, now began to vibrate where it sat. A hum that made his horse snort and back into Kama's, came from it.

Along with the hum came an excitation of the air that Randal had long come to associate with the Storm God's lightning and thunder.

"Perhaps Tempus is coming out to see the dragons, firsthand," Nikodemos postulated halfheartedly, rubbing his bare arms.

Kama said, "I don't like this."

"They're almost here," Randal observed mildly, considering what sort of spell might protect Jihan and Straton from anything untoward.

As he started to cast one, he finally saw the dragons. Far, far off, were they.

No human eye could ever have seen them when the Drekka did. No magical eye could have seen them either, until Randal's did.

Behind him, the Drekka who'd announced the dragons' return was driving his wagon into the cave's mouth, and another wagon was getting in line behind that one. Of the twelve Drekka wagons that had come out to meet them, only five remained.

In the back of the last wagon, the man tending the humming crossbow shouted, "I'll handle this here. Everybody else go ahead."

"When my people catch up," Kama said and crossed her arms in a gesture reminiscent of her father.

Where was Tempus? It was unlike him to leave any confrontation—even only a potential one—to others. If he was too busy to come and greet them, surely he'd have sent someone, at least as far as the gates.

But Tempus had not appeared by the time Strat herded Jihan back among them.

And by then, the dragon shapes in the sky were clearly visible.

And the Drekka in the humming wagon was swearing vilely in a language more suited to cursing than Randal had first believed.

The remaining Drekka said, "Go *on*, you! Hey, on the horses! Get inside where it's safe. *Now!*"

Kama looked at Niko. Niko shrugged, and looked past her, at the faraway dots in the sky.

"Safe?" Randal wondered. Did these Drekka understand what a pair of dragons from hell could do, when one was a witch? And one the child of the Froth Daughter?

But he followed Kama, reining his horse toward the cave where the doors were open, falling in behind the wagons.

Jihan's horse was blowing hard, and she and Strat were arguing about whose orders meant what, here.

"You'll obey the Riddler. When his daughter's given orders, you'll obey those orders," Strat was telling her. "And sometimes, you'll even obey me. And I don't give a damn who your father is or what that dragon is. If you're here with us, you'll do what you're told."

A dragon screamed, far off.

Randal twisted around to see what he could.

And he saw, as he looked, a bright blast of light spit from the remaining wagon into the sky. It was blue-white, painful to look upon, and filled with dust. For an instant, it made a beam miles long, from the wagon to the first of the dragons.

Then it was gone, and Randal heard a scream that chilled him to his very bones. A scream of agony, or fear, or rage, or challenge—which, he wasn't sure.

But he knew that voice from his own worst nightmares.

So did Niko.

His leftside leader nearly wheeled his horse. Randal caught its reins beneath the bit. "Niko, you can't go out there alone."

"It's here. I—"

"You what?" Their horses were squarely between the open doors, where the walls of sandstone cave turned glassy and smooth and a manmade tunnel went down into the bowels of the earth. "You what, Niko? Have you lost your senses? Again? Just because she's calling you, you don't have to go."

Niko shook his head as if to clear it. "Thanks, Randal."

"Don't mention it," Randal said. "I put a spell on Jihan and Strat to protect them, but not on you. I think you know that if you happened to ride in front of the wagon's beam, there'd be no magic strong enough to save you from Drekkan magic."

Randal kneed his horse and, still holding Niko's sable by the reins, moved on. Straton and Jihan came wordlessly after, both angry and pouting, both on sweating, hard-blowing horses.

Again, behind them, the wagon's giant crossbow spat light.

Again, the sky erupted with hell-spawned fury.

And this time, flame followed.

Randal could see a wall of flame envelope the wagon as the doors started to close. The last Drekka jumped from the wagon, running for the doors.

Too late: a gout of flame caught him. He ran, aflame, for two steps—three—screaming and beating himself. Then he fell where he was, writhing in the sand.

The doors shut with a clang of finality.

All was dark. Randal's eyes strove to adjust as Strat swore and the horses reared and plunged, neighing loudly.

Even over that neighing and the echoing of fright-

ened horses' hooves and wagon-noise, Randal heard
the shut doors bang as something hit them, hard.

Once. Twice. Three times.

Up ahead, the Drekkan leader called back, "Hurry,
damn you."

And damned they surely were. There was no need
for the local magicians to try to make things worse.

Chapter 15:

PRAYING OUT LOUD

Trekking across the desert was easier for the Stepsons this time, thanks to Faun's knowledge of Sandia and the Storm God's favor.

The god was showing off for the Sandian Shepherd. As soon as their horses nosed out into the desert, distant thunder rumbled. The sky scudded dark with clouds, and a steady drizzle started. *Enlil, Your despicable womanizing will get You nowhere,* Tempus warned the god in his head. Faun might be easily wooed by soft rain, and even the horses and men put in a better humor, but Tempus was worried and angry.

Leave it to the god to get besotted with a woman when Tempus really needed His full attention. As they rode through the soft rain, a bank of cloud traveled with them, keeping the bright sun from beating down upon them.

This was a wonder and a joy to the Sandians, and Tempus couldn't warn Crit in time to keep his first officer from saying, with his quick grin, that rain was the province of the Storm God of the armies.

"So thank the god Enlil, Shepherd, for your rain and your thunder and your lightning," Crit told her.

The Sandians rode on platforms that sighed like contented women and puffed up little waves and wakes of sand, as if their prows were boats' prows, and their sterns were boats' sterns.

These platforms had canopies that could be raised or lowered. The Sandian Shepherd had lowered hers. She had her face turned up to heaven and was rubbing the rain against her cheeks as if she were bathing.

This was too banal. The god would come a cropper, so fixated on a human woman when there were dragons in Sandia's sky and a flotilla of platforms, obviously armed for battle, headed toward some unknown Drekka stronghold.

Tempus's Tros snorted whenever the sand from the Shepherd's platform eddied around its legs. Nevertheless, the Tros kept pace, one eye warily on the moving, wheelless thing that barely reached its knees.

A dozen more platforms were strung out among the Stepsons. As well as war, these Sandians were prepared for trading: "negotiation," Faun called it.

Tempus had no intention of negotiating with the Drekka if the Drekka, who and whatever they were, had hurt or detained any of his people. He tried repeatedly to make this clear to the Sandians, who merely murmured inconsequential strings of words meant to soothe him.

Thus they traveled along, Tempus and Faun continuing these noncommittal conversations whenever Tempus would call a rest for the horses.

In addition to the god's rain and cool storm clouds, the traveling party had Sandian water in barrels and grain. During a rest stop, the Tros snuffled up the grain greedily, as if it were home grown, while all along the valley floor, the god-given rain made plants sprout between Tempus's feet while he watched. Telling his men to graze the horses, Tempus climbed a hillock by himself to talk to the god and learn the lay of the land.

He looked back once and saw Faun, with a hand on Crit's arm. Bark up that tree, and she'd get splinters. But Tempus's jealousy was not shared by Enlil.

Your fighters are My fighters, Meddler, Enlil announced, when they were alone on the hillock and Tempus could see how the storm clouds ended only a thousand yards beyond and behind their party's extent. *If these Sandian sluts wish my fighters' good seed for their orchards, then let the Sandians have it! This I decree, and you, mortal, will not interfere.*

Are you so flattered, he yelled back at the god in his head, *that you're blind, O Mighty Loins of Heaven? Can You not tell when You are being shucked? These Sandians want Your power and Your glory and Your storm to be theirs, eternally! They'll make an end to me and all my Stepsons, just to keep You happy!*

So? They are worthy worshippers, far better than you, who disobey me whenever the whim strikes you. Perhaps I will forsake you for these grateful folk, and turn their land into a garden of earthly delights!

When the thirteen sons of heaven we gave the Shepherd are born here, You Idiot among Deities, what do You think will happen? You have already populated a heaven for these fools. Unless we destroy those offspring, there'll be no more room for You here than for me—or for any mortal folk but slavish worshippers, when that clutch of godling brats starts shaking little red fists!

And then the god grew canny: *Ah, mortal, thou art jealous indeed. Why say to me such things, unless you want to destroy the seed that we have sown among these Sandians, to have Me and My Glory all for yourself? You are getting old, mortal. Perhaps it is time to replace you with more virile, younger avatars after all. Some hot young men who'll rape their way through Sandia will put the fear of Me into them.*

Tempus gave up. The god didn't understand what Faun had shown them. The god wasn't ready to become civilized. And if He thought He could make these people god-ridden and uncivilized, Enlil was underestimating the power of frozen embryos and 'non-live' cover.

But Faun loved the rain. Perhaps the god would win her folk with blandishments of nature. He knew well what Enlil could do when the god wanted to. So he said: "God, my men need me, in the Drekka stronghold. As You say. I am getting old. I tire of trekking. Make me a cloud-conveyance of Your finest sort, one big enough and bold enough to bring us right into the midst of the Drekkan stronghold, without having to traverse all this sandy ground. It's surely easier than wetting down all the miles between here and there."

Having said this aloud, he looked around in case someone had heard him praying out loud on a hilltop. Praying out loud on a hilltop had gotten him into this situation in the first place, long ago and far away.

Since the god did not immediately answer, he sat down there, blanking his mind from Enlil's mind as best he could, waiting for the Storm God to decide both their fates. The less time Faun and her sort had to sidle around his men and stroke their arms, the better. And the less he heard of "sensoring packages" and sorcerous intelligence reports of the Drekkan enemy, the better.

As for the dragons, Tempus was sure the dragons would find him, wherever he was. So he'd prefer to meet the dragons in the stronghold of the Drekka, Sandia's enemies, since they were now his sworn enemies.

Otherwise, the Storm God might have to show the Sandians how He could protect their fragile hold on life from ravening dragons.

Tempus didn't know it, but his lips drew back in a feral grin at the thought. His eyes scanned the wet and gray sky for hints of dragons.

But all he saw was deep cloud; gray cloud lounging

upon black cloud; thunderhead bulging into heaven; white-edged cloud and wispy cloud flying low, bringing the soft rain that unceasingly drenched them.

Could the mere introduction of Enlil into this place bring it back to life? Lemuria had given Sandia living seas, but Faun had not asked for gods. Or had asked only Tempus for a god. He kept trying to remember exactly what she'd said, and he'd said, that night in Lemuria, but he couldn't. He'd had too many women in his life to pay much attention to what he said, courting one; or to what they said, being courted.

His hands, without much direction, fished in his belt purse. He could slip back to Lemuria for a bit, see if Cime was there, or here with the Drekka, and get out of this blasted rain. Do all that, and still be back by the time the party was rested and on its way again.

His fingers found the little black oblong that he carried when he was away from Lemuria. To get back, he merely designated how many, by turning a ratcheting wheel, and depressed a stud. Even Enlil had never dared dispute or decry the usefulness of this particular bit of Lemurian magic.

When Tempus had gone into the future once before, he'd learned to call that magic 'technology,' from the folk he'd met. But Lemuria's magic was a deeper and more sorcerous technology than any other, anywhere Tempus had been.

So he'd gone back to calling it magic, and Cime had too. Thus they reminded themselves that what they'd thought the world to be was not the world at all: the world was not defined by a battle between good and evil, magic and gods, or any other single thing. The world was all of these, every venture of consciousness, on all its planes—in the body and out.

The god in his head proved that truth, as much as

the Tros he rode here, or the Lemurian magic oblong in his beltpurse.

If the world were not so full of wonders, he'd have found a way to kill himself to alleviate the boredom of it, long since.

But the world was full of wonders, and Lemuria's were the dearest and the finest wonders of them all. He truly did want a respite there, if only for an hour. Then he could use the Lemurian windows to look in on the Drekkan stronghold, prepare a battle plan. He could see how his fighters were faring: Niko, Randal, Straton . . . he'd even check on Kama.

If Cime was in Lemuria, and not the extra woman with Niko's party, Tempus could ask her what she thought Faun meant, and the god meant, by all this fuss over reproductive rights. Reproduction came as naturally to Tempus as eating. Reproductive rights, as he'd known them, were usually reproductive *rites*: you took a woman in the heat of battle, for the god's pleasure, or in ritual coupling to ensure a harvest, or for some other purpose under heaven.

This whole Sandian matter confused and distressed him. He felt as though he'd been tricked. Worse, raped. His willingness to father children was no longer central to the event. It rankled in his gut. It made his mind uneasy. It made his heart sore.

Had he not won control over his lusts, for just such a reason? Was he an animal, or a plant, to be harvested? Was it not a matter of will and purpose, to bring a child into the world?

Tempus, who had spread his seed so widely, was sure that the rights to that seed were his. And even though he'd had women by force and put children in their bellies out of the god's rapacious need, he'd always known that those women could rid themselves of those children with just a midwife or a potion.

Only slaves were bred. It was that simple.

Humans were never meant to be slaves. A eunuch was better off than a breeding slave in every culture he'd ever visited. What if, in a place like Sandia, where customs were so different, a whole host of Tempus's children were raised up? And these became a ruling class of tyrants, because of the god in their blood? And these children of his, all with his temperament, started wiping out normal folk? Then what? Would living interminably be normal?

Would having a god in your head be the standard of the day?

He pushed the button, decided that he must talk to Cime, who'd have a woman's view as to what this could come to mean. Steeling himself for her cynical glee and the teasing he'd endure when she found out what was troubling him, he closed his eyes, waiting for the tug and bump that meant that the trip home to Lemuria was completed.

Nothing happened.

He opened his eyes to the same wet sky, the same sodden hillock.

Well, then, he must have done something wrong. Usually, he walked through space as the transport worked. He would do it the normal way. He started striding over the hillock, and pushed the button again, between steps.

Nothing happened. He took out the oblong and looked at it. Its little green eye was blind, no longer shining.

He shook it. The light didn't go on. The eye didn't open. He put it back in his pocket and tried again, still striding back and forth as if pacing in worry.

And worried he was, now.

No matter what he tried, he couldn't get the oblong to take him to Lemuria.

Now his time was up. Down on the flat, the platforms were rising and the horses were snorting.

Why had nothing happened? He rubbed his arms,

telling himself he was merely chilled from the wet rain.

Still, to be stuck forever in Sandia . . .

He heard a laugh, and then he thought he knew: "You!" he growled aloud. *Pillager, this is no game. This is not funny. Don't stand between me and Lemuria!*

The god said nothing, just made a sound that seemed somewhat commiserating.

Again, Tempus tried the oblong, this time putting the god on notice that if Enlil interfered, his godbond was forever broken from that moment on.

And again, nothing happened.

Well, not exactly nothing happened:

From the west, on a harsh wind, a cyclone began to well up from the land. It rose up and up, and arched high, and ate all the clouds along its way.

By the time the funnel of it was snaking its way around the hillock, Tempus realized it was no cyclone: Enlil had made a cloud conveyance, a funnel of cloud big enough and long enough and strong enough to bear the whole Sandian traveling party, as well as his Stepsons, to the Drekkan stronghold.

He refused to thank the god, as he hurried down the hill to explain to Faun what was approaching.

A cloud-conveyance could seem threatening to the Sandians, who'd probably never seen one before. They wouldn't know that its lightnings and its thunders were tame and soft; or that, inside, all would be warm and dry and safe.

"Safe for all your platforms, and your people, Faun," he insisted when the Shepherd disbelieved him, holding her hair off her face against the rising gale. "You wanted a god among you. Now you have one," he reminded her. "Don't refuse Enlil's blessings. If a mortal spurns the signs of favor of a god, then ill befalls that mortal. You'd better get used to this, if you're growing thirteen of Enlil's babies in your artificial wombs."

"Oh, Tempus, stop! We're not taking the hovercraft into—"

But of course, in the end, the Sandians did. It was either that, or be left behind, shamed by the bold Stepsons and their brave horses, who stepped gingerly into the cloud-conveyance without complaint— once Tempus's Tros had gone first, snorting and prancing, his tail flagged and his head held high.

Perhaps Lemuria could not be found today. But the Drekka stronghold, by the grace of Enlil, was nearly Tempus's already.

Since the Storm God, Enlil, was obviously trying to make amends, Tempus relented in his silence and little lightnings sparked around him in the conveyance, stroking his cheek like overhanging leaves as he passed.

He'd try Lemuria again, as soon as he dealt with the Drekka and the dragons, and reunited his band with their lost companions.

Once they'd feted in joyous reunion, then maybe Kama could talk some sense into Faun. Otherwise, with the god behaving Himself once again, Tempus would have to get Cime to come all the way from Lemuria to do the job.

Maybe the god had been right: opening himself to Cime's sharp tongue was a move that should be undertaken only when all others had failed. If his sister found out that he and Enlil had thirteen offspring soon to be born in Sandia, they'd never hear the end of it. Slaying dragons was often preferable to letting Cime get the upper hand.

The god had remembered that, when he had forgotten. So he would go carefully in among the Drekkans, and see if he and Enlil could help him make this matter of the Sandian babies right.

Having decided, Tempus waited for the god to

approve this plan. But Enlil was ominously silent in his head. It must, Tempus decided, be the complexity of keeping not only the whole band of Stepsons, but all the Sandian platforms from falling through the clouds to the ground below.

Enlil? Tempus tested. But only a grunt answered him, from somewhere far away in heaven, beyond the tube of cloud through which the Tros picked its careful way, high above the desert.

Chapter 16:

BODY SWAP

Roxane's pride hurt most of all: more than her singed dragon hide, more than her bruised and battered scaly ruff, more than her shoulders, feet, tail and claws from throwing herself against the stout steel doors of the human stronghold.

Now she was lying on her side, her head in the sand, panting. Her tongue trailed desultorily out of her mouth, its forked tip making little curlicues in the sand.

Beside her lay the thing, on its back. Its hind legs were spread wide, as if it were sunning its huge testicles. Once in a while, its tail would lash. Its breathing was stentorian.

The thing had fought well, Roxane had to give it that. It had broken itself against the enemy, and even against the steel doors behind which the enemy lurked, with as much abandon as Roxane could have desired. The fire from its jaws still flickered weakly.

They'd nearly killed themselves, and what had they gotten? Bruises, burns, and a few roast bits of human to fight over. Those bits were covered with charred, foul-tasting clothing made of some sticky substance that smelled like rotten eggs.

Roxane had let the thing feed first, not because she was afraid of it but because she was afraid it might die out here. To get to her beloved Niko, she needed the thing, now that it had proved itself biddable.

The thing kept one dragon's eye on her, its protective membrane half-closed, giving it a dead and staring look. She couldn't quite remember when she'd discovered she could communicate with the thing in more detail than a scream of rage or a warning blare of fire and smoke.

During the battle, when she'd been distracted by Niko, only the thing's quickness had saved her. When again they'd attacked, and the light weapon had sprung from the cave's mouth into heaven to assault her, the thing had dived at her and butted her out of harm's way.

Just in time. If not for the thing, Roxane might now be lying broken on the desert floor with a charred wing and the life draining out of her.

The thing had saved her. Of course, it really was trying to save itself. It knew it needed her.

Whatever the bond between them was, Roxane never refused a worthy minion. And this thing had great power, great passion, great tenacity.

None with less could have kept pace with her.

She half-snored, drifting into exhausted sleep there on her side before the cave of her enemy. The thing raised its head protectively.

She batted her inner eyelid at it: *don't worry*. She grumbled to herself and pulled in her tongue. The thing relaxed.

Roxane was too tired to eat. She could trust the thing to keep watch while she slept, surely.

If it still wanted to kill or ravage her, it would have attacked by now. It, too, was simply too tired to fight an ally when adversaries were at hand—adversaries who desperately needed to be taught a lesson.

If the humans with the light weapon had done no more than attack Roxane, she still would have been intent upon their doom by now. But something else spiced the brew.

Niko was with them. She could almost hear her beloved calling her name. Calling, *Roxane, help me. I'm trapped. Help me.*

She sat up in a flurry of sand, tail and limbs. Had he truly called? Or had she dreamed it?

Lumbering on sore feet, she approached the leftovers of human on the ground. Cold, now, and probably tough; greasy, stringy, and bony.

But sustenance was here, nonetheless. The thing had cracked the cadaver's skull and eaten its brain first, then its heart, stomach, liver and entrails—and left all the muscle meat for her.

Roxane looked back at the thing. It was quiet, a great white dragon smudged from battle, lying on the sand with its balls in the air.

It had left her the haunch and the flank of this human. And though the clothes stuck to the corpse skin made its skin unpalatable, the meat was white and firm. Her dragon's jaw found the loin tender, not tough in the slightest.

She kept an eye on the thing the whole time she ate. No sense in turning your back to it. It was still the thing that had chased her across three worlds: it could not be trusted. When her rumbling stomach attested that she'd nearly eaten her fill, she began planning a second attack, as best her dragon's brain could plan.

This skull of hers was too thick for certain niceties of tactics. But even in this skull, she could hear Niko calling her. She could see him in her mind's eye: beloved Nikodemos, man among men, paragon among humans.

She would marshal her strength and try the doors again. She would get the thing to help her. This time, the combined fire of their bellies would be too much for those blackened, steely doors. Together they would melt the doors, charge inside, find Niko, and carry him off.

Roxane would fly high with Nikodemos cradled tenderly in her great, protective jaws. . . .

She smelled cloud, right through her daydream. She smelled storm, disturbing her musings.

She smelled the hateful, hideous, hotblooded Storm God, Enlil!

Up on her hind legs, Roxane reared and roared a baleful blast into the sky. There, fast approaching, was the telltale of the god: a snakelike, phallic tube of black wind filled with lightning and evil.

Again she roared. This time, the thing roared with her.

She'd forgotten about the thing. It, too, stood tall on its hind legs. It, too, balanced on its tail, the better to scrape the vault of heaven with its fiery breath and its sharp claws. It shook its great white head and roared.

Then it looked at her, like a child, or a puppy, head cocked—waiting for approval; waiting to see what it should do next.

Roxane sat back on her haunches, glaring at the travesty in the sky.

Here was an unnatural horror among horrors: the Storm God bringing rain to the desert. And probably His accursed minions with Him.

She should have known: where Niko and some Stepsons went, the rest would surely follow.

Should have known—but she hadn't, even though she'd seen Niko's companions. She knew them well enough. Roxane, a connoisseur of hate and conservator of revenge, had flown over Niko's party and recognized each hateful Stepson: the mageling Randal, an inept adept; Jihan, pawn of power; Straton, Tempus's most indefatigable officer; and the Riddler's miscreant daughter, Kama.

Naturally the god and the godbearing Tempus must be close behind.

Roxane shook her head, to clear all passion from it and banish all dragonly urges to fly off and sear the moist clouds from the very sky.

The white dragon aped her every move.

She looked at it and hissed.

It hissed back.

Roxane blew a perfect ring of fire, the size of a bracelet for her dragon wrist.

The thing blew a fire ring to match.

She looked into the thing's eyes, and saw there rapt attention.

She crouched down on the ground. It crouched down just the same, its tail pulled in tight to its haunches, just like hers.

This thing's provocative behavior set her to thinking, hard.

Roxane looked over her shoulder once. Yes, there was time. If she could just manage to do what she had in mind, before the clouds and their awful cargo got here. . . .

If the thing followed her lead—mimicked her exactly, did everything she did—then she might save its bacon too. They could go on fighting together, if it did as she did.

If it didn't follow through; if it couldn't . . . Well, then, a dragon would be there for the god's soldiers to slay.

But that dragon wouldn't be Roxane. It would be the great, white thing.

Roxane would be sorry to sacrifice the thing. Its bemusing nature was something she was growing quite fond of; the thing had its moments, as long as it wasn't chasing you headlong.

She crawled slowly over to it, trying to communicate with it as she felt she'd done before. She stared into its eyes as she crawled closer.

It held quite still, its gaze unblinking.

It was *the thing*, after all, she cautioned herself as she neared its jaws: the ravening thing that had chased her up the side of one sky and down another. It could lunge at her and lock her in a death grip, this close. . . .

But it didn't. It stared unwaveringly into her eyes.

She snuffled at it, blowing a little puff of smoke that said: *try this*.

Neither of them had been a dragon long enough to really know dragonness, to be adept at dragon signals and dragon conversation.

But as Roxane turned herself inward, to the shard of power now in her belly (which she'd swallowed in order to protect it when she'd been an eagle), she no longer cared what the white dragon did.

She cared what she would do. She must make this transformation perfect, and timely.

She must. She must. She must . . . shrink. Sluff off substance. Forget dragonliness and remember womanliness, in all its guises.

Roxane must become a beautiful woman of the desert, with the skins of a lizard for her clothing, and the teeth and claws of a lizard for her jewelry.

She must absorb all the power of her dragon flesh and bone and sinew and keep it in a human form. She could not afford to be found wanting. She could not waste a bit of the dragon substance she'd accrued.

She hunched down, and down, and down, and a smell like sulphur came from her dragon skin. A hiss like cooling lava came from her melting bones. A complaint like settling timbers came from her changing form.

And she screamed in horror at the pain, in wonder at the glory, in joy at the delight of pouring all her power into woman form once again.

Dust and sand rose in a flurry around her as she changed herself.

And when the dust and sand subsided, there sat a beautiful, lithe girl on her haunches, in a lizardskin desert suit, with long black curls cascading down her back.

She stretched her arms and moaned in pleasure. She wiggled her toes and giggled in anticipation. She shook her hair and shuddered in delight.

Roxane was a woman again! She raised her perfect hands to heaven. Light glinted off her fingernails: a woman to the nails.

Those fingernails were . . . a little special, a little different. Harder and thicker than women's nails, they resembled dragon's claws, an opalescent white.

But in a strange land, she would pass for human among humans. In a moment of need, those nails and what they signified could be worth her life.

She leaned back on the sand, stiff-armed, and stretched, testing her voice in a throaty laugh.

And something laughed with her.

She turned her head and beheld *the boy*.

The boy was light-skinned and green-eyed. He wore lizard clothing, like hers, of fine white skins. His arms were bared and these were muscled like a god's. His legs, within their pantaloons, were long and straight. He sat upon the sand in a double of her position, mimicking everything down to her laugh.

And his face . . . Roxane's breath caught in her throat when she beheld the face of the thing.

The thing's eyes, as green as the deep sea, had long lashes as thick as seaweed on a beach, as gold as sunlight on the horizon. His smiling lips were generous; his teeth were straight and as white as coral.

"You're beautiful," she said.

"*You're* beautiful," he said. "I've been trying to tell you that for . . . how long? Days? Weeks? It seems forever."

So he knew how to speak like a man.

"How can you speak to me as men speak?" she asked him.

"I ate the brain of the dead man. I know what he knew—for what it's worth."

"You do? Then teach me what you can about these folk, quickly. And follow my lead when the cloud arrives."

"Cloud?" The beautiful thing looked up at the lowering cloud in the sky and a furrow creased his perfect brow. His skin was nearly transparent, so fine was it.

"Cloud. More men come, in that cloud. Trust me, I know the ways of men. And clouds."

"I trust you," he said, with a limpid look tʰat made her buttocks tighten. "I'm Cyrus."

Could he be giving her his true name? Somehow she thought he had. "True names aren't for this place: you give someone power over you when you give him your name. Quickly, make up another name."

"Uh . . . You do it. What can I call you?"

There was no time for this. But she must make time. She was acquiring a powerful servant, here. "I will be Sibyl and you will be Mandrake. Can you remember?"

"Yes, I can remember. What about . . . ?"

"Hush. You must do as I say, when they come. We'll use these fools to sneak inside and get—"

"My mother, yes. My mother's in there."

That made no sense. What was his mother? A rat? A lizard? A desert spirit? The bowels of the earth? Thinking he was speaking allegorically, she said, "We'll go see your mother, then. And we'll find a friend of mine who needs to be rescued. I will not stop until I have him out of there safely, no matter the cost in human life."

"Then I will not stop, either," Cyrus said proudly. "If you'll have me. . . ."

"Of course—Mandrake. We'll fight together. Haven't we been doing that, all along?"

"Yes. And afterwards . . ." He smiled a broad smile like sunrise over a tropical pool. . . .

"Afterwards, you'll tell me how it is you have such power, whence it came, and what you're doing here."

"Here? Following you. I thought you realized that I was—"

"Yes, yes, I think I know."

She reached out to touch his cheek. It was cool and moist. He kissed her fingertips, as softly as the kiss of a wave.

Mandrake, she thought, was a foolish name for such a being. Firedrake would have been better. But it was too late.

The cloud conveyance was already dipping over their heads.

And the thing was on its feet, wide-eyed, stumbling backward. As Roxane suspected, it had never seen such a sight as this before.

"Hold firm," she told it. "Stay with me. I will protect you."

The thing called Cyrus, who was now the human youth she'd named Mandrake, ran over to the sooty wagon and jumped atop it, straddling the light weapon there.

"No!" she commanded as loud as she could, when he leaned against it with his shoulder, trying to aim it at the cloud-snake dipping their way.

"But why not?" The thing's voice was petulant. "I ate the brain of the man who used this weapon. I can use it, now. I can fry everything in that cloud to nothingness. . . ."

"Mandrake, no!"

There. She'd used the name.

He came up straight, on the wagon.

At least he'd responded—acknowledged his name, her power.

And now she knew that he could use the weapon. A fact that might come in handy, if the weapon itself still worked.

"Get down from there. Come here to me," she told the thing.

Mandrake jumped down from the weapon on its flatbed with all the grace of a dancer, and trotted to heel like a faithful dog.

He stood there, beside her, radiating energy and youth so that she could hardly concentrate on the cloud-conveyance and the heinous things coming out of it in a miasma of dirt and dust and fog and mist.

Soon enough, the mist evaporated. And there, in the midst of his minions, rode Tempus on a gray Tros horse.

Roxane shivered so that Mandrake said, "What's wrong, Sibyl?"

His question reminded her of where she was and what she'd promised herself. Niko awaited. Niko had called on her for aid. She was sure now that she hadn't dreamed it.

To anyone but Tempus, Roxane might have gone honestly for help. After all, Tempus was here looking for his strayed men. Why else?

Sure enough, up he rode, straight to her and the thing, who was quivering now with excitement at her side.

The mounted avatar of destruction looked down at them from his saddle and said, "Tell us what happened here, woman. Quickly. In simple words."

"I— My husband was taken captive by those inside." She didn't know how much Tempus knew. How much could he know? She saw a tawny woman, behind the Riddler on a magical divan, conferring with one of the Stepsons' lieutenants. And she saw many men she didn't know: new blood, that her soul had not tasted. A hunger began to grow within her for men's hearts and men's souls. "I couldn't stop them," Roxane continued. "I beat on the doors. . . ." Truth would ring right to Tempus. Roxane did not underestimate the power of this ancient enemy.

"And were there other prisoners?"

"Other . . . strangers," she said. "I don't know. Oh, I'm so worried." She swooned back against Mandrake, who caught her and held her, his young face full of concern.

"You, boy. What's your name?"

"Mandrake. And this is Sibyl."

"Sibyl." Tempus tasted the named doubtfully. "Well, go find some shelter. Once we're inside, we'll find your husband, madam, and free him. What's his—?"

Tempus was going to ask for a name. She couldn't say "Niko." She didn't want to lie. The god would smell the lie. She said, "Take us with you. We know how to fight. We know the workings of that device there. . . ." She pointed at the light weapon. Tempus could be no more familiar with such a thing than she.

Critias came up beside his commander. His horse snorted at Roxane and flattened its ears, smelling sorcery.

"Yes, Crit?" Tempus said. And: "Woman, boy. If you wish to join our party, go to the rear. We have our own experts with such weapons."

And so it was done. She was safe among her enemies, although Critias wondered, "Are you sure, Commander?"

Tempus growled, "Do I look sure of much to you? These Sandians want to trade *what* for the hostages?"

Roxane heard Crit say, "Ah, sir, a frozen . . . baby, if I have it right."

"And whose baby might this be?" Tempus's voice carried all the way down the mixed cadre of horsemen and floating divans.

"Uh . . . yours, sir?" Roxane heard Critias say, as if he were guessing a riddle.

An argument broke out among the horsemen and the riders of the divans, about whether there were prisoners inside, or not.

Roxane heard her new name used, and Mandrake's, as evidence of foul play.

Then the Riddler gave an order, and one of the men from the divans hopped off and ran over to the light weapon.

As he climbed aboard, the honey-haired woman, who argued with Tempus, left her divan, saying, "Commander, you're going too fast. Let me just talk to them."

"No more talk. You go up to those doors. If they open for us, fine. If they don't, get out the way quickly, Shepherd, because, by god or magic, we'll melt them down before nightfall."

The woman strode past Tempus with an ill-considered curse, over to the steely doors, where she yelled and pounded in vain.

"Out of the way, Faun," the big immortal cried in his gravelly voice. When she didn't heed him, Tempus cantered his Tros up to the doors and lifted her off her feet like a sack of spelt. Carrying the woman, the Tros horse backed up carefully, its neck arched, snorting its disapproval. When all the horses were well clear, the man at the wagon turned its weapon on the doors, and three floating divans came up to join it. These had weapons on them also.

"See," Mandrake whispered in her ear with his moist, cool breath, "I told you. All we had to do was turn one of those weapons on that door, and we could have gotten in on our own."

"And then what, Mandrake? This is a formidable raiding party, complete with hierarchal powers, if I don't miss my guess. Among them, we'll last much longer. Going in secretively, we'll bide our time. When we find our quarry we'll—"

"Mother. Mother may not be too happy with me, but I can't turn back—"

Mother? "I will talk to your mother, when the time comes. We'll find my husband," she told him, "and be on our way."

"Husband? Sibyl," said the thing, who was a little behind her, holding her around the waist, "I must tell the truth."

"If you really must . . ."

"I wish your husband was dead. I wish I was your husband. All this time we've traveled . . ."

"A husband is a term, my dear Mandrake, that can be applied to more than one man, and to different men at different times. Do well for me on this gambit, and I promise you a reward such as you've never dreamed. Give me your heart and soul, and I'll show you the gates of wonder."

"It is yours," said the besotted thing, as if intoxicated by the perfume of her human shape.

"Just like that?" This was serious business. She knew her new minion didn't know what he'd offered. But she still could take it.

"Just like that. All my strength, my obedience, my love . . ."

"Young lover, I accept. But we will still save my . . . other husband from his peril."

"Oh, all *right*," said Mandrake, who seemed a trifle disappointed. "But we could leave now, just us two. Mother will surely be well enough, with all these men to help her. I'm looking for my father, actually. Perhaps you've heard of him? He's called Lord Tempus."

"Ssh!" Oh, what luck! Sweet fortune! Fate's own joke, that no one had yet called Tempus by his name where the boy could hear. Tempus's son? By what demon? "I've heard of him. A formidable enemy. A difficult taskmaster. A murderer and a soldier—"

The boy interrupted: "I knew it! I *knew* it! He left my mother, and . . ."

"Ssh, Mandrake. There'll be time to savor every sweet moment of revenge, for both of us. I promise."

And that promise, Roxane fully intended to make good. As soon as she'd rescued Niko, she'd begin it.

This thing who sought his father might be the weapon that fate had given her, finally, to make an end to Tempus.

She looked sidelong at the beautiful body the thing now wore, and remembered the white dragon. That ravening dragon had struck fear into her own, fearless heart.

Properly guided, what might it do to Tempus, once its young ire was aroused?

The right tool for the job might at last be hers. A world without Tempus was a world in which Niko was free of his accursed soldier's oath: free to come to her, as she knew Niko really wanted to do.

Up ahead, the light weapons started to hum and whine.

The air grew charged. Mandrake held her tight. She shivered, remembering how it had felt to have that weapon trained upon her.

And then she closed her eyes against the unbearable brightness of its fire.

The doors lasted through three onslaughts before they melted into a heap of slag, glowing pink and orange.

All around them, soldiers cheered and floating divans moved forward with deceptive speed.

"Into the tunnel, Mandrake," she said to the thing. "Don't worry, I'm right beside you."

And she was, as they entered the stronghold cut into the bowels of the earth.

Roxane could smell Niko everywhere, now. She

smelled sorcery, too, and the reek of Jihan, the Froth Daughter.

Then it struck her, who Cyrus's mother might be. But she told herself that this could be no child of Jihan's. And if it were, all the better.

The thing called Cyrus loved Roxane. It had declared its fealty. It had given her not only its heart, but its immortal soul.

There was nothing heaven or earth, Jihan or Tempus, or all the magic of the desert folk could do about that.

Roxane was not just any witch. A bond to her could not be sundered. A promise to her could not be broken. Love of her could not be shed.

Nikodemos, when she found him, would attest to that.

Chapter 17:

A DOG'S LIFE

In the lemon and lavender light of a Lemurian sunset, Cime stared down at the sea blankly, her shoulders slumped, her proud chin quivering.

She had tried and tried, but she couldn't get the window into Sandia to come alight.

She had replaced its magic eye with another from Lemuria's stores. She had learned to connect the proper wires. She had read the documents over and over again.

Still, the eye of the Sandian window would not come alight. If there was something deeper wrong, Cime was not yet expert enough to fix it.

And time was running out.

A servant came up behind her saying, "Evening Star, you must eat."

"Not until I get this fixed," she said, running the back of her hand across her brow. Her spine ached from so much sitting. She was not a sedentary person. She had sat or crouched or hunched, motionless, over this inanimate or that, for days now. And all she had to show for it were sore muscles and a growing sense of frustration.

She wasn't about to eat. She had to think.

One of the dogs came up and nuzzled her knee. The poor dogs were howling every night. They knew something was wrong. This one whined and butted her thigh.

Without looking down, she said, "Dog, go find me some help. Don't just stand around here crying. I need somebody who can make the windows work!"

And the dog slunk away, making the little disgruntled noises a dog makes when you won't play with it any more.

She didn't have time to play. Tonight, she was going to begin trying other windows, looking for help. In some time she could access, there must be a civilization—a person was all she needed, just one man or woman—who could fix what was wrong here.

With the exception of Sandia and one other venue, she could go anywhere, access any of mankind's knowledge.

If she'd known where to look for help, Cime might have solved her problem by now. Tonight she'd face her own ignorance.

Tonight she was going into Lemuria's great library to read of times beyond her own. Somewhere, in all that history, she'd find the clue that would lead her to the wisdom she sought.

She'd thought this out. Short of falling asleep and dreaming the answer, this was her only recourse. But unless she was inordinately lucky, finding help in the library would take a very long time.

Cime didn't feel that she had much time. And she didn't want to go to her ex-husband, Askelon, entelechy of dreams, and ask for his help. She'd solve her brother's problem without the aid of the dream lord.

Tempus would never forgive her if she went to Ash for help. So she wouldn't.

As Lemuria's Evening Star, everything she needed to chart mankind's course was purportedly at her disposal. She had been chosen to correct errors in the very fabric of creation. She ought to be able to fix this one window and bring her own brother home.

Sometimes she wished that Tempus was really her brother. If their love wasn't so strong, then perhaps emotions wouldn't be standing in the way of clear thinking, here and now.

She was afraid for Tempus, as she had never been before. She was afraid for herself, in case she failed him. What would life be worth, without their love? Together and apart, they each had always taken strength from the knowledge that the other existed.

One does not fail such a loved one gracefully. In a world where too few knew love and even fewer knew how to nurture it when they had it, she and Tempus had fought long and hard to have this life together. They deserved it.

Nearly in tears, she turned from the seascape. The ocean was eternal; humankind was not. She had lived a long life, an endless one of men and magic and monsters and mistakes.

In this one instance, she must have perfection from herself, or she truly did not know what she would do. Could one go on, without one's heart? Could she face this eternal gift of Tempus's, knowing she'd trapped him in a blasted land full of unknown peril?

Could she . . .

Cime blinked, and rubbed her eyes. She was so tired she was seeing things. She rubbed them once more, and saw a clearer shape.

A woman was coming through the great hall, toward her. The step was imperious. The bearing was sure, not the carriage of some servant.

She had never seen such a woman.

She had never seen such a ghost of a woman, she amended.

For Cime could see light and furniture through the shape approaching her. The woman's form was translucent, and glowing.

When it had reached the doors to the balcony, the

ghost stopped and put a hand on the frame in a gesture of ancient familiarity.

Cime could only stare. Her mouth was half open, but no words would come out. Beyond the ghost woman, the great hall was completely empty. Not a single dog was there.

The ghost woman said, "Ah, now I see what the Riddler saw in you." The ghost smiled out of a haughty, imperious face softened by compassionate eyes. The lips were . . . a bit thick. The chin was . . . a bit square. But the bearing was a queen's.

"I . . . you see what . . . You know my brother?"

The ghost put out a hand and Cime took it.

Despite its translucence, it seemed solid. Yet when Cime shook the hand, it was like shaking the paw of one of the great dogs: the hand was horny on the palm and had short fingers with long claws.

"I know your brother," said the ghost of the woman. "I am Chiara. I was your predecessor. You're in need of help. I suspect. So I'm here."

"I—ah. Help would be great. Help would be, that is, much appreciated. I've got a broken window, and—"

"A lost Tempus. Yes, I know. Let's hurry, child. You have much to learn and I'd prefer to make this materialization as short as possible. I'm very tired of being a human, you see. That's why I gave it up."

"Tired of being a human. I think I know what you mean, Madam Chiara," said Cime through dry lips. She scolded herself for being taken aback; she tried to shake the superstitious trill that traveled her spine.

Cime had been many places, in and out of time, but never seen anything stranger than this ghost woman walking the halls of Lemuria. Somehow, the woman's weariness made Cime sad.

She said, as the ghost woman led her into the library, "Will you tell me why you left? Where you've come from? How I can repay you? What this is going to cost me?"

The ghost woman turned then, and smiled at her through thick lips. "Be good to the dogs, dear. Tend the fates of all the earth's creatures. Remember that humans are animals, and that all animals are part of nature. Keep the place clean and keep the place welcoming. Keep the earth as she keeps you. Don't forget your brothers and sisters on four feet, or on the wing, or in the sea. And when you're as tired as I've become, then you too can live among the wild things, a free life, without all the cares of humankind."

"I don't understand."

"We're the caretakers of nature, dear. I was. You are. Your Riddler is. And when you're done, you'll find others to take your place. Nature made us to keep her glory, her profundity, her varied splendor, without preferential treatment to this creature or that. So those who serve here have been among man at his worst, and at his best. We harbor no illusions, but we bear no grudges. Now do you understand?"

"I think so," said Cime somberly. She'd known, of course, what it must mean to live here in Pinnacle House. But she hadn't known any more then than she could bear to know. She said, "I'm sorry about the dogs getting hurt in the fight with the dragons—"

"Unnatural enemies breed unnatural results, dear. Pick your enemies more carefully, next time. The Evening Star doesn't need enemies. She is impartial."

"Ha!" It slipped out of her.

The ghost woman turned. "You will learn to be, dear. You and Tempus have earned the right to try. That's all nature asks, child: try your best; do right; tend to creation's needs as it has tended to yours."

"I . . . we're doing the best we can."

"And now," said Chiara, handing her a book with that translucent hand, "you'll do better. Here's your index, dear. When you're more secure here, you can use the windows to find information. Right now, you'll just have to look it up."

"Wait, don't leave me to fix that on my own. I tried and failed so many—"

But the translucent woman form was walking away, fading as she did, either unheeding or unmindful.

And the dogs were coming back.

One especially big bitch came right up to her, stood up with its paws on her waist, and nuzzled the book.

The book dropped from Cime's hands. Before she could reach down to grab it, the dog picked up the book in its giant mouth and trotted toward the great hall, where the dead-eyed window was.

Cime followed the dog, who carried the book, to the blind-eyed window into the future.

The dog was sitting before the black plinth when Cime caught up, the book under one paw, its tongue lolling out of one side of its mouth, waiting for her and whining softly.

Time to begin in earnest.

Chapter 18:

CULTURE CLASH

A shudder shook the Drekkan stronghold as if a dog had it by its scruff. A tremor ran up through Niko's feet. His sable whinnied, somewhere down the long, straight corridor.

The glowing strips overhead flickered, then steadied.

"She's in here," Niko whispered aloud. He hadn't meant to say it. The shock of feeling Roxane so close numbed him to the effect of his words. In that instant, he wasn't sure whether the shudder and flickering of the world about him was a warning from his maat, or whether the others felt it too.

The Drekkas guiding them to Tempus surely felt the tremor and saw the flicker. The Drekkas ahead of Niko's party stopped. Then those behind stopped. They all conferred among themselves.

Beside him, Kama asked, *"Who's* in here?" narrow-eyed and arms akimbo in the midst of their honor guard. The way she looked at him reminded Niko of her father.

"The *witch* is in here," Randal said, to make the matter clear. "Roxane." His nervous eyes darted everywhere, over the heads of the slight men and women around them in the tunnel. Yet there was compassion, even pity, in his voice.

Niko didn't want Randal's pity. He didn't want Strat to grunt as if gut-kicked and stare at him. He

didn't want Jihan to murmur, "I will protect you,
Stepson."

But his friends all knew what this meant as well as
he. Niko fought the urge to run. Run away. Lure
Roxane somewhere. Anywhere. Finish this matter
hanging between a man and a witch where his friends
wouldn't be witnesses.

He'd come looking for her, hadn't he? He'd come
seeking revenge for Nino's death, even though he
knew revenge was self-indulgent, ultimately fruit-
less, and only begot more of the same. He told
himself that he should sit down here and refuse to
move. The others would go on without him. The
witch would come. Life as he'd known it would end.
And then, a true servant of maat, he could sleep in
peace.

Maat wasn't revenge. It was justice. But sometimes, Niko lost sight of where he ended and maat
began. Justice in the world—balance, truth, and
integrity—were the province of nature, not of man.
Of history, not of fathers grieving over lost sons.
Niko, in the world, was maat's instrument, not its
wielder.

Niko slid past the Drekkas who were chattering in
low voices and talking into little boxes, and leaned
against one of the smooth corridor walls.

One Drekka looked at him warningly, but they
were too busy among themselves to bother him. At
the corridor's end, a red light had begun to flash like
a winking star.

Kama followed him. "What's wrong, Stepson?"

She would push him to the ends of the earth, to
the limits of his strength, to the edges of his tolerance, just like her father. But she was not her father.
She had never saved his life, tested his mettle, or
shown him what it was to be a caretaker of men.

He said, "What's wrong? A couple of dragons,
Jihan's face, Randal's fear . . . all because I went

seeking the witch in vengeance." He slumped against the sorcerously smooth, glassy wall. "I never should have come. She killed my son. . . . I'm sorry. I thought—"

"I, too, lost a child battling sorcery," Kama said in a husky voice and squeezed his arm.

Niko almost shook her off. Cold fury rose in him, at this arrogant woman who thought she knew how he felt. How could she? Kama had nearly destroyed Crit, and Strat, with her unthinking passion. . . .

As he rounded on her to tell her so, his eyes filled unaccountably with tears. His arms grew weak. What strength remained in him drained away. Nino was dead and nothing would change it. His boy's soul was lost to a witch and only the god of the armies could make the matter right. Niko was just a man who'd lost a son, chasing phantasms of remorse and penance.

Kama's bright eyes locked on his, and somehow she was holding him. Her arms were around him and he could feel her body tremble against his, her breath puff against his neck. "No one could ask any more of you, Niko," she murmured. "You're not alone anymore. It's all right."

He almost lost control then and there, hearing simple words from the Riddler's daughter. It was as though his soul had been hungry to hear them ever since the witch in eagle form circled high above the palace walls. Or even before. Release and relief washed over him, as though Tempus himself had given Niko absolution. And he found himself holding the Riddler's daughter tight.

His lips found her eyelids, her cheek. Something welled up in him that melted all the ill feeling between them and turned it into something else, much stronger. How long had Niko been alone, truly? Maat made you singular, in the world.

Kama shifted her head and their lips brushed. She

pulled back and met his gaze: "Niko, we'll come through this. Then we'll talk. We can heal each other. I know it. Promise me you'll try. For my father's sake, if not. . . ."

Kama had looked right into his soul and saw the wish for death there. "So you know me too well, already." He let her go.

"I know myself, and how I'd feel . . . what I'd do." She stepped back.

Jihan and Randal were staring at them. Strat was looking at his feet, a dour smile on his dirty face.

And the Drekkan leader was coming toward them, hands in his pockets, frowning uncertainly. "You done?" he said in their abrupt, impolite language. "Cause we've got trouble you can help with, maybe. We got to get you all over to the main quad—"

"Trouble?" Kama repeated, listening with her ensorceled ears and answering in the tongue Randal's magic had enabled.

"I know," Niko said at the same time. "The lights, yes? The tremors? It's the witch."

"The what?"

"Never mind," Kama said. "Take us to my father, as you promised."

The Drekka's face screwed up as if he'd tasted something sour. "That's not going to be a problem, ma'am. If you'll just come with me. . . ."

Something was so wrong here that Niko's whole body was reacting as if that wrongness was blowing through his very soul.

And yet, in the middle of all this, he'd found a friend where he'd thought sure he'd had an enemy. How could he never have noticed what Kama was really like? How could he have misread her so? He was so aroused from the imminent danger and the revelation of Kama's true nature that his maat haloed every living being in the corridor with a nimbus of color, allowing him to read hearts and minds as easily as Randal's spell allowed him to understand and speak an alien language.

Strat's nimbus was all readiness and aggression, red and gold, underlined with the yellow of fear.

Randal's form was limbed with pure wizardly power—green and blue and red—but the compassion and protectiveness of an honored friend made the wizard-light benign, even welcome.

Jihan was radiating a copper cloud that reached to the very ceiling, in which seafoam and restless tides surged. Never had Niko forgotten that the Froth Daughter wasn't human. Yet, seeing her aura so great and imperious made him blink.

And Kama's . . . He closed his eyes. This was the Riddler's daughter. The blood of both Tempus and the Storm God ran in her veins. She'd lost a child on the battlefield, an unborn baby—and gotten up and fought again long after, right alongside the men. He should have looked more closely at Kama long ago, when there was time to do something about it.

Now . . . the witch was on his track, as he'd wanted. He'd brought this upon himself. And he'd brought destruction upon Shaga, and upon Lemuria, and upon this blighted desert world of Sandia, to assuage his grief and guilt.

Everyone who'd died here in the dragon's fire had died on his account. Every benighted Shagan soul, too, was dead because Niko hadn't had the courage to meet the witch, one on one, on any roof or street or hill.

Had he shamed maat, or only himself? There was still time, he told himself, to go to Roxane and trade his soul for his son's. If his maat counseled otherwise, then he must try to understand why it did.

And quickly. The moment when he could make amends was coming near.

Kama was truly the Riddler's daughter. She'd freed him, as best she could. She'd showed him, with those few words, that he wasn't alone. And she'd reminded him that he was still a man, no matter what else he was.

For that, he would always be grateful. He fell in beside Randal, and the adept said, "What was that, back there? Are you making peace all around, or getting ready to die?"

"There's no peace in life, Randal," Niko said, "nor should there be. There's life, in life. As for dying— why should I worry about dying, with you and Jihan and Kama here to see my soul to heaven?"

"Niko, we've known each other too long for you to fool me. . . ."

"All right. If I die with the witch, Randal, see what you can do to make sure my son's soul isn't trapped by evil magic." He turned. "Promise me."

"You won't die with the witch," said the little mageling, puffing out his chest.

"You're so sure?" Strat, behind them, grunted, sticking his head over Randal's shoulder. "Are you now a soothsayer, as well, witchy ears?"

"Hush," Jihan said from in front of them. "Pay attention. Can't you hear it?"

They had mere human ears, not like hers. But everybody listened hard. At first Niko heard only the shuffling of their own feet and the rap of the hard-heeled Drekkan boots against the floor. Then he heard a low rumbling he thought was the heart of the Drekkan stronghold, beating.

And beneath it, he heard a deeper sound, a whine as if the very fortress was keening a death knell.

One of the Drekkas turned to another and said, "Emergency power."

Whatever that meant, Randal's language spell wasn't strong enough to tell them.

As they looked at each other, the lights flickered again above their head. Jihan murmured under her breath, "If they aren't taking us right to Tempus, we fight our way out of here. I will lead us. We will survive."

No one argued. But Randal said, "I smell her too," and Niko knew that Randal meant he could scent the witchsign, seeping through the walls and floor of this place as if seeking Niko.

In a short blink of darkness, Kama reached out to him again. He caught her hand for just a moment. If there were time, they could have talked about what it was like to lose a child.

If there were time, they could have talked about whether caretakers of mankind could be impartial if they had children of their own.

Niko's maat was seeing a balance in Kama's loss and his. That sight gave Niko strength such as he hadn't known since Tempus left him in the city at the edge of time.

Perhaps he could outwit the witch, one more time. Perhaps he could even outwit himself, and see beyond Roxane, to a real future in the world.

After all, Kama was in the world. And she was her father's daughter.

Chapter 19:

A FROZEN BABY

Once they'd blasted through the doors of the Drekkan stronghold, Tempus had expected pitched resistance. He'd galloped his Tros ahead, with his sword in his hand. And that god-given sword was glowing pink in reaction to fielded sorcery.

But there'd been no men in the corridors, no light weapons spitting over their heads. . . . just another pair of closed, steely doors.

These doors opened to Faun's command, though Tempus was already telling the men to spread out, in case some trap door behind them came down from the ceiling to imprison them between the two.

Crit, having noticed the color of Tempus's god-given sword, sidled his skittish horse up beside the Tros. Stroking its neck, Crit asked, "What do you think, Commander?" His eyes swept over the floating hovercrafts and horses in the corridor, the second pair of doors opening before them, and the strange lights above their heads.

"I think," Tempus said, "we follow where we're led." He sheathed the sword decisively. Crit's eyes stayed on it.

Tempus added, "It's been like that since we found the woman and the boy."

"That 'Sibyl'?" Crit's lips quirked. "You know what I think about that, Commander."

"I know, Crit. One enemy at a time. Let's get Niko and the rest of the band back among us."

Crit's face cooled and hardened in a set, professional mien. "Kama, Randal, Strat. . . . Yes, sir. One enemy at a time. But you won't mind if I ride back there with the . . . camp followers?"

Crit's instincts were always unerring. Tempus himself suspected sorcery in the person of the woman called Sibyl. Whose sorcery, and what kind, remained to be determined.

"No, Crit. You're not expendable. Let's not tempt fate. We'll have Randal back soon enough, and he'll tell us what kind of enchanters we have back there. After all, they needed us to get through the first set of doors. . . ."

Which were now blown wide open. Crit looked up from under his dark brows at Tempus. "I have a bad feeling about this, Riddler."

"Any suggestions?" Crit was about to face his own demons, Tempus knew: Straton and Kama, who'd been traveling together for so long, had made Critias the bone of contention between them.

"Just . . . I wanted to keep an eye on those two, that's all."

"Keep an eye on the Sandian with the frozen baby."

"Joe? He's . . . comprehensible, at least." Crit's horse snorted as a hovercraft passed by its haunches, brushing its tail, which the horse switched wildly.

"Here where not much else is, eh? Hold firm, Crit. Stay close to me. I might need you."

Tempus urged the Tros forward before his first officer could respond. But he saw Crit straighten in his saddle.

Critias couldn't be blamed for caution. But Tempus saw more danger ahead of him than behind. . . .

Faun was up at the head of the party, sitting in her hovercraft with her legs crossed. She had a pensive smile on her tawny face by the time Tempus had threaded the Tros horse through close quarters to reach her.

"So, Riddler," she said. "Now we see what can be won by negotiation, yes?"

"I—"

The lights went out. Something clanged in the dark. Horses screamed. The hovercrafts hissed, squealed, and spewed bright white light.

"I told you," Tempus nearly roared over the confusion, "not to trust these Drekkan enemies."

They were in a sealed length of corridor. There was no going forward. There was no going back.

And the tail of their party had been separated from the rest by doors that had come out from the walls to slam shut behind them.

Crit, two hovercrafts away, struggled with his rearing horse in a pool of bright lights. "Commander," Crit called: "The camp followers . . . They're gone. Beyond the doors."

The witchy ones, he meant.

"I saw. Not our problem, now."

If the camp followers were chance-met folk, and nothing more, then Tempus might be doing them a disservice. But he hadn't sworn to protect them; he'd only said he'd get the husband of that Sibyl back, if she wished. But she wouldn't give his name. . . .

He tried to forget about the witch-tainted pair. The boy had looked somehow familiar. Tempus had knottier troubles at hand.

Faun was ignoring him, talking into a little oblong connected by a snaky thong to her hovercraft's floor.

Tiny voices were coming out of it.

He clapped the Tros with his knees and urged it forward until its head was so close to hers that froth from its bit dripped on her hair.

Any closer, and the Tros would start climbing the

hovercraft. He said, "Faun, talk to me about 'negotiation.' "

"Don't panic, all right? This is just . . . where we're having the meeting. They'll bring your people down here, and we'll receive them in good shape, and then we'll leave."

"And that's the whole of it?" The Tros threw its head and nearly brained her with its bit. Foam spattered her like rain.

She raised an arm. "Will you *get* that horse out of my face? Can you blame the Drekka, for losing faith? You galloping at the head of these . . . ruffians . . . with your sword drawn and your antique armor? I knew it was a bad idea to blow the doors. I should never have listened . . ."

"Howsoever," he said, from deep in his throat, because the god was stirring in him and he was having trouble paying attention to her. "What are the Drekka asking in return?"

Let her say it to him. Let her admit the truth.

"Ah . . . oh, *all right*. One of the frozen embryos."

"And whose baby is this?"

"Mine."

"Ours," Enlil corrected, using Tempus's voice with so much power that Faun shrank back.

"Look, you don't want them anyway, right? You wish to destroy the embryos. You've made that clear. What's wrong with trading one for the soldiers you want, and losing no lives—no blood—in the process? I don't understand you at all, Riddler."

Nor did he truly understand himself. Enlil, who purported to understand all things, prompted him to tell the Shepherd that this was acceptable: *What is wrong with the Drekka having one of Our children, mortal, if the Shepherd's people have the others? If we are populating a heaven here, should not all peoples have their own gods?*

Tempus didn't answer Enlil. "I didn't sanction

more than a single child. I don't want these raiders raising a son of mine."

Faun replied: "You mistake the situation, Tempus. The child is mine. The sperm was yours. You have no rights in this matter, under our laws. Our laws apply to our citizens—you're not one. Neither is the fetus, until it's born. The living citizen's rights outweigh those of the potential citizen."

"There are the laws of nature," he warned.

But these Sandians and their Drekkan enemies had flouted every law of nature, and lived with the daily result. So what was the use?

Tempus leaned on his saddlehorn and glowered, while the Tros dribbled foam on her, waiting for the negotiating party to arrive with his people.

At his side, his god-given sword was heating in its scabbard, sensing magic deploying close by. But where? And whose?

They'd brought something into the Drekkan stronghold, he was now certain, that might change everyone's plans.

At that moment, he did not regret what he had done. The Sandians had destroyed nearly all of nature's blessings—so many that they'd had to find a way to send the Shepherd to Lemuria, to beg for a second chance at life.

He was among desperate people, guilt-ridden beyond comprehension.

How must it feel to dig a hole in the ground and pull it in after you? To live away from the sun and wind because you've destroyed your very sky, and the sun is no longer a friend to you? To never know rain, to never hear thunder, never sit on a hill and watch the glory of sunset, which the gods have decreed is never twice the same?

What must it be like to know your sky is empty of eagles, of hawks, of cranes? To forget the splendor of watching masked swans mate in a reed-filled pond?

To never hear the geese fly over in autumn, or watch the trees turn colors, or see clumsy ducks catch their wingtips on landing and tumble into an icy river, quacking?

What must it be like to have the murder of nature upon your very soul? To have sacrificed all the world's creatures for your own kind, and thereby lost your souls more completely than by any evil magic?

In their burrows, these folk tried to breed a new race, from remnants whom the gods despised.

Perhaps Enlil was right to want to give these folk new gods. But if He could not give them reverence for nature—or for one another's rights—then what good were gods to them?

If Tempus had been Enlil, he would not have been anxious to help Sandia reassert humanity's rule so quickly. The desert spoke too eloquently of what kind of rulers these folk were.

Barrenness of the heart could not be remedied by Lemurian gifts of renewed life in the seas, or by Tempus's sperm in the Shepherd's artificial wombs. The world these Sandians had made was the world they deserved, in Tempus's estimation.

But then, he was trapped between two sets of stout steel doors, feeling foolish—breathing dead, dry air that hurt his throat and waiting for an enemy who'd caught him in a trap to come lord it over him.

Right now, Tempus would have traded all life in this barren place for one slim chance to get his Stepsons home to Lemuria. He fingered the oblong in his pocket. Not the time, or the place, to try it. He had to get his missing soldiers back first.

To do that, he'd even trade his frozen baby. But of course, he'd never let the Shepherd hear him admit to it.

When the trading party arrived, opening the doors up ahead and coming through in a cadre of lights, wagons and splendid banners streaming in the dead air, Crit was right beside him.

They both saw their missing fighters at the same time, and Crit said, "Thank the god."

Tempus was not so certain that Enlil, who was pouty and silent, had any part in bringing his fighters back to him: Jihan, the Froth Daughter, was with them! With some questions answered, others burned brighter: Where was Cime? Why couldn't he get to her in Lemuria? Something still rang strange to him.

All the Drekka wore strange helmets. Their faces couldn't be seen. His soldiers, in their midst, looked worried, too.

Jihan waved uncertainly. Niko gave a signal meant to convey caution. And Strat, more bold still, ran a hand across his throat.

Only Kama seemed unconcerned. She was talking to two of the Drekka in strange helmets, pointing at Tempus and gesturing.

The Shepherd was talking into her little oblong, and low voices spoke from her hovercraft's bumper whenever she subsided.

The Tros horse trumpeted a greeting to Niko's sable, and the sable mare answered.

Before the echoes of the horses had died away, the Shepherd looked up at him and said, "There's a complication."

"Why am I not surprised?"

"There were two more in our party when we arrived, according to Drekkan count, than there are now. They're worried."

"Only two?"

He'd assumed that some of the Sandians had been cut off with the camp followers.

He'd been wrong. So had Crit. They'd seen that no Stepsons were missing, and not truly cared about the rest. "Gayle," Tempus called over his shoulder.

"Did you see what happened when the doors came down behind us?"

"No sir, Commander," called the big Stepson from between two hovercrafts. "The frogging thing happened so fast I couldn't do more than get out of the way. . . ."

Tempus translated that for Faun, and she said, "Well, we have to account for them before negotiations can proceed."

Tempus nearly drew his sword, to show Faun the antimagical glow upon it. He refrained. "Those are wizards, who were with us—not part of our band. We neither know nor care what became of them."

"The Drekka do."

"Have them send my daughter over," he ordered the Shepherd.

The tawny woman blinked. "Your . . ."

"Kama. She's talking to the men in front."

"I'll try," Faun sighed. "I can't promise anything."

But Kama was soon riding slowly toward them, with a Drekka walking by her horse, holding its bit.

Jihan caught Tempus's eye. Her bronze skin glimmered in the artificial light. She signaled an alert.

He knew that. He could nearly smell the trouble on the air. It was a smell of mould and cold, of dank and wizardry: he'd smelled it too often in the past.

Whatever these desert people thought, those sorcerers were not missing. They were right here, among them.

The horses knew it, too.

When Kama reached them, she said, "Tempus, this is Calder, who speaks for the Drekka. Calder, this is my father, Tempus, the Riddler, Lord of Lemuria."

It sounded strange to hear her say it.

Faun turned in her hovercraft and motioned: "Joe, bring the cylinder."

The small man came scrambling over, a metal urn in his hand.

Inside must be the frozen baby. Tempus could tell by the way the god leaped up into his eyes to look, and by the effluence of steam or mist from the urn's top.

The Drekkan named Calder said, "We're anxious to make the trade, Commander. Shepherd." He nodded his helmeted head. Below its glass visor, nothing could be seen of his temper. "Commander, the Shepherd says you'll explain the missing persons."

"What difference? If you've collected two of our persons, you can trade them back to us later for more frozen babies, can't you?" Tempus said, leaning on his saddle horn.

"Tempus, please. You promised," said Faun in a stricken voice.

"What's this crap?" said the Drekka. "I thought we were here to cut a deal?"

"I promised nothing," Tempus reminded Faun. Twenty-five yards away, Jihan was whispering in Niko's ear. Niko seemed well enough. Randal was flushed but waiting patiently. Strat was watching Critias in dour contemplation. There was not a mark on any of them.

"Shepherd," said the Drekkan Calder, "are we making a deal, or not?"

Joe had the urn cradled in his arms. He stood next to Tempus's horse, where Calder could see it.

Kama said, "Father, please . . ."

The Shepherd said, "Joe, let Calder examine it."

Joe handed Calder the urn with the frozen baby in it.

Tempus was looking at Jihan. Jihan was so beautiful, there on an odd horse not entirely horselike, that Tempus couldn't imagine why he hadn't guessed that the extra woman with their party must be she. The

Froth Daughter sat among these Drekka with all the quiet of a force of nature.

Now that he'd seen her, his strategy was plainer. His heart was lighter. Perhaps Jihan could get them back to Lemuria, if Tempus failed on his next try.

Knowing that none of his were in any mortal danger, with Jihan among them, made him bold. Seeing Jihan and Niko there made him want to get this over with, leave this accursed place and go back to Lemuria. And seeing his daughter looking from him to the urn made him uncomfortable.

So he said, "Calder of the Drekka, do you know what you have there?"

"Yeah," said the man in the helmet. "One frozen, viable fetus, of a . . . rare . . . genetic strain. New blood."

"Blood indeed. Blood of the Storm God. Do you want to raise a pillager, a ravener, a part-immortal like the woman beside you?"

The helmeted head turned and the glass-eyed Drekka regarded Kama. "Looks good to me," said the muffled voice coming out of the helmet.

"Kama, would you recommend your—"

A huge blare and a blast of light cut off the rest of his words.

Kama staggered back, a hand thrown over her eyes. The Drekka reached for a weapon at his belt, and went to his knees, rolling almost under Faun's hovercraft. Faun threw herself full length across her hovercraft's floor.

When the lightning had subsided, and the thunder rolled away, only Tempus and the Tros horse were truly calm.

In all the tunnel, every fighter was deployed for battle. The hostages, taking advantage of the confusion, bolted to Tempus's side of the clear space.

Jihan called, "Tempus, I need a word with you," as she passed by.

"Stay back," he told her. "Up," he told the rest. "The Storm God of Heaven wishes you Drekka to know whose son you have there." It had to be said. "As for what your lives will be like henceforth, you have only yourselves to blame." He turned to Faun: "Get off your belly, woman, and finalize this exchange. I want to be out of here, now."

Before the sorcery he smelled manifested itself in close quarters, Tempus meant. But he couldn't say that to people who threw themselves to the ground at the mere hint of the presence of a god.

He wasn't going to argue with Enlil about this. Since the Storm God felt so strongly about His rebirth into this paltry nature, who was Tempus to deny Him?

Maybe the god would leave Tempus's flesh and stay here, dwelling among the Drekka and the other Sandians, among the endless dunes that needed a Storm God's tending.

Maybe I will, mortal, said the god in his head. *Maybe I will stay here, where I am needed.*

Chapter 20:

MY FATHER, MYSELF

Hiding under the divan's fender, Cyrus couldn't believe his tiny ears. Tempus! The great Lord Tempus was here, with his daughter, whom he loved; with his men and his horses and even his sorcerous minion! And Cyrus's mother!

Cyrus was beside himself with joy, and with fury; with embarrassment, and hurt pride.

Only the canny Sibyl had kept him from falling immediately upon Lord Tempus there and then, and demanding a full accounting while the humans argued about impenetrable human affairs.

But Sibyl was right: in the form of a scorpion, under a fender of one of the divans, what attention would Tempus have paid to Cyrus?

And if he had made himself a man, there and then, what good would that have done?

His father was busy, Sibyl assured him. And, she cautioned, what if his mother saw him as a scorpion, or in the shape of a man, and Tempus made a fool of him in front of everyone?

The changeling creature, who had taught him everything worth knowing and brought him to his father, was never wrong. Now she counseled patience. So he was patient. He crawled and hopped where and when she told him, safely riding out of the Drekkan stronghold on one of the divans.

She'd said she'd tell him when.

But when they rode out of the subterranean stronghold into the desert, she dropped off the divan, into the sand. Though Cyrus tried to follow her, Sibyl buried herself too quickly.

So there was Cyrus, a tiny scorpion in a vast desert, lost, watching the divans and the horses speed away.

And then something picked him up and put him in a dark box. He crawled all over the box, but he couldn't get out of it. He felt himself being carried along. He cried, "Oh, Sibyl, where are you? Why have you forsaken me?" in his tiny scorpion voice.

Then a great voice in his head echoed silently, "Bide your time, Mandrake, pet. Bide your time, Cyrus, and be patient. We wouldn't want your mother to find out you are here too soon."

"But she knows I'm here. She must! I flew over her in my dragon form, and—"

But the voice in his head was unconvinced, and using any voice in a scorpion's body was tiring.

Cyrus curled up on the floor of the box and he wept.

He should be able to turn himself into a dragon again, but he'd forgotten how. Or else his scorpion brain was too small to hold the magic of it. Or, worse, he was too weak to perform the transformation, tiny and lost, here in the dark box, away from the wind and sun and any hint of the sea.

So he jounced around in the box forever and ever. And when forever and ever was done, he felt his box come to rest somewhere.

How had he gotten into this predicament? He'd been so *close* to confronting his father, he could just taste it. His tail twitched with anticipation at the thought of it.

He stung the floor of the box weakly—once, twice. No use. No good, either. He was stuck here until whatever had him let him out, or until Sibyl found him and rescued him.

He knew she would, if she could. But where was she? Where was the great black dragon he'd chased over so much of creation?

He slept and dreamed scorpion dreams of tender insects, sand crabs, and human flesh.

In the dream, Sibyl came to him as a beautiful woman of the desert. He crawled up her arm and nestled next to her cheek, his tail arched over his back.

And when he woke, that was exactly where he was.

He looked around: it was night. The stars were sparse and distant. The desert was cold and the cold made him sleepy. And Sibyl's voice reverberated throughout his chitin as she told him tales of Tempus.

So that he would be ready. So that he would make the right judgment.

After all, Sibyl was sure, Cyrus's mother would defend her lover. Worse, she might grab Cyrus by the scruff of the neck and spank him and haul him off to his cave beneath the sea, where he'd then be imprisoned again forever, without having met his father face-to-face and aired his grievances.

This made his tail-tip twitch. "I want to get him," he said in his scorpion voice. Scorpions didn't have much vocabulary.

"Good, dear Mandrake Cyrus. Remember that you do. Remember that you can, if you evade your mother. And remember that you have given me not only your heart, but your soul."

Even a scorpion knew what to say to that: "I do, I do," squeaked Cyrus. "Make me big. Help me get him. Put me in his bed. I'll sting him, sting him. . . ."

No, that wasn't right. He wanted to talk to his father face-to-face. He wanted to look into the eyes that had spawned him and spurned him; find out why he'd been born, and then discarded.

Tempus had made his daughter a master of the armies. She was an officer, respected. She traveled with him.

Jihan had never said why Tempus had deserted them. Sibyl thought it was because Jihan was not human.

But his father was not human, either, was he?

"More human than not. An immortal made, not born. A favorite of the reprehensible Storm God," said the great voice of Sibyl through huge lips that Cyrus watched as best he could. A woman's lips are full of secrets. These were full of deep, dark creases, nearly big enough to climb.

"Back in your box, now, Mandrake Cyrus," said the voice.

Almost, he stung her. Almost, he remembered what it had been like to be bigger than she, to be a mighty dragon chasing her everywhere. But it was dark and he was cold and weak. And anyway, he had given her his heart and his soul.

Cyrus, at least, valued his word and honored his commitments. Not like his father, the reprehensible Lord Tempus. Not like that at all.

Sometime later, the box stopped rocking and daylight poured in on him. This daylight warmed him. It gave him strength. It gave him courage. He uncurled his tail and tottered out of the box.

There she was: a mountain of power, sitting on the sand before him. Sibyl!

She put her hand down flat, and he climbed it. The urge to sting her was almost impossible to control. He was so hungry. But he did not sting. He held perfectly still.

She said, "Good. I had to test you. Now, I am going to give you strength. And you will be even more mine."

A monstrous white fingernail, opalescent and sharp, came down in front of him and ripped the skin of Sibyl's hand. Blood came welling from the slash.

"Drink, Cyrus. Drink and be mine," she said.

The blood was full of power. It warmed him. It intoxicated him. It buoyed him so that he could barely think, so full of pleasure and power was he.

But he heard her words, and his body obeyed her orders, though his tiny scorpion brain didn't really understand what it was doing.

When the pain of transformation came, he understood that, though.

And when he was again a man, he wiped her blood from his lips and thanked her, as a man thanks a woman.

This thanking was very pleasant. Cyrus had never thanked anyone as skilled in acknowledging thanks before.

They thanked each other in the sand repeatedly, until the sun was high. Then Sybil said, "You may know my name, now, for my enemies know it, and you will hear it. You must promise to listen to none of the lies they spread about me; to heed none of the awful things they say of me, even though some are true."

"I promise," he panted. "Am I not now your husband?"

"Oh you are, Cyrus. You are. My name is Roxane. Say it: your mistress's name is Roxane."

"My wife's name is Roxane."

"No: your *mistress's* name is Roxane."

"As you wish: my mistress's name is Roxane."

Then she roared a laugh like a gale and her eyes grew huge and glowing and those eyes swallowed up his manly form and flung him about in them as if he were caught in a whirlpool in the sea.

When the spinning stopped, he staggered to get his footing. Then he looked around.

There she was, beside him. But where were they?

Cyrus blinked human eyes, then saw a dark, cool place with pillows on the chairs and pictures on the walls. One of the pictures was of the ocean. He walked over to it, tapped it, and said, "I must take you to meet my grandfather, Stormbringer. He is lord of—"

"Hush, Cyrus," said his mistress Roxane, who was still in the form of the beautiful desert woman, Sibyl. "I have brought you to the lair of your father, where he cavorts with a foreign slut while your mother sleeps with soldiers. You will have your chance to stand face-to-face with Tempus, and learn all you need to know. If, when you are finished, you are still angry, then I will help you take your revenge. After all, you are my husband. Whatever hurts you, hurts me."

"You will?" This was good. "Um—my mother . . . does she know I'm here?"

"Not yet. So we will stay in this room until Tempus comes. When he does, Mandrake Cyrus, you will make your feelings clear."

"Oh, I will," Cyrus promised Roxane. "I will." He had not come all this way and had all these adventures to quail before the travesty that was his father.

Cyrus was sure he was ready. A mirror he found on the inside of a door there confirmed it: he was a strapping, fine youth, as beautiful as his mother in human form, but manly.

No father worth the name would not be proud of such a son.

Why, oh why, had Tempus forsaken him?

His gut burned to learn the answer. His soul quivered with pain. If not for Roxane, he might have slunk away, to hide forever, disheartened, disinherited, disenfranchised.

But his beloved was here. His wife and mistress,

Sibyl Roxane. And she was the most powerful female he had ever met, except for his mother.

Even Mother must listen if Roxane pled Cyrus's case, he was certain.

Once he'd confronted his father, he was going to ask Roxane to help him make peace with his mother.

Of course, if he had to kill Tempus, then it might not be the time to ask Mother to forgive him. And right now, it seemed that was what he would have to do. He had known it when he was just a scorpion. If something offends you, or abrades you, or insults you, you kill it. Even a part-immortal like his father could be killed by such as he.

If Cyrus killed Tempus, he could eat his father's brain. Then he would know everything Tempus knew, including why his father had forsaken him.

If he did not kill Tempus, whatever story his father told him, no matter how good a story, might not be the truth. Men lied. He didn't need Roxane to teach him that.

And men were cruel to women. His father had offended his mother's honor so grievously, Cyrus could not stand to think of it. How could she stay here, under the same roof with him, when he was sleeping with someone else and she was sleeping in with soldiers?

Cyrus wanted desperately, then, to see his mother, and talk to her.

But Roxane was right: if his mother found him, she'd banish him to his prison under the sea again. Then he'd never get to kill Tempus and eat his brain and know everything that Tempus knew.

Chapter 21:

BLOODHOUNDS

Cime sat before the Sandian window in Lemuria's great hall, her face smudged with weariness, her eyes circled with strain. The window was still not working. At her back, the rising sun poured in the repaired windowwall, washing the room in the warm light of another day where days were without number.

She leaned back, one hand to her spine, and glared over her shoulder at the magnificent vista. Pinnacle House offered the most majestic views that Cime had ever seen. Outside, where tree-dotted cliffs spilled to meet the ocean and waves with frothy heads on azure necks broke against pure white sand, the folk of Lemuria lived in harmony with the world.

Their homes and farms bejeweled terraces. White-washed walls glimmered peach and gold in the sunrise. Clay roofs marked the pattern of man in Lemuria, and softened the eternal ocean that held up the heavens with its mighty shoulders.

Yet, with Tempus gone, the view was lonely, empty, and somehow cold.

How could she be so dim-witted? How long had she been trying to reopen the window into Sandia, with no sign of success? Somewhere in Pinnacle House, the dogs began baying for their breakfasts. Someone would feed them.

But who would feed her heart, with her brother

gone? Eternity wasn't a pretty sight when you were lonely. She looked away from the ocean, rolling in from the horizon forever. The universe, her ex-husband Ash would have scolded her, didn't care if she was happy.

She had to find her own happiness in life. And with all her advantages, she'd let that one true happiness slip through her fingers.

The dogs bayed again, like bloodhounds on a track. Tempus had gone off like some manic hunter in search of fresh quarry, and now look what the result was. Cime held her hand out in front of her and turned it in the Lemurian sunrise. Only the slightest tracery of lines marbled her fair skin, even in dawn's harsh and unremittingly honest light.

Cime had come here soon enough to live forever, content with her body and what she was—if Tempus were with her. Human beings lived a span and died of loneliness, as much as anything else, once their friends were gone. She and Tempus had fought their way through a dozen hells to have this time together. Even the Storm God had averted his face to give them peace at night. They'd fought every battle without complaint. They'd endured the worst that mankind had to offer.

One night, when they'd been here long enough for the newness to have worn off but not truly long enough to be acclimated, she'd asked Tempus in their bed, "What do you think we're doing here—really?"

He'd shrugged, playing the taciturn soldier, as if she didn't know what kind of mind hid behind those armored eyes. Then he'd said, finally, "Maybe putting the 'being' back in 'human being.' "

She'd never forget what he'd said, so much more honest than his protestations of carnal power. He played the avatar of the Storm God all too well, when really he was a sad philosopher trying to understand why people couldn't take life as a gift and live it, instead of as a burden and destroy it.

He'd gone among the armies of the world, and she'd gone among the most foul magicians of the underworld. They'd fought the same battle: she on the arcane plane, with power brokers of the soul; he on the material, with kings and generals and the lord of murder, Enlil, residing in his head.

They'd both searched so long for the answers they sought that, by the time Lemuria was given to them, they'd almost forgotten how to live the life they'd once dreamed of. Humankind had so disheartened them, they'd spent nearly all their energy trying to come to grips with what they couldn't understand.

Cime had wanted to wipe out evil where it was exalted for its own sake. Tempus had wanted to lend right to might's side, where he could—to learn to love the things he wished men were not, and thus find compassion through comprehension.

Did they want peace, or only freedom? Freedom brought harder battles than either had yet fought: great freedom led to greater responsibility.

And so, feeling that he must act, rather than simply be, Tempus had gone right back to throwing himself bodily against the most terrible enemies he could find.

Maybe it was man's way in the world. For many years, it had been hers, as well.

But she'd never had this chance before. She'd never thought that peace was anything but death in disguise. She'd never been free of self-imposed limitation. But then, she'd never met Chiara, her predecessor as the Evening Star.

Sitting there, watching the sun rays play upon her hand, Cime toyed with giving up on restoring the Sandian window. She'd done everything Chiara had suggested. The window into Sandia still would not come alight. Her brother was beyond it, somewhere, and dragons from hell were on his track.

Did something in Tempus, and in herself, court destruction? Could they not be happy, now that they had the chance? Was happiness a habit that, once forgotten, could never be relearned? A dim and illusory memory of childhood, a thing that never was, except in retrospect?

She wanted to know what happiness was, now that she knew what love was. She had enemies who'd never love her, but enemies were the price of morality in a world built on greed and convenience. If her ancient enemies had sent those dragons, then she'd . . .

What? Go out from Lemuria, seeking revenge? Leave her appointed task? Belittle everything for no reason under heaven except to bury the pain in her heart under newer, less guilty pains?

If she could cajole the mind in her skull into solving this problem, then she would go personally to Sandia—just briefly, long enough to fix whatever mess Tempus, his men and their magic had made this time.

Since the mess was no doubt manly and surely one in which courage was tested, her brother would be stuck in it like a frog in amber. That was the problem with Tempus, with all men. The Riddler he was, and always had been. It was in women's nature to love the childishness in men and call it manliness; to see their most primitive acts as inscrutable and glorious; to sustain the fantasy men shared to make sure that they needn't grow up.

She got up from the floor, nearly toppling a pile of books she'd taken from the library. On the top of the pile was the index Chiara had given her.

It fell open to the carpet.

A ray of sun shone off it, making it glow as if it were possessed of an inner light. A dog bayed again.

She went to her knees, to see what the page said.

The page in the light said, *BlOODHOUNDS, LEMURIAN, breeding of; feeding of; fielding of; training of; types of; uses of.* Beside each subentry were book and page numbers.

Cime got to her feet, the index in her hands. Of course! Tempus, the arrogant fool, didn't like dogs. Dogs were unclean. He'd only tolerated the dogs in Lemuria because they'd come with the place and Chiara had told him to take good care of them. But had he bothered to learn about them? No, he hadn't.

No more than he'd bothered to tell Cime anything she'd need to know, in case he got lost out there— such as how to find him or how to retrieve him. She'd been reading these books all night, long enough to know that only a self-important avatar such as Tempus would have settled in here, all indolence and ease, assuming he could learn as he went.

Her brother had been using the Lemurian windows with no more skill than a battle-axe or a short sword. . . .

Well, now she thought she knew how to save him, one more time. She looked at the window, still dark despite all she'd tried. And something she'd read finally made its way from her pool of new knowledge to her conscious understanding.

She bent over and searched through the books for the one that had an entry on *DISPLAY, enabling of.*

Holding the index against her side with her elbow, she flipped through the pages. When she'd found what she wanted, she opened a panel she'd cursed a hundred times during the long Lemurian night, and tripped switches.

The Sandian window blinked its eye at her.

So she'd already fixed the window, only not understood how to make it show her that she had. The window was working—had been, for some time. She knew now that she didn't have to see what the window could show to use its abilities.

But she wanted to. And now, she could set about finding Tempus. In all of Sandian time and space, he was still lost somewhere. To find him at the right time, she must work quickly.

She half-ran down the hall to the library, to find the bloodhound book before it was too late.

There was so much about Lemuria that Tempus didn't know. If she ever got him back here she was going to forbid him any more hubristic wandering until he knew, for once, what it was he was doing.

There was no need to go jouncing around the universe like some drunken king in a chariot, looking for trouble, not knowing where you were going, or why, or even, really, much about how.

When Cime found Tempus, she was going to talk to that god of his, seriously, about just what rights the god had to her brother's soul—especially now that Tempus was the steward of Lemuria.

That was one discussion long, long, overdue. And if anything dire had happened to Tempus, so far as Cime was concerned, it was the god's fault. She'd tell Him so. And, if she could, she was going to exorcise that spirit out of her beloved, once and for all.

Who could tell? Without Enlil jerking Tempus hither and yon, her brother might finally begin to act like a man, rather than an overgrown boy in constant need of rescuing.

As she reached the library, the dogs began to appear.

By the time she'd found the book she wanted, there were thirty dogs in the library: lolling on the rug, biting each other's tails, licking their paws.

And staring at her with their great, brown, wise eyes.

If Tempus hadn't been so unreasonably prejudiced against dogs, maybe none of this mess would have happened in the first place.

The big dog with the burned flank trotted up to her and wagged its long tail, pawing at the bookshelves and whining.

"I know," she told it. "I'm sorry I'm slow-witted. Just be patient with me. As soon as I find out how, we're going for a little stroll. Won't that be nice?"

The big brindle dog barked, and the others took up the call, filling the library with their cacaphony.

Oh, Tempus, you eternal dolt. When I find you . . .

But when she found him, she'd be content—she'd thank even the foolhardy Enlil—if she had a lover to scold, and not a corpse to bury. Even the favorite of Enlil could die in a foreign land if his god died with him.

The burned flank of the big brindle reminded her all too well how powerful those two dragons were, who had gone chasing after Tempus into Sandia.

Chapter 22:

WITCH HUNT

Crit kept trying to get Strat alone, so that they could talk. But the gods themselves seemed against him. All the way back to the Sandian warren, Strat had one set of orders, Crit had another.

Crit was still Tempus's first officer. He couldn't let personal matters intrude on his attention or his time, not when the Stepsons were moving.

All the horses were flighty around the hovercrafts. And the Riddler was sorely displeased about the frozen baby.

If that had been Crit's baby, he'd still have been fighting to keep it, or have died in the Drekka stronghold, trying.

But Crit had only ever had one baby he knew of—with Kama. And that had been a travesty under heaven, which fate had decreed would be stillborn.

Crit knew now, had known for a long time, that he never should have touched the Riddler's daughter. As much as he'd like to forget that it ever happened, Kama wouldn't. And Strat had been caught between them.

Kama was riding with Niko now, it seemed. Once they got back inside the Sandian fortress, and the horses were stabled, the men billeted, and Tempus had gone off with the Sandian Shepherd and Jihan, Crit could begin to wonder what Kama's interest in Niko might mean.

He was going to go see Strat, he told himself. As soon as he checked these last few stalls. . . .

Tempus didn't need him right now. The Riddler had said, "Crit, get some rest. I'll see you at dinner."

And he'd been on his own. The Riddler didn't usually need him when Jihan was around. He tried not to let it bother him. But Crit was always at loose ends without an assignment, even if it was something unimportant.

And Tempus knew it. Giving Crit free time was telling him that Crit had things to see to that Tempus wouldn't order him to confront.

But they both knew what had to be done.

Crit fiddled around his horse's stall. These makeshift stalls weren't meant for horses. They'd put soft pads against the metal stall partitions, but still . . . if his horse kicked hard, he'd crack a hoof, or worse. Crit decided he'd bandage his horse's legs, just in case.

No use not paying attention to detail.

A shadow fell over the stall door.

Crit looked up from the foreleg he was wrapping, then back to his work, carefully feeling the horse's pastern before he got up to face the waiting men.

Straton was regarding him dolefully from behind the half door. Randal's freckled face was peeking over the door, too, just his eyes visible.

"What is it, Stepsons?" Crit said with a grunt as he rose up. There was no straw here. They were bedding the horses in something that resembled wood shavings, but wasn't any wood Crit had ever seen: it was white and filled with bubbles, as if someone had shaved snow.

"We wanted . . . Never mind," Strat said.

Randal's frail hand came down on Straton's forearm. "Your partner, here, wants to talk to you, Critias—and so do I . . . privately."

"Something this horse can't hear? Why not?" Crit

pulled the stall door from their hands and slid out, then closed it carefully, paying close attention to the lock until he was sure it was fastened.

His neck was aprickle.

He didn't want Randal hearing the things he had to say to Straton.

He faced Straton and the flop-eared mage: "Talk." He crossed his arms, looking exaggeratedly up and down the makeshift corridor of stalls. This place still made him nervous. He didn't like being so far under ground. All that sand might cave in and bury them any time, and then no magic of Randal's could avail the band. "There's no one here but us."

"She's here." Randal shivered.

"Who's here?" Crit's question snapped around the stable corridor like a whip. "That pesky witch?"

"It's no use, Randal. He won't listen." Strat's face was positively mournful now.

"Straton, you look like you've lost your best friend." It had to be said. "And since that's me, I know it isn't true. Now, if the witch is here, so what?"

"So what?" Randal stared at him, aghast. "She's after Niko."

"Then let her have him. Tempus is here. Jihan is here. You're here. I'm seeing to the horse barns." Crit shrugged. "Not my assignment, Randal. Understand? The Riddler said I should get some rest. So that's what I'm going to do."

"What about the Sandians?" Randal wanted to know.

"Crit," Straton said simultaneously. "Listen to us. It's everybody's problem if the witch is here."

Crit kept trying to forget what a disastrous hold a witch had once had on his partner. He kept thinking Strat would want him to pretend it never happened. He ignored Randal: "Strat, I'll do anything you want. About the witch, about anything else. Are *you* asking me to do something about the witch?"

"I—" Strat shook his head. "It's trouble."

"There's always trouble. I want to know if it's *our* trouble, so far as you're concerned."

Randal said, "Strat and I think we should warn the Riddler that she's—"

"Shut up, Randal. Straton can speak for himself." Strat and Randal had been in Shaga together, Crit reminded himself. Just because Crit had a prejudice against enchanters didn't mean that two Stepsons who'd shared an exile couldn't have grown close.

Straton growled: "I just need to know where I stand with. . . . Niko is Randal's partner, that's all."

The first thing was the one that had to be answered. "Strat . . ." Crit couldn't find the words.

He wanted to hug the big man, but he couldn't. There was still too much witchtaint on Straton, too much suspicion on both sides. "You stand on my right, Strat, unless I'm mistaken," Crit said formally. Straton was still his rightman, his sworn partner. "That doesn't change while we're alive." A man's given word wasn't something to be interpreted, reconsidered, or changed as circumstances dictated. A man's word was his bond, or he wasn't a man. Regardless of performance, Strat was Crit's partner until life fled from one of them, as Crit saw it.

Strat's face screwed up. "Randal needs our help with the witch." Bright-eyed, Strat stared at him.

A test of honor was as good an assignment as any for this interval, Crit told himself. "Where to, Randal?"

"To find Jihan, Critias. She'll listen to you."

"And not Niko?" Niko was with Kama—probably more the real problem than any witch.

"I'm not strong enough to take the witch on my own," Randal said with downcast eyes. Then he lifted them and they burned a weird blue where their pupils should be. "But with Jihan's help, we can make an end to Roxane. She brought the dragons; I know it."

"She is the dragons," Strat muttered. "I saw it in a dream."

Crit closed his eyes. His sworn rightman might never be free of the witchtaint; he'd had his soul sucked by a vampire. And Crit was bound to Straton, to the death, shoulder to shoulder. . . .

Crit exhaled a long slow breath and shook his head, "Okay, Stepsons. Let's go find the Froth Daughter and see if she'll freeze us a witch."

He was going to regret this. But he probably wouldn't regret it more than having too much time on his hands to wonder about frozen babies and Niko's interest in Kama and what, if anything, the commander wanted to do about those dragons, whoever they were.

Finding Jihan in Sandia wasn't as simple as it sounded. But at least they were together, Strat on his right as if everything separating them had been only a bad dream. The little mageling went first; the freckle-faced, huge-eared Randal was ready to protect them from any magic encountered in Sandia's underground halls.

"I hate this place," Strat confided.

"We'll leave it soon enough." Either Tempus would take the band home to Lemuria, or they'd die here.

"Are you sure?"

"As sure as Randal is that the dragons are Roxane's doing."

"Ssh," Randal warned, walking backwards for three steps. "Don't use her name. Not here."

Strat rolled his eyes. "Witchy-ears, don't overplay this, or I'll send you to bed without your dinner."

Crit was beginning to relax, with his partner beside him. Maybe he and Strat could make things right between them. There was no man he'd rather have with him in a battle or on a night-stalk than Straton. They'd entrusted their lives to each other for years before sorcery intervened. A man alone in this business—in any business—was a fool. You had to trust someone.

But Strat stopped them twice in the halls, unaccountably, imagining witchery. Even Randal knew that Strat was seeing things.

And then Strat wanted to take the lead, sword drawn. Crit couldn't stop him. At Crit's side, Randal said, "Look, Critias—he's had a terrible time. Awful shocks. He's—"

"I can see what he is, Randal. If you've a potion to fix it, or a spell, I don't want it—and I don't want him to have it. Time will heal my partner, once we get all the magic out from among us."

Randal turned red and his eyes couldn't meet Crit's.

"Except yours," Crit growled into too long a silence, while everyone moved stiffly and the tension rose. "The Riddler's chosen you, Randal. I never go against my orders." He wouldn't apologize—couldn't, not for the truth.

Then three Sandians in their desert camouflage came around a corner and stopped, facing Straton, huge and with sword drawn.

One Sandian put up his hands. A second touched his belt. Crit darted forward in two strides and put a hand on Strat's sword arm. "It's okay. It's all right." He spoke quickly, first in Sandian English, then in Straton's own birth tongue, before he continued so that all could understand: "My partner's jumpy, with all that's been happening. Strange turf."

"No open carry, okay, fellas?" said the Sandian with his hand on his belt.

"Put it away, Strat," Crit muttered under his breath, almost pleading. Tempus would be furious if there was a confrontation. "We're looking for the tall woman that came in with the new arrivals: Jihan. Well-built, red hair—"

Strat put the sword away and all three Sandians relaxed. The one whose hands had risen in the air said, "Yeah, you go down this corridor, take two lefts, a right, the next left. Door 23A."

Crit was watching Strat out of the corner of his eye. His partner might not be all he once was, but he was struggling to be the best he could. Crit wanted to take Strat under his wing and tell the bigger man that everything would be all right

But that was up to Straton. Crit had seen men this tired from battle once or twice. Some made it back to full competence; some never did. It was a matter of personal strength, and nothing anyone could do would change the way things would go for Strat, or anybody like him.

As the six men cautiously passed by each other in the sterile, eerily bright hallway, Randal said, "If you men hear or see anything strange, I'd like you to come to me with it right away."

"Yeah? Who are you, fella?"

"Randal, the staff sor—"

"Sortie officer for foreign venues," Crit interrupted. Didn't Randal know enough not to say "sorcerer" to these folk? The gibberish he'd made up satisfied the Sandians, who went on their way.

Crit waited until they'd turned a corner, and then said, "Randal, don't talk about magic here."

"Or anywhere," Strat said, with a grimace.

"It's over, Strat," Crit said.

"If you say so," replied his partner doubtfully.

But Crit had no right to say so, not in the face of Randal's surety, the dragons they'd seen, and the way his own horse had been behaving.

When they found Jihan's quarters, the Froth Daughter was another testament to the fact that magic wasn't out of their lives yet.

Not by a long shot. Every time Crit saw Jihan, he wondered how anything that magnificent could live. Then he wondered if she was truly living. Her size, the muscles on her, the beauty of her—she was some gilded temple statue of a foreign goddess come to life.

They'd all seen Jihan freeze enemies in their tracks, and call down her father's wet whirlwinds from heaven.

"Yes?" she said, when they'd stood speechless in her doorway far too long. "Critias?" She knew who he was, oh yes. "Is there a message from Tempus?"

The Froth Daughter had naked hope in her voice. Could this creature be lonely? Could she be as vulnerable as she sounded?

Jihan's brow creased when Crit couldn't find an answer quickly enough: "Come in, please. All of you."

So they went inside, with the daughter of the primal power who ruled the seas.

Strat rubbed his arms. His eyes were nearly pupilless. Randal closed the door.

"Ma'am . . ." Crit began.

"I hope this isn't about my son. . . ."

"Son?" Crit echoed.

"We haven't told him, Jihan," Randal interjected.

"Tell him, Jihan," Strat said wearily.

"Told me what? Tell me. I'm allergic to subterfuge, my lady."

"The dragons. You saw them, I know: one was my son. By Tempus."

"Oh." Her son, by Tempus. Crit looked for a place to sit. No wonder Tempus had been worried about giving frozen babies to the Drekka and the Sandians. He knew he should say something else. "Which dragon was that? Randal, here, says the dragons were the witch's . . ."

"The witch?" Jihan frowned again, and added, "Please sit." But she didn't sit. She moved around the room like some huge cat. "What witch do you mean?"

Crit and Strat looked at each other, then at Randal.

"Well, tell her, Witchy-ears," Straton finally demanded.

"Well, Roxane, ma'am. I'm sure it's Roxane. Actually, that's why we're here—"

"No, oh no," Jihan, the mighty fighter, sank down like some serving wench on the floor and buried her face in her hands.

Crit stood up, walked halfway to the Froth Daughter, and stopped. What was he going to do? Comfort this force of nature that could turn him into a human icicle?

He couldn't touch her. His hand was half outstretched. He pulled it back.

She looked up at him: "You know what this means?"

"Nope," Crit said. "I'm in over my head with this. That's why we're here." He hoped.

He kept trying to watch Strat. With men in Strat's condition, anything could set them off. . . .

But Strat was taciturn, his dirty face set.

"May I speak freely, Jihan?" Randal piped up in his nasal whine. "We—I—we need your help, against the witch."

"Of course," Jihan said. But it sounded dull and shocky. She looked up and her eyes were pinwheels of molten copper. "The witch . . . this creature, you think she's done something to my son?"

"Done something to your . . . Perhaps," Randal said slowly. "Almost certainly. We need to—"

"Easy, Randal," Crit advised.

Jihan had buried her face in her hands again. Her shoulders seemed to be shaking.

"Jihan," Straton said, and everybody looked at him. "If the witch is here, she's got to be destroyed. No use wondering who she's got her hooks into. Nobody's safe." Naked emotion made Strat's words raw. "Niko—she's likely after Niko. But she'll use anything and anybody. I know. So if your son's what you care about, the only way to save him is to make an end to the witch, once and for all."

Crit held his breath. Jihan stared straight at Straton for so long that Crit's lungs started to ache.

Then she said, "Of course. I wasn't thinking. Ever since I realized Cyrus was . . . hunting Tempus, changing shape . . . being so awful, I've been trying to warn his father. I couldn't think of anything else. But you're right. To save Cyrus, we must destroy the witch." Her face brightened. "It's all her fault. I will—"

She rose up in a ripple of more-than-human limbs.

"Hold on," Crit said. "You said 'trying to warn.' Doesn't Tempus know one of those dragons is—?"

"Your commander has had no time for me." Jihan sniffed. "So I was waiting, as he ordered, until he could speak to me."

"God's balls! Look, Jihan, he's got to be told," Crit said, forgetful of his place.

"Then you tell him, soldier. Randal, let us go destroy the witch. Where is she?" Shaking her copper mane, Jihan strode across the room to tower over Randal.

"Ah—around. Somewhere. Close. The best place to start is with Niko. Surely you'll agree. . . ."

"Crit," Straton said, "let's go with them. They might need us."

"Somebody's got to tell Tempus."

Straton came over to Crit and put a hand on his shoulder. "It's your call, leftside leader."

Crit looked around. Randal and Jihan were already headed toward the door. Kama and Niko had gone off together. Now Randal and Jihan were going witch-hunting in Sandia. . . .

"Strat, you come with me. Randal," he called to the little mageling, headed down the hall with Jihan. "Once you've found Niko, stay there. We'll tell Tempus and join you presently. You hear? Don't go off in Sandia on your own. And don't start anything—"

Jihan looked back at him. "Critias, tell Tempus I

am come to help my son—his son. Randal and I will do what we have to do."

"Don't start anything until I can tell him and—"

But Jihan was already striding down the hall, with Randal half-running to keep up.

And Strat was hurrying him along. "Come on, leftside leader. Now we've got to let Tempus know, before Jihan tears Sandia apart looking for Randal's witch and her son the dragon."

A glimmer of the old, black humor shone from Straton's eyes.

Chapter 23:

FIRST BLOOD

Roxane was enjoying herself, exploring in the Sandian stronghold, full of power and bloodlust. Her woman form was perfect, but she'd soon realized that her perfect beauty and her lizard skins were wrong.

They made her too special as she walked the Sandian halls, exploring and exulting and letting her nose and her power lead her to Nikodemos.

He was here. She knew he was. She was in no hurry. She need look no farther. This body felt good to her. It would feel better as soon as she had Niko inside it. She would envelope him entirely, she'd decided. She was going to change herself again, and spirit him away to a private place where she could teach him what Niko had long needed to learn.

The first woman she saw didn't look at her the way the men did. Whenever a man would see her in the halls, he would stare. Once he stared at her, he was hers. She mesmerized the men—first with her body, next with her touch, and last with her sorcery. She'd passed ten men and all them were now hers to command. She hadn't killed a one, although she was getting hungry. Powerful magic demanded an expenditure of energy.

She'd taken half the souls of the ten men she'd ensorceled, but these souls she could only sup on gradually. She needed a kill. And she needed the right shape, the right clothes. Her minions were going about their work in Sandia. When she looked through their eyes, she saw what they saw. She was becoming wise to the ways of this place. And the wiser she got, the more cautious she became.

It was good to be a woman again, to have the wiles of a woman and the brains of a woman. To the right woman, all men were perfect instruments. She had ten instruments, five stronger than the other five.

Now she needed a full soul to eat in a sitting. And for that, she wanted a woman. Once she'd found this woman, she'd eat her soul, don her aspect and her clothes, and continue on her way.

But as her ten minions knew, there weren't as many women in Sandia as men. This had to do with historical prejudice and something called genetic manipulation. Sandia, she was learning, was more like a society of bees than of men as she'd known them. Here many men serviced fewer women.

And yet women were not ruling here like queen bees. The whole place was dying. They'd all lost faith in life. Now the men here had some hope that Tempus—the egregious, disgusting bull of the Storm God, would renew them.

What rot! What foolish, arrogant human pride. What these people needed was a little magic. If the Sandians could serve her well enough, Roxane could turn their barren deserts into a garden of delights. And what delights!

But first she needed a sacrifice. And her new minions, who'd once been men, were becoming adjusted to the thought of sacrificing others for their own betterment. This was always easy with the right sort of man.

These Sandians were definitely the right sort of men. They were frustrated and relatively powerless posturers. They resented the freedom and the physiques of the Riddler's Stepsons, on their great horses.

They coveted the horses and the gear of the visitors, as they coveted the power of Tempus's stupid little genital god.

So they were selling out their whole society to the carnal deity Enlil, without realizing they might entertain another bidder.

Roxane would be that bidder. Her minions were already teaching her what she needed to know and setting the scene for her official entrance into Sandia. All she had to do was destroy the Storm God's progeny, and this would be a world so ripe for magic that Roxane might be able to pay all her debts to the accountants of evil with its bounty.

Yes, she could even free herself from eternal damnation by delivering a horde of amoral humans such as these into the service of the dark forces.

In each of them, the life force was already sufficiently dark. Not one of her minions cared for anything beyond his own betterment, and the possibility of reproducing. Progeny were at a premium here.

What a perfect place for Roxane! She could bring a clutch of horny demons up here and breed an army such as the universe had never seen. . . .

Nearly reeling with intoxication, drunk on ten tasty souls and the promise of more, she'd all but forgotten Cyrus.

But she hadn't forgotten Niko. Oh, no. Niko was the finest prize in all this charming place, where no one cared for morality, only law; where everyone wanted everything, at any cost; where no one worked but in the service of personal gratification.

Roxane was the queen of gratification. Here she would be empress of the whole dustball world. She would supplant the Sandian ruler, who was a weak and foolish woman, and crush rebel settlements such as the Drekka in a heartbeat.

Once she'd eaten all the dead's manna, she would be unstoppable. Then she could go right back the way she'd come, with Niko as her piteous hostage, and wrest control of Lemuria from Tempus.

Tempus was basically flawed: he believed in honor, in personal worth, in morality and love and righteousness. To win this game, you could believe in nothing but yourself and expediency. You must deserve everything, regardless of the cost to others. Then you would have everything.

Roxane, who'd nearly lost everything pursuing that course, knew now that she'd been right all along. She'd only made a few . . . missteps.

Now she could rectify them. Through the halls she went, nodding hello to the few people she encountered, waiting for a woman who'd be the first blood she'd taste tonight.

It was hard to hold back. It was difficult not to jump on these short, white, slight men with their big heads and their thin necks, and devour them.

But she refrained. These were her cattle now. She wanted to fatten them up first. They weren't even frightened of her. A frightened, suffering soul is much tastier than a shocked, uncomprehending one.

She would give them something worth being afraid of, before she was done here.

She would be Roxane, queen of power, once again. And Niko would sit by her side, a golden collar around his neck, and massage her toes for her. She couldn't wait!

But she must wait. She was stalking these white, clean halls looking for a woman to sup upon, some female whose death would inaugurate the enslavement of a race.

She must choose a nice, fat soul. If she couldn't have a tortured one, then a fatuous, self-satisfied one would do.

One of the minions she was monitoring seemed to have the glimmer of an idea. It was a nasty idea, born of personal grudges, and she liked it because of that.

It was a dangerous idea, perhaps. But she was near enough to the dwelling place of the Sandian Shepherd that she was willing to at least investigate the possibility.

The closer she came, turning left and climbing ramps and turning right again, the more she thought how delicious it would be to destroy the Shepherd first.

But she must make the Shepherd come to her. Otherwise, she'd spoil Tempus's surprise. And Niko's.

This was going to take a little doing. For this, she needed to concentrate.

Roxane searched for an open door along the hall, and finally found one. Into a closet she stepped, and there she sat and composed herself.

In her belly was still the shard of power she'd eaten when she was an eagle.

While she was a scorpion, it had been uncomfortably large inside her.

Now, she must have it in her hand.

She began trying to regurgitate the stone. She stuck her finger down her throat and choked. She bent over and retched.

And there it was, lovely and glowing in its slimy puddle of stomach acid and bile. Oh, if only she'd have eaten some real food, what a fine slop would have covered it!

But she sat down on her haunches and began to chant.

She chanted over the stone, and picked it up, holding it in her marvelous fingernails, so sharp and opalescent. Bile dripped from the stone and it began to glow brighter.

The brighter it grew, the more tenuous Roxane's womanly form became.

But it was worth the strain, the pain, the risk, to make the Shepherd of Sandia come to her.

Sitting there in her bile, Roxane concentrated as hard as she could. She found the Shepherd in her mind's eye, and she entered the woman's heart and looked around.

What was there was unremarkable, but serviceable.

While sitting inside the Shepherd, who was busy with her staff in the wake of the Drekkan incident, Roxane simultaneously ordered one of her minions to send a message requiring the Shepherd's presence at the place of artificial wombs.

The message came to the Shepherd's hands, and Roxane prompted the Sandian woman to excuse herself, alone.

Walking an as-yet uncontrolled human down all those halls was exhausting.

The hunger building in Roxane, though, was great enough to make her risk all her newfound strength. She'd never been short on will power. She brought the Shepherd closer, and closer.

Roxane prompted the woman to go visiting those disgusting god-spawns. She lured the Sandian Shepherd into self-absorption and distraction.

As yet, this was the best that Roxane could do.

When the Shepherd came past the closet in which Roxane lurked, she gathered herself and sprung out the door in a flurry of lizard skins and bile and claws and teeth.

Her eyes, by then, were huge. They dominated her person, which was otherwise thin and ethereal, as she enveloped the Sandian Shepherd in her arms.

For a moment she saw herself through the Sandian Shepherd's eyes: a ravening ghost with huge claws and sucking black eyes from hell.

Oh, good! The fear of her victim came pouring forth, strengthening Roxane and confirming how sweet this victory would be.

The Shepherd staggered back against the wall, already too deep in Roxane's power to scream.

From the Shepherd's throat came a tantalizing mew of terror. Her bowels voided, and shame mixed with her fear.

The ecstasy was nearly unendurable.

With all her skill, Roxane maneuvered the Shepherd of Sandia into the closet.

The woman slipped on the bile and went down in a heap, cracking her head.

Then Roxane fell upon her straightaway, unable to wait a moment longer, even if delicious fear was wasted.

Now was the time to inflict a painful death and grow strong. Her nails bit into the Shepherd's face, eyes first. Once the eyes popped, the rest was easy.

Roxane didn't know it, but she sighed as she fed. And fed. And fed. She ate every bit, even the body, of the Shepherd of Sandia, even the Shepherd's clothes.

Never the mind the clothes. At this level of power, Roxane could materialize the Sandian clothes she needed. She materialized a fine suit, just like the Shepherd's. She donned it and stepped out of the closet.

Before she closed it, she looked back. Inside, there were only a few bloodstains and strands of hair to mark where the Shepherd of Sandia had died. And Roxane now knew everything she needed to make Sandia hers—even how to become the exact image of its Shepherd.

As the Shepherd of Sandia, she strode down the halls, imperious, looking for Niko.

Once she'd found her Nikodemos, and made him her love slave again, the true carnage could begin.

Sandia was going to be hers, lock, stock, and frozen embryos of the god.

Let's see what the Storm God did to protect Tempus when Roxane had Enlil's own sons as her hostages!

Walking the quiet, clean halls of Sandia, Roxane began to chuckle, and then to laugh a sweet, throaty laugh.

Chapter 24:

SONS AND LOVERS

Jihan knocked on the door where Niko was, and the Riddler's daughter answered.

Kama was disheveled, flushed and wild-eyed, so Jihan pushed peremptorily past her, thinking the battle for Nikodemos's soul was already under way.

Randal the magician followed.

In the room, on the bed, Nikodemos covered his virile nakedness and jumped up, holding his blanket. "What's wrong?"

He, too, was flushed.

"The witch," Jihan demanded. "Where is she? I have come to make an end to her."

"Randal!" Kama slammed the door and said, "Randal, I'm going to kill you."

Kama, too, Jihan now realized as she looked at Tempus's daughter a second time, was wearing only a blanket.

Randal said, "Kama, we apologize for breaking in like this. But the witch—"

"Pork the witch, if you dare, and leave us alone."

"We will not," Jihan said, crossing her arms as Tempus did when he gave an order. "Kama, your father is meeting us here. We are laying a trap to destroy the witch when she comes for Niko."

"Oh, for—"

"Kama," said Nikodemos, fixing his blanket around

him as he came forward. "Get dressed. They're right. We shouldn't be . . . thinking about ourselves."

"Now look what you've done," Kama said in a voice shaking with rage, and flew by Randal toward a second door, which she slammed.

Jihan frowned. "What is wrong with the Riddler's daughter? Where has she gone?"

"To dress. Sit down, Lady Jihan, and tell me whatever you think I should know," Niko said in a courtly fashion, bowing low and snagging his undershirt from the floor as he did.

Randal said, "Jihan, maybe we should go until he's dressed. I'm uncomfortable—"

"Nonsense. Lives are at stake here. Sit down, wizard, and compose yourself. I need you to alert me when the witch is coming."

"Yes, ma'am," said Randal with a sigh and a beseeching look toward his Nikodemos, his partner.

"Niko," Jihan said, "you have maat. Your rightman, here, has magic. I have my inheritance: power over water, even in the veins and flesh of creatures, and over the wind and sea. Do not fear. We will triumph over the witch."

Niko was pulling on his shirt. He dropped the blanket. As he buckled his swordbelt on, he said, "I appreciate anything you can do, Jihan, but why. . . ?"

Niko's maat saw right through Jihan's facade. "The witch has ensorceled my son, so Randal has explained it to me." She tried to sound brave, but she was not brave. And she was very angry. Even in this place of dead winds and tame water, a breeze began to stir and the air itself grew moist.

"Bide your time, Jihan, if you will," said Nikodemos in an odd voice.

Jihan had forgotten how bold Niko was. The only thing on earth he respected was Tempus. She said, "If you mock me—"

"I? Never, Lady Jihan. It's just . . . You've . . .

upset Kama. I have to see to her. I'll be right back. If the witch comes at me in the bath, you'll hear me or Kama scream. Do I have your permission?"

Jihan was uncertain. She looked at the human adept. "Randal?"

"Of course; of course." The mageling was beet red. "We're here, now, Niko. We'll handle it."

"You do that . . . partner." Tempus's favorite Stepson left them, through the small door where Kama had gone, to tend to the Riddler's daughter.

Jihan could feel them, behind that door, doing what humans did. And she was suddenly very lonely, alone in that alien dwelling, beneath dry sand, with Tempus's staff magician, when what she wanted was the Riddler's arms around her, his comforting voice in her ear, telling her everything would be fine, the way Nikodemos was telling Kama things would be.

Tempus should be here with Jihan, now, in this moment of their mutual trial. After all, Cyrus was the Riddler's son, too.

Book 3:

CHILDREN OF THE STORM GOD

Chapter 25:

SON OF MAN

"Commander!"

Crit's voice rattled off the glassy walls of the corridor like stones down a well.

Tempus looked over his shoulder. Critias had his rightman, Straton, with him. That was a good sign.

The looks on their faces were not. Tempus blinked and looked again, at Crit's dark mien and Straton's nearly blank countenance: when Strat approached destruction, his face was always scoured of emotion.

With the god in Tempus's head ramping like a bear and growling as inarticulately, Tempus could barely keep them in focus.

Since the god wouldn't—or couldn't—tell Tempus what was wrong, the only solution was to ignore Him. The god had wanted to see his gestating offspring. They had just done that. All was well with His children. Now, the affairs of living men have priority. Tempus said silently, *Leave off, You nattering nanny of a god! If Thy children take precedence over me and mine, then get You out of me, and see to them, if you must. But let me do my work, which should be Thine, if Thou couldst think straight!*

Enlil was worse than any pregnant mother, these days.

And Tempus's two officers wanted to know where he'd been. "We've been looking everywhere for you, Commander," Strat all but croaked.

243

"Come," Tempus said, and bent to open the door to the room the Shepherd had given him. "We'll talk in here. This place has more ears in its walls than a provincial palace."

"Riddler," Crit said, "Wait. Listen to me. . . ."

Tempus straightened up and looked closer at his first officer. Crit was nearly undone by something.

"If you can say it here, Crit, say it," Tempus said, one hand going instinctively to his swordhilt.

Crit seemed to shiver once. Then the careful soldier said in a rush: "Jihan and Randal are with Niko, awaiting you, ready to fight off the witch, Roxane, if she strikes meanwhile. Jihan wants you to join them. She says . . ."

"Yes, Crit?"

Strat jostled his leftside leader. "One of those dragons was Roxane, Randal's sure. And the other—"

"Sir, Commander . . ." Crit interrupted, then stumbled over his tongue.

"Out with it, Critias. You and I knew there was magic about us out there. What's the surprise?"

"Jihan says the . . . second dragon . . . mage, witch, whatever, is in here too, somewhere, with Roxane. . . ."

Tempus turned back to the door, to push it open. "Come in here. Both of you need a drink. . . ."

Strat blurted, "The second one's Jihan's son—and yours, Riddler. So she says—"

He pushed the door inward.

Something white blew through the open door. Something huge wrapped Tempus in a tentacle of fire and brightness, and sucked him inside. The door slammed shut.

He hit a wall, hard. The impact knocked the wind from his lungs. And in his head, the god was roaring so that his ears rang and he could hear nothing else.

White fire was all around him. Enlil was up in his skin, meeting that fire with His own supernal might.

Never had Tempus felt such pain. He was seared and roasted. His flesh melted from his bones. His eyes boiled and popped. The liquid danced on his fleshless cheekbones like drops of water on a hot iron skillet.

His whole body seemed about to collapse in a clatter of white, burned bone.

But the god wouldn't let him fall. Enlil manifested new sinew, new muscle, new blood and new skin upon his skeleton. Enlil put new eyes in his head and a new tongue in his mouth. His god clothed him anew in power and made him terrible in fury.

His god-given sword was somehow in his hand when he again had eyelids to blink and hair to shake from his eyes.

The smell in the room was the first thing that hit him: it was the stomach-turning smell of burned human being, laced with the choking odor of carbonized hair and bone.

Yet he stood. Stood, sword in his hand, facing a dragon so big that its ruff scraped the ceiling of the room and its tail lashed against the walls around them.

The smoke coming from the dragon's nostrils threatened to choke him as Tempus tried to breathe. The god in his head was silent, but gasping, as if Enlil had already fought to the end of His strength.

The the dragon cocked its head at Tempus. Fire licked at the corners of its great jaws, but didn't stream out to envelope him again.

In his head, he tested the god, asking Enlil: *What now, Pillager?* The Storm God was silent, but for his panting. Tempus's own chest rose and fell greedily, despite the pall of smoke.

The dragon was making his new eyes tear.

It was making its own eyes tear.

Its head snaked toward him, and Tempus raised his antimagical sword.

The sword wasn't glowing pink from close proximity to magic.

In this moment of calm before a second round of battle, it struck him as strange that this was so.

The dragon's nostrils widened, as if it were taking a great sniff of him.

Its head swayed to and fro on its great neck.

Then it reared back. Its wings beat, to steady it. Its forelegs, one of which was pinkish, pawed the air with human hands.

Tempus braced himself against the wall. This time, Enlil was tired. The god couldn't even spare him a word. Was this the way of it, to die under the earth in a place he'd sought to bring to life? To die, sword in hand, fighting the unknowable with your god dying with you. . . .

No, Mortal fool. This travesty is Ours, Enlil gasped.

Then Tempus almost remembered the last thing his ears had heard before the fire took him: one of his Stepsons, telling him . . . what?

He looked at the thing before him and it seemed to waver. Maybe he was already dead, just a simulacrum Enlil had made, some final consequence of the bond between them. His brain surely had boiled and blazed away with the rest of him.

If it had not, he'd surely have been thinking more quickly than he was now. Where was his god-given speed?

The thing that had been a dragon was shimmering. He steeled himself for another blast of flame. This next one would take him straight to heaven or hell, Tempus knew.

Cime would be lonely, in Lemuria, and curse his name for leaving her. . . .

His eyes were streaming tears in the smoky room. Enlil had been so concerned over his offspring that Tempus had been tempted to think that the Storm

God of Heaven actually cared about something more than His eternal pride.

But even the sword in his hand had lost its power. It was a sword, but it couldn't recognize the witch before him.

For witch this must be. It was changing shape before his eyes. It was a horrid, glowing miasma of stuff, having a dozen heads and a hundred eyes.

In the cloud were the eyes of men and the eyes of eagles and the eyes of dragons. Guilt was there, and horror, and fury and misery and murder, blazing out from all those eyes. Hands were there, and wings, and claws with bright talons. Scales shone and tails lashed. Fists curled and hair whipped as if in a great storm.

Then the whole cloud of flesh turned bloody, and expanded toward him.

He raised his sword arm to strike, knowing that no sword cut would harm it, when it shrank back.

And back. It turned in on itself with an awful roar.

This roaring grew as the cloud spun round and became the size of a man, like a dust devil in the desert with a thousand eyes.

Tempus's own eyes were too blurry to make sense of what spun there. All the horror of hell and the glory of heaven whirled together before him. An awful, tearing cry like the cry of a newborn world rang in his ears. If a man were born full-formed, with all his knowledge of all his sorrows intact, that man's cry might sound like what he'd heard. It made his limbs grow weak. Or the god did. He lowered his sword and stared.

Enlil, too, stared, but from a great distance. The god had withdrawn from Tempus's skin, and dwelled now in the farthest reaches of his person, as far away as possible from the death spinning before them in the room.

Come, God, come meet this death with me, Tempus told Enlil. *All our days, unnumbered, have come to this. Have we not had a full life, doing Thy will upon the earth? Canst Thou now not face an end to life, and give up flesh? Can't we go to Your heaven, where so many of my men have gone, and be there forever, without regrets?*

He'd long known that Enlil was a coward in the face of dissolution. But then, gods expected to live forever. Men did not. And Tempus, a man made more than human, caught between the fates of men and gods, knew full well that even he could not give up life without regret. Cime still lived. His men still needed him. There was so much left undone. . . .

And Jihan had had a son who turned into a dragon and now wanted to hold him to account for it. . . .

He wiped his eyes with the back of his hand and looked again at the whirlwind that had him trapped.

In it, now, was a form, discernable as the form of a man. From it came sounds, as if a man were trying to speak with a volcano's voice. Or the voice of the crashing waves.

Tempus put his sword away. If this was not sorcery, the god would determine his fate. If this was his child, out of Jihan, he didn't want to meet it with a sword in his hand.

He'd met too much in life that way.

Having sheathed the sword, Tempus let his hands hang at his sides, just staring into the whirlwind. It was bright, still, but not so bright that his new eyes burned to look upon it.

And it was getting smaller. It seemed to be coalescing. As it shrank, the shape within it grew more discernable. The man within it was almost solid.

But so bright. Too bright too look upon and say, "Son, let me explain to you. . . ."

So Tempus waited, calmly now—for this thing was of his making, he was nearly sure.

Jihan had wanted to talk to him, but he'd had no

time for her, being caught up in the matter of the
god's frozen embryos.

Inside his head, Enlil was slowing coming forth.
Tempus wanted to ask the god what He thought of
this creature they had made together, with the Froth
Daughter, but he did not.

This was no time to bicker over who was at fault
and what was wrong.

The thing that was becoming a man before him
had the blood of Stormbringer, who ruled the seas,
in its veins. It had the legacy of Enlil, the Storm God
of Heaven, in its soul. And it had come from Tempus's loins, into the changeling Jihan.

Whatever this was, was clearly their shared responsibility.

The cloud was almost entirely gone now. A strapping youth stood there, Tempus's size, with fine,
glowing skin like his mother's and Jihan's pinwheel
eyes.

Tempus leaned back against the wall, his new skin
stinging and every new hair on him standing up on
end. "Welcome, son," he said carefully. "What took
you so long?"

The youth before him was of an age to begin
soldiering. This probably was part of the problem.
He tried to envision what a childhood with Jihan in
her realm might have been like. He couldn't. He
waited for an answer: death, life, love, hate.

The choice was the boy's, and Tempus didn't even
know his name.

The boy who'd been a dragon took one hesitant
step forward. His fine jaw worked. His lips tried to
form words and failed.

He raised a naked hand.

Tempus started to duck reflexively, and caught
himself. He wouldn't shrink from what he'd wrought.
He took a step forward, forsaking the wall's support.

Tempus raised his hand as well.

The boy extended his. Tempus matched the gesture.

"You're mother's here," Tempus said.

"I . . ."

"Yes?"

"I . . . I am Cyrus."

"I am Tempus."

"Why have you forsaken Mother and me?"

"I have not. She brought you when you were ready."

"Liar! I escaped. She followed me."

"Test of manhood."

"Why don't you love us?"

He couldn't think of a thing to say.

Enlil took his tongue. "*We love you. Listen to no lies about us. The Storm God of Heaven, and of the Armies, and of the Weather, blesses you, son of Ours.*"

Aloud, through both their voices, the sound made the youth take a step backward. Then he recovered. "*She* told me not to be fooled by you. I must decide if you deserve to die."

"No one deserves to die, or no one deserves to live, Cyrus," said Tempus in his own voice, wresting control of his tongue from the god. "Who's 'she?' Not Jihan, who knows better, who loves life and gave up so much to be human long enough to come to me and make your life with me."

"My wife—my mistress, Roxane." The boy's head lifted rebelliously.

So that was it. "A little magic? Playing with wanton evil? And you think I'm angry? I've done worse. You're a man—"

"Sometimes."

"When you're a man, you'll do what men do. But since you're more than a man, you'll do what men do . . . somewhat more forcefully. You've seen me. The god. Your mother. Your grandfather. Who do you think could really be your mistress?"

"She's . . . I love Roxane. I have given her my heart and my soul."

"Take them back!" The god's fury nearly made Tempus strike the boy backhanded across the mouth. By the time Tempus had regained control of his body, he was less than an arm's length from the youth who'd been a ravening dragon.

"I'm not sure if I can," said Cyrus very softly.

This close, Tempus's flesh remembered being seared from his bones by the boy. It quivered. Yet he forced his hand to extend, once more, to Cyrus's.

"Welcome, son. I know you have many questions. . . ."

"Just one."

The boy took his hand and Tempus felt the thrill of contact, so intense, with such flesh. "And that is?"

"Why did you not die in the fire of my dragon's breath?"

"Because you didn't want me to," Tempus said. On that clever turn of phrase, he knew, his life depended. He was absolutely sure that he could not—would not—kill this child of his in battle. He felt no anger, just sorrow for what must have brought Cyrus to him this way, at this time.

"I . . . didn't. You're right. Roxane will be disappointed. And she has my soul. . . ."

"No, she doesn't."

"She said you'd lie to me."

"My men call me the Riddler. Souls belong only to themselves. What you've given, take back. Give it to me. I'll use you the way you want to be used. But if you do, you'll have to obey orders, like any other soldier of mine."

"Like your daughter? Why did you take a woman over me, and make her an officer in your army?"

"Kama came to me, the way you did. Endured trials, found me, the way you did. And proved her worth—without any witch's help."

Could Roxane have a hold on Cyrus's soul that would be disastrous for all of them? Jihan might know if an immortal changeling could be compromised by a witch. Looking at this child of his, Tempus didn't think that any force could hold Cyrus against his will for long. So that will must be tempered well—and tempered now. Loosing an amoral force upon the universe wasn't something he wanted on his conscience.

Even Enlil was touched and disturbed by what they'd seen.

"Have I not proved my worth?" Cyrus demanded. "More than any other? I *should* kill you. You're *lying* to me!"

The boy's hand began to squeeze his. Tempus squeezed back and held his ground.

"You've proved you can destroy. Men are not evaluated by what they can destroy, but by what they can create. By judgment. By honor. By community. By purpose and sacrifice. Tell me if you think you've proved yourself that way."

Cyrus dropped Tempus's hand. The bones in it ached and burned.

"I came here to have an accounting from you. To learn why you've left my mother and me and chosen others. . . ." Cyrus's lips quivered. His bright eyes seemed to glow as Jihan's sometimes did when she was gathering power to strike.

"I've told you the truth. If you come into my service, I will teach you what it is to be a man. But I can't teach you what it is to be a superhuman power. Your grandfather and mother must teach you that. Let's ask Jihan what she wants for you."

"Mother's . . . probably mad at me." Cyrus made a face and put his hands on his naked hips. "But I'm not sorry. They kept me locked up beneath the sea so long. I had to get out."

"And the witch beguiled you." Tempus thought he

understood, now. "Perhaps it would be good if you learned what it is to live like a man. I will say that to Jihan, if you'll go with me to see her."

"I . . ." Cyrus looked down at himself. "You won't let her take me back to my prison?"

"No son of mine lives as a prisoner. Do you believe that?"

Cyrus looked at him a long time. "I believe that. I don't love you, you know. I love Roxane."

"That's your choice. But if you side with a witch against me, we'll resume our battle. Is that clear?"

The boy took a step back and said wonderingly, "But I will kill you in any such battle. You know I will."

"No battle is fought before it starts. Now, we'll get you clothes. You'll agree to put them on and walk with me as a man. To be obedient before my soldiers, as befits a son of mine. Respectful to my officers. No changing into a dragon whenever you want—or into anything else."

"All right," said Cyrus doubtfully. "For now."

The boy wasn't stupid. "And when the witch comes to you, before you defect to her, you'll give me the honor of fighting me fairly, in this form you now wear, to the death. In my army, the men who call themselves the Stepsons say, 'to the death, with honor.' That's how men live, if they are worthy of the name. Fully. Facing everything—their mothers included—without quailing."

"This army, can I lead it?" Cyrus said.

"You may join it, if you pass the test. The men say, when they meet their brothers, 'Life to you, and everlasting glory.' If you say that to my officers outside, they'll know you're a man of good will. The rest, we'll see as we go along. Now, shall we try it?"

"I— Yes, we'll try it. But . . ."

Tempus moved slowly and carefully to find the boy something to wear. "But what, Cyrus?"

"What do I call you?"

"In public? Any of my names. In private, do as you please . . . once we've settled this matter of the witch—and you've decided that you don't want to kill me, of course. One never calls one's victim by a familiar name. Remember that."

"Um— I'm . . . Father." The powerful creature behind him said it very softly, as Tempus turned with an armload of army clothes.

"Yes, son," he said. Any ploy was fair in a war for survival. Whatever Cyrus was, he was Tempus's son. Time to own up to it.

Whether it was a mistake, as the god now insisted, time would tell.

Outside, Crit and Strat still waited. And Cyrus said to the Stepsons, "Life to you, soldiers, and everlasting glory."

Crit stared at Tempus before he murmured, "Life to you, Stepson," with a raised eyebrow and a quick assessment of who and what this youngster might be.

"I assume Jihan is still waiting," Tempus said, to make the matter clearer. "We must take Cyrus to see his mother, witch or no witch."

And Strat said, "Boy, are you going to help us with this witch?" in an undertone as Crit fell in beside Tempus and Cyrus followed behind.

"Whatever my father wants."

Tempus hoped it would be so easy. But his body still trembled from Cyrus's fire and his heart knew that boys were not men, who meant what they said, or even understood what they said.

Jihan had better have a good explanation, when he got there, for how this demigod had escaped from her care under the sea. And some suggestion or two that might help Tempus decide what to do with the boy who was also a dragon.

Cyrus could kill them all yet, if the witch got the better of his naive heart again. She already, according to Cyrus, had control of his soul.

Chapter 26:

BROTHERS AND LOVERS

Waiting for the witch to come for Niko, Kama regretted everything: getting involved with this fighter, who was so inarguably unique; letting his sorcerous partner, Randal, find them in bed together; being anywhere near Jihan when the Froth Daughter was preparing for battle.

Why couldn't her father have had a normal army, with normal men in it? If Tempus had, then Kama might have been good enough to attract her father's attention.

In this whole room, Kama was the only one awaiting Roxane, magic's queen, who had no superhuman attribute or special relationship to universal forces that she could call upon for aid.

It made her feel common, an outsider, some trollop caught up in the business of her betters.

If Tempus's patron god hadn't been such a misogynist, then maybe the blood in her veins might have meant something.

But it didn't. She knew it didn't. She was just a plain woman, whose father had begotten her on a whore some night the god was absent from his loins. And she was in too deep with Nikodemos, even without everyone looking at her as if she'd defiled an altar or gotten into heaven on a fluke.

She puttered around, wanting to make the bed but

unwilling to play the chamber maid before Jihan.

The Froth Daughter sat in one corner, watching them out of eyes that glowed from within, her back against a corner, half entranced.

Niko was little better. His eyes were half closed; Kama could see the whites of them. He was meditating with his maat, or whatever he did.

And Randal, Niko's rightman, was cross-legged before the door in wizardly concentration, as befitted the staff sorcerer of the Stepsons. His lips moved silently, repeating some spell or other meant to protect them from the witch.

Maybe Randal could teach her to do something. Anything. Some parlor trick she could pull out at moments like these, when everyone else was seeming so damned special.

Something to amaze Tempus, and make him pay attention to her. Something to convince Critias that she hadn't fallen into bed with Niko on the rebound. Because Crit would soon know what had happened here. All the Stepsons would know. Randal was no good at secrets, and . . .

Kama wanted people to know. She was proud of Niko—and of doing what she could to help him, in her way. Even to help herself.

The witch was coming. How many times had they been the loser in confrontations with Roxane? She was indefatigable. They were, except for Jihan, mortals.

Her father ought to be here.

"Tempus ought to be here," she said.

She didn't say it loudly, but Niko jumped as if startled. Randal looked at her as if she had uttered a curse. And Jihan said, stretching those muscled arms, "He will, child. He will."

"Don't call me 'child.' I'm not your child. We might all be dead by the time Tempus gets here. . . ."

"Kama," Niko said. The single word silenced her.

A knock on the door followed the word like a punctuation mark.

She was up. She wasn't busy communing with higher powers. "I'll get it," she said, and nearly lunged for the door: at least now she had something to do.

Kama pulled the door open, expecting her father. She saw the Sandian Shepherd instead. Kama hadn't liked the Shepherd, who was bedding her father, from the moment they'd met.

She stretched one arm across the doorway, barring it. "Yes, Shepherd? We're really busy right now. . . ."

"Ah, the Riddler's daughter. . . ." The voice was a purr of sensuality, very different from the Shepherd's usual brusque demeanor. "Surely not too busy to discuss . . ."

"Shepherd!" called a voice from down the corridor.

"Yes, Joe?" said the Sandian woman, and then: "Excuse me. I have other duties. I'll see you all later, when you're not so . . . busy."

And she strode away with a roll in her hips that Kama hadn't seen before, either.

Closing the door, Kama backed right into Randal. "Randal, don't crowd me like that. You scared me."

"That was very interesting," Randal said, but shook his head when Kama asked, "What was?"

Niko was up now, wandering around the room slowly, as if in a daze. He looked at her keenly when she'd closed the door and left Randal making passes over it to reinforce its antisorcerous wards.

"Kama," Niko asked, "what happened there?"

"I didn't want her in here," Kama shrugged. "I don't like her. She's pushy. Nasty. I disapprove of the frozen—"

"That's not what I meant." Niko came close and lifted her chin with his fingers. Standing so near him, she felt protective and invulnerable, malleable and deferential, all at once. And it wasn't uncomfortable. It felt right. She wasn't embarrassed, even before these gossipy Sacred Banders.

"What did you mean?" she said softly. Would he take her in his arms, in front of everyone? She half dreaded it, half wanted it to happen.

"Have you ever, in all your time in Tempus's service, confronted Roxane directly or been attacked by her?" Niko demanded in his quiet, intimate way.

"No. But we've all fought sorcery and been hurt by it. You know how I lost my child."

"I know. We have that sorrow in common. But look: you barred the door with your arm and the witch backed off."

"The witch?"

"Or my maat's been fooled."

Niko knew Roxane better than anyone. Still: "That was the Shepherd."

"Not any more," Randal said, so close behind her she jumped.

"Randal, stop sneaking up on me."

"I will go after her, children," Jihan said, getting up. "You stay here."

"Better take Kama with you," Niko said in an odd tone.

Kama's eyes flew to his. Was he trying to get rid of her? Joking? "What are you implying?"

"Maybe nothing. Maybe she had other business, after all. But you and I. . . ." Niko ducked his head. "You know," he half whispered.

"No, I don't know."

"Niko's saying that Roxane is a jealous, fiendish witch who loves revenge. She would have been able to smell what you and Niko have been up to—"

"Randal!" Kama flared. "You need your ears pulled off!"

"Nevertheless, it's true. She should have attacked you, then and there. You stood between her and Niko. You've . . . been intimate with him—"

"Kama," Jihan interrupted throatily. "Come with me. This is women's work. Let the men huddle here, where they're safe. You and I will find your father and see what he has to say."

"I can't leave him—Niko. . ." It came out of her almost like a moan.

Jihan was at the door. "The Riddler's daughter wouldn't quail before all the storms of heaven," Jihan said softly from the door.

"Go," said Niko. "If she comes, she comes. Jihan is right. We can't hide here, all of us, because of me, when Tempus has other troubles. If she's not—"

"What if it's a trick?" Kama wailed.

"Then it's a trick." Niko shrugged, then turned his back on her and continued, "She's my problem, in the end. Maybe she's bashful. Maybe she'll wait till I'm alone."

"I'll be with him," Randal said.

"Randal, I'm not a goat," Niko said, "to be tethered where the wolf will come. Why don't you go too?"

Jihan, looking at Kama, slowly shook her head, and motioned.

"Randal stays," Kama decreed as if she had her father's power. "I'm going."

Outside the door, Jihan looked down at her with a crinkle of humor around her eyes. "You are in love with Nikodemos. Tell me, how does it feel?"

"Jihan! You can't just ask something like—"

"Why not? I want to know if it's like what I feel for my son."

"Not what you felt with my father?"

The Froth Daughter started down the hall, taking Kama with her. "Your father and I were not . . . what you and Niko are."

"I . . . don't know what love is," Kama said, then admitted, "No, I do. I loved Crit, I thought. But this with Niko is different . . . deeper, as if it had always been the driver in my heart and I'd just never real-ized it was there."

"So love is always with you?"

"I . . . I'm not sure. Jihan, why wouldn't you let me stay with him?"

"We may have underestimated you, little sister. Or him. The witch must not be frightened away by you. Niko must settle this on his—"

Kama turned to run back the way she'd come. Jihan's hand gripped her arm like iron. Kama almost struggled to free herself. But it would be useless, fighting Jihan.

"And, too," said the inhuman Froth Daughter who was so fascinated with humankind, "I want you to meet your brother." The way she said it made Kama shiver.

"The dragon?"

"My son, the dragon." Jihan sighed. "Did you know," she said, as they rounded a corner, "that when I first came to your father I raped him?"

"You what?"

"I did. You can't imagine what it is like to hear the supplications of humans and see the misery of hu-mans and wonder what it would be like to go among these beings of unimaginable fealty and deepest feeling—and then do it. So when I found Tempus, and he was worthy, I showed him who was stronger and made him service me."

"You—" Kama giggled. "You didn't?"

"I did. But he would not give me a child. He and his spiteful god withheld that privilege from me for many years. At last, I tricked him into it. And this is the result."

"What, the dragon?"

"Kama, my son is running wild. When you first came to Tempus, were you angry?"

"I tried . . . so hard to find him. I think it was, anticlimactic. He put me to work. I thought the doors of heavenly love, dignity, family honor, and joy would open and my life would come pouring out to wipe away all the loneliness. You know him. He's not . . . demonstrative."

"Oh, he is. But not where tender feelings are concerned. You have helped me, Kama. I thank you."

"How?" She was puzzled.

"I need to understand how my son may feel, and his father may feel. I must take Cyrus back with me, you see. He can't stay among these creatures."

"You mean, among creatures like me?"

"I mean . . . frail human beings, who call upon the gods to give them what they have not. For we must answer, Kama. And you must only ask."

"Jihan . . ."

'Wise humans ask of themselves what they need. I saw you in that doorway, Tempus's daughter. You have strengths you haven't tapped."

"I'm nothing special."

"So you think. Thinking is being, dear. I thought I could come and walk among men. None of my kind had ever done such a thing. I did it, because I never thought for a moment that I couldn't do it. I thought for many moments how I could do it."

"You're not telling me that I can do things like Tempus does, because if you think that, you're wrong. His god is a soldier's god, a man's god, a god of—"

"Are you not a soldier? Do you not belong to the race of man?"

"I meant . . ."

"We'll need your help, Kama. Niko knows you're something special. Let yourself be what he knows you can be. It's better than losing more than you can afford to lose."

The Froth Daughter finally took her hand from Kama's arm. "You know, Jihan, you talk as if all this were simple. Don't you ever react out of hurt feelings, rather than reason?"

"All the time, as a human."

'Don't you ever find yourself doing the opposite of what you should—or what you want, to spite someone or something?"

"Frequently, in human form. But that is the human struggle, is it not? To control the animal nature and use it to soften the intellectual nature, thus becoming the eyes of all nature on this world the gods have made? Without you, little human with a god's blood in your veins, where would the gods be, do you think?"

"What difference does it make what I think? I'm lucky: I found Tempus. A place in life. Now Niko. I can make amends to Strat, and Crit. I'm thankful to the gods—"

"Thank yourself," Jihan advised, and slowed in the corridor, putting up a hand in the Stepsons' caution signal. "He comes."

"Who, your dragon son?"

The bronze head nodded. The beautiful profile of the Froth Daughter turned from her. "And his father." Her voice was as low as the rumble of waves on a beach.

Jihan pushed her hair back from her face and Kama found that primping ludicrous. She watched the Froth Daughter straighten up. If humanity was Jihan's study, she'd learned it.

Judging from the look on Tempus's face as he came around the corner, Jihan was a master.

Shock widened her father's eyes. Then caution hooded them. He touched Critias, who was looking at Kama as if she stood before a bright light.

Behind them, Strat was beside someone Kama had never seen before—a long-legged youth with fair hair and skin, who had to be Jihan's child.

Tempus was suddenly walking backwards, talking to the boy.

And Kama felt Jihan take her hand and squeeze, hard.

The youngster hesitated. All the men stopped and conferred.

Then Crit hurried toward them, a sour look on his face.

Kama was sure it was because of her, until Crit said, "Jihan, Tempus says tell the boy you're not angry, and come with us. No personal discussions. The Drekka are at the gates, and the Shepherd is threatening to give them the rest of the embryos to keep the peace."

"And Tempus doesn't want her to?" Jihan asked, falling in beside Crit.

Kama watched her ex-lover's back for a moment. It had been as if she didn't exist for Critias.

Then she shook off her hurt feelings and ran to catch up: "Crit!"

"Not now, Kama," he said, not slowing.

"Crit!" She caught up. He looked at her askance. She plowed on: "Jihan and Randal both think that Roxane is around, wearing the Sandian Shepherd's face as a disguise."

"Terrific. Come tell your father that. Why aren't you with Niko, by the way?"

Jihan answered before she could: "I brought her. To meet her brother."

"By Enlil's sharp point, I'll never understand women. Who's with Niko?"

"Randal," Kama said, feeling faint, suddenly dizzy. "They told me to come. . . ."

"And here you are." Crit clapped her on the back as if she were Straton. "We'll work with it. Watch it with the—with Cyrus. He's . . ." Crit grinned fleetingly. ". . . unpredictable."

They were too close to the others for Crit to risk saying more.

Tempus's eyes flicked past Kama, to Jihan's face, and his was very grave. "Jihan, say something to him," the Riddler whispered.

"Cyrus," Jihan began on a rising note. Then took a deep breath. "It's good to see you safe with your father. This is your sister, Kama." All in a rush, it came out.

And then Kama was shaking hands with a boy who, reputedly, had been a firebreathing dragon that nearly killed them all.

With eyes like his mother's, Cyrus looked her over and said, "Walk with me, sister. Tell me all your secrets. I'm, uh . . . going to be a soldier, just like you."

Ahead, Jihan and Tempus were arguing, sotto voce.

And Crit, on Straton's left, turned to Kama and said, "Tell the Riddler about the Shepherd, when you get a chance?"

"You tell him, Crit," she said. "I'm busy getting to know my brother."

The thing beside her was as strong as Jihan and as intense. His face was hard to read, but he seemed as eager to please as he was shy.

So she said, "The secret of getting along in the armies is not to be too pushy. Because of blood, I mean. . . ."

All the while, she listened to Strat and Crit talk about the Drekka at the gates and tried to make out what it was that Jihan and Tempus were arguing about.

But she couldn't. And the boy at her side was so wide-eyed and innocent that she said, "You've got to ask me questions, whenever you're confused, Cyrus. I was confused when I first came. The men will tease you and test you. They mean nothing by it. You mustn't get angry."

"I mustn't? How do I stop it?" Before she could answer, Cyrus leaned close to her, saying on a breath that smelled like the ocean, "Is my mother mad at me?"

And she whispered back, "No, Cyrus. Just concerned. We're in a battle for our very lives, here."

"Here?" He looked around. "Don't worry. My mother and I will save you. After all, it's a matter of blood, isn't it?"

"Yes, Cyrus," she said. "A matter of blood."

What had Tempus and Jihan wrought?

Chapter 27:

TWO PLACES AT ONCE

Although the halls of Sandia were peaceful yet, the Drekka were at the gates. Roxane cursed the Drekka to a thousand hells, upside down with their feet sticking into the air, forever.

She'd just found Niko, and now this. . . . Even the Queen of Hell was hesitant to bilocate with so much at stake. Ten minions she had. Without direct supervision, ten were hardly enough to gather all the fetuses and frozen embryos, prepare the Sandian flock, and create a doom here fit for fools.

Niko was waiting for her!

Roxane could feel him, his calm, his maat extending out from him so far that it blew around her like silk curtains on a marriage bed.

And here she was, carting metal flasks of frozen babies around Sandia's glassy white halls. It just wasn't fair!

She said to her most powerful minion, "Find Joe. Tell him I want to go over the plan."

The minion scurried away, but she had to send a portion of her attention with him to make sure he did things right. You could never tell with humans, especially soul-sucked humans. They tended to botch things up, to misconstrue, to be clumsy. Clumsiness could lead to failure.

There was too much at risk here to chance failure.

Through the halls with the gathering war council of the Sandians she went, all the unborn children of the god—even the Shepherd's own child—collected in a cart that one of her minions drew.

A procession of fit irony, it was, as she led these fools toward the destruction of their last, best hope.

One of the councillors approached her deferentially: "Shepherd, are you sure that this is the wisest course?" asked the fool, peering imploringly at her.

One moment's eye contact. Two. Three. A blink, and the fool was hers. Eleven minions now. But she said, for the sake of the others: "Of course. Let the Drekka have these cylinders, if peace is the result. And the fetuses as well. Isn't that what we all want—peace?"

"But the fetuses—" objected a voice from the crowd around her.

"No one says we have to guarantee *viable* fetuses. Just to hand them over."

A distraught mutter went through this crowd of gutless wonders. They venerated life too much. She would teach them the glories of death.

"Listen, Councillors of Sandia," she snapped in the Shepherd's most commanding, abrupt manner. "You've seen those dragons in the sky. You've heard the Riddler's talk of his god and how these fetuses are the god's as much as his. What kind of fetuses do you think we have here?"

People made confused noises. Some said, "What do you mean, Shepherd?"

Roxane opened her Shepherd mouth and said fiercely: "Any of those fetuses you hold could become a dragon, if it wills. A destroyer. I know it seems strange to you, but I'm the one who went to Lemuria. And now I'm sorry. Any of those fetuses— including my own—could destroy what's left of our world, if we don't destroy them first. Or do you want our few remaining children to become like Tempus, possessed of delusions of godhood and uncontrollable rages?"

They buzzed like the bees they were.

She added, "The father of a dragon shouldn't father Sandian citizens. But of course, it's up to you. Take a vote. And quickly, before it's too late to poison the canisters."

Joe was jostling through the crowd to get to her. He reached her, his face suffused with rage. "What are you doing, Shepherd? This is crazy. We need those fetuses—and the embryos. Even if we didn't, what do you think the Drekka will do when they find out they've been tricked into a treaty? If you murder the trading goods, what—?"

Look at me, fool. Look at me, Joe.

But the Shepherd's second-in-command wouldn't look at her. He was staring around at the confused Sandians, breaking ranks in the hall like any mob shorn of its purpose.

"Look at me, Joe," she said aloud.

"There's no time. I disagree. I'll never vote for destroying one embryo, one fetus. I can't believe you could. Your own child . . . dragons from human sperm. . . ."

"Joe! Tempus's god is hardly human."

"Come on, Sally," said Joe, using the Shepherd's birth name.

If there'd been a shard of the Shepherd left in this body, it would have reacted to its birth name, and Roxane might have been fazed. But the body was a true simulacrum. Still, she'd eaten the Shepherd's soul, and the name gave her pause.

When she recovered from the shock, Joe was striding away, back to her, his little, misshapen head bobbing on its thin neck, talking to this Sandian or that.

Her word must hold here by consensus. This she

knew. To assure it, she must spread herself very thin.

Yet she was hesitant to leave this body and go, wraithlike, among the crowd. Better she should touch each canister and personally destroy the life inside. But if she did that, too early, Tempus's despicable god might track her by the act.

If Enlil came raging forth to confront her, too soon, all could yet be lost.

She bumped the cart beside her, in which the god-spawn rested. All of them were her greatest enemies. Any of them, allowed to mature, could be her destruction. Any of them might vie with her for control of this ripe, febrile world.

She wanted to use them as hostages, to make the god give her Tempus, and let her destroy the Riddler, most tenacious of her antagonists.

Then, with Tempus dead, she'd destroy the god's children and chase the distraught, grieving little Storm God out of her. This place would have no heaven, only a hell in the sky as well as below the ground.

She would see to it.

She must.

But these creatures went so slowly about their business. They were afraid of everything and anything, all things except the right thing.

As she listened to them squabble, she realized that they did not truly believe in Tempus's immortality, in Enlil's godhead—or in gods at all.

If they did not believe in heaven, then they did not believe in hell. If they did not believe the evidence of their own senses—not even when those senses were assaulted by dragons—then what *did* they believe in?

Then Roxane knew that she had handled these folk wrong: she must show them clear advantage, a prize worth dying for. And she knew that she could barter for their souls with beads and trinkets and silly things like human fertility. She could be the fertility goddess of this place, if she wanted. She liked that thought so much, she smiled as she accompanied the cart with the god's spawn upon it.

How many witches had become goddesses?

This was truly worth holding back her hunger to accomplish. Even her lust for spilled manna, blood, and warm, sweet death paled before the thought of becoming a goddess.

She was all but a goddess here already, she realized. And then she thought that Niko would be much happier by the side of a goddess than by the side of a witch.

Her beloved Niko would welcome her with open arms, once he realized what Roxane was about to become.

So excited was she then, so buoyed by the revelation of total regency soon to be hers, she decided to risk it.

She would go now to Niko—keeping this body moving meanwhile; keeping it herding her cattle to their doom with one part of herself, while the rest took her beloved to her bosom.

Roxane had time. And she had power. She had glory. And she had desire. What else, really, mattered? And what could stop her, now?

The Riddler and his primitive little god, who sought to woo these people with gifts and impress them with a piddling little thunderstorm?

No, she was already too powerful to be worrying about some trap laid by the Riddler and his puny little Trickster god.

A goddess in the making needed a godling to be her consort. This was what Niko had been born for, she now knew. Once his maat was transmuted into a hunger for the purity of absolute power, instead of some ethereal justice, Niko could no longer resist her.

Was she not Roxane, in full flower, once again?

She was flowing out of the Shepherd body she'd made before she consciously decided. No problem. These folk couldn't see aura, or soul, or manna, or essence, any more than they'd been able to see their destruction in their hands.

Among the blind, she would rule with her clear eagle's sight. Forever, with Niko by her knee.

It remained only to teach him his place.

Chapter 28:

SWEET SOUL'S PEACE

Niko could feel his doom near. No matter how he cleared his mind, his life paraded by his inner eye. He saw the day he'd come to Tempus's band, so raw, mourning for a lost partner. He saw the weapons of the gods that the lord of dreams had given him, when he was frightened of what the dream lord sought to make of him. He saw his island home, and the sorrow in the face of the adepts there as Niko wandered farther and farther from the paths of tradition.

And he saw Randal, circling as a hawk over Niko's meditation pond, once long ago when magic had sought him as an ally, and he'd agreed.

He opened his eyes. He'd lost himself a dozen times and always found his center once again. Why was this different?

Randal's face was sweaty from concentration, by the door where the adept sat, trying to protect Niko bodily if he must.

"Randal, come away from the door and sit with me." He'd been too hard on Randal, through the years. Maat was kinder than Niko, its instrument. "I want to talk to you."

"Niko . . ." Randal's slight, awkward form rose up stiffly and came to sit beside him. "What is it? You look like you've seen your . . ."

Even the wizard couldn't say it.

"I want you to know, Randal, what a beloved friend you've been. I honor your wisdom, and your bravery, your honesty and your steadfastness. Though you serve through magic, you serve the same ends as I." Formal speech was hard for Niko. He touched the wizard's knee. "I'll always love you, and hold you in my heart. Friendship such as yours is denied most men. I'm the richer for it."

"Niko," Randal sniffed, batting at his nose. "Stop this. Don't give up. We'll win this yet."

"I couldn't give up if I tried, don't worry. But part of my training tells me that death comes when it wills, and we must make sure we're ready. When the end of life comes, so we believe, a man should go free of regrets, content with what he's done. If death came to me now, I could meet it without flinching."

"Niko!"

"Life is everlasting, Randal. Everything we've ever done together, been to one another—that's eternal, written in the record of time itself. Nothing that ever was can ever cease to be. Do you understand? I know you have a different faith."

"Faith . . ." The mage's nose was red. He sniffled and blinked rapidly. "I have faith that life is life and death is death and I'm happy right here, staving off the latter in favor of the former. Don't go so hastily into death, Nikodemos. It lasts a long time."

"The witch has my son's soul, Randal. I'm going to trade her mine for his, when she comes. I want you to ask the Riddler for me if he'll do the rites for Nino. If Tempus beseeches heaven, surely the Storm God will make a place for an innocent child there. Mine will be empty, waiting."

"Niko, get hold of yourself. No one's going to die here."

"Your nose is stuffed up, Randal. A sharp-nosed

wizard like you should be smelling the death all around us. It's in the air."

"It's in your heart." Randal glared at him. "You give up too easily, leftside leader. When your heart is wounded, you lie down and say, 'Death, take me, I am ready.' Well, you're not, you know. No man worthy of the name would leave his brothers to mourn him and clean up his messes. And if you knew what I know about eternal unrest with your soul in a witch's clutches, you'd shut your mouth and pray to your god to protect you. There's no valor, no glory, in giving yourself over to evil—even in sacrifice." Randal clamped his mouth shut. His chest was heaving.

"Get out of here, Randal. A man deserves to be free of argumentative fools before he dies. Go tell Tempus my last wish. Make yourself useful somewhere else. I'll meet this with my maat. I respect what you believe, but I mustn't believe it. Not now. I'll meet my fate as I have lived. It's my way."

Niko knew he was hurting Randal very badly, but he could feel the witch approaching. He couldn't let Randal sacrifice himself to save Niko. Not from Roxane. Too many had died in Niko's stead because of Roxane. It was time they settled things, one on one.

Randal's freckled face was so white that the blotches on it looked like a spattering of mud. "You can't mean this. You can't—"

"Out, wizard. Your kind has made my life a misery. I hold you responsible for none of it, but evil cannot be supplanted by evil. Go find the Riddler, and make clear to him what I've said." *Before I have to lie and hurt you more than I can bear, to keep you safe.*

Life was so dear to him then, that Niko nearly wept.

The anguished mage got clumsily to his feet and Niko got up too, following him to the door.

When Randal undid the wards to open it, Niko pulled the frail, brave soul against him and kissed Randal's head. "No man ever had a better partner, mage or not. Life to you, Randal, and everlasting glory."

Randal pulled away from him and swept out the door, his bony shoulders hunched, without a word.

So be it.

Niko closed the door and leaned back upon it. Revenge was now beyond him. He had chased it away for the sake of his rightman's life.

To the death, with honor, shoulder to shoulder. . . .

No man wants to die alone. And die he would, somehow, rather than let Roxane make him an undying mockery of all he'd struggled to embody in life. He wished he could see the Riddler, one more time.

His maat was filling the whole room with wisps of Roxane: with glowing trails in which contorted faces gleamed. He knew he was seeing the witch's horde of tortured souls, who made up her army of the damned.

"Roxane," he gritted, "at least come alone, for this. You owe me that much."

His son Nino had never known fear, or hardship, or prejudice, or grief, or greed, or hunger, or death—not even the death of a goldfish or a puppy. Niko had never pretended that such a life was right. But he'd let it happen, because Niko had never known any of the joys that made up Nino's days in the city at the edge of time. Maat had let him pretend that, if he could give utopia to his son, there was no harm. He'd paid in advance.

Nino must have been so frightened, in the clutches of the witch.

A frightened child was the cruelest joke of heaven. Niko's childhood had been awash in blood and fear. He'd tried so hard to keep Nino from it. . . .

He'd never wanted to bring a child into the world

whom he couldn't protect. But what the world wanted from Niko, it took. He never should have had the child. He knew that now. He'd known it then. But the city of placid wisdom had beguiled him, whispering that it was not in the world at all. . . .

The room was thickening with Roxane's spoor. Niko closed his eyes again. He saw green grass and his sable mare running for the joy of it, her tail flagged high. He saw white clouds in a blue sky so clear his throat ached. He saw all the beauty of the world. And he forgave it for having death as its final gift.

Could life be so sweet without death at the end of it? He and his brothers went abroad in the world to soak up all the death they could, all the violence they might. Then there was less misery for humble folk, who weren't strong enough to fight their battles on their own.

In his head he heard a bird sing, and a baby laugh, and the wind rustle the leaves at springtime.

The world was so wonderful, which the gods had made for men. He could hardly bear to leave it. He heard his blood in his ears then, a sound like the sea against the shore. No one lives forever. His son deserved a place in heaven. Niko had done all he could do for others. He would do this thing for Nino—for himself, so that his maat, at least, would be at peace.

He opened his eyes and the witch was there. This bond between them was something as ineluctable as the passing of the seasons or the rotting of man's bones.

"Roxane," he said, nodding his head just slightly. She appeared to him as he'd first seen her—an ethereal, lovely girl with a face of pure innocence, and long hair tumbling down her back. But she was thinner than he remembered, almost translucent, delicate and . . . somehow old.

"Nikodemosssss," she hissed through a mouth that had eaten the soul of his son. "I have come for you, my love."

She held out her hand.

He kept his eyes on her face. His maat was questing, testing, touching her black heart and finding . . . nothing.

"You killed my son," he said.

"To free you, beloved. To bring you out into the world again, where you belong. To make you—"

"I know." He sighed. "I can't even hate you. You're lost, witch. And I can't save you. But give me the boy's soul back—free it, to go to heaven in my place, and I'll give you mine without a fight."

There. It was done now, all but for enduring the consequences of striking a bargain with rampant evil.

"Niko," the witch said, her face flowing and her eyes widening, "my beloved, you mistake me. I am about to become a goddess. You must come to me—"

"Willingly, I said. Just show me Nino, and set him free. I'm what you want, aren't I? All the deaths to get us here, all the misery you've spread over the world . . . isn't it time we stopped? Just stopped." Now he extended his hand, not touching Roxane's, but almost.

He couldn't bear to touch her. The repulsion in his heart was too great. The revulsion of his maat was making his muscles twitch. He wore his ancient battlesword, in its scabbard wrought with likenesses of the elder gods—but he wouldn't try to hack this evil thing apart.

She'd chased him too far. There was no maat in even one more death.

"Stopped?" The witch cocked her head. Her eyes were glowing red. "I can't . . . stop. You'll learn to love my service. You'll grow strong again—I'll help you. We'll rule the whole world—"

"There's no world for me with my son's soul in

hell. I don't care what you do with me, is that clear? I'm your creature. Take me. Just give up the soul of Nino, and I won't fight you further."

The face of the witch began to spin. She snarled, and he took a step backward. He wanted to close his eyes, so as not to see his death come—and what would be after it. But he could not.

Maat looked hard at the witch: a shape within a shape, a form with no form, a thing with a woman's eyes and a hole where its heart should be. And then Niko saw her heart there, after all: a wizened thing, a sad little raisin that thought it beat. It thought it was right. It was quivering with disappointment, unhappiness, confusion. And loss.

"What?" he said, into the face of the hesitating maw from hell in front of him.

It made full-formed breasts, young and rosy.

They hung in the air, inviting, but there was no young body around them. Then the breasts were gone, back into the glow of the face wrapped in souls, and from it he heard:

"I can't give you your son's soul. I ate it. It is a part of me. It will live inside me forever, as long as I am living. Come to me, Niko. Unite with me. Forget that spurt of your manhood, made in an instant. I will give you children untold, an army of children."

"No!" It tore out of him, unbidden. Nino's soul was in that maelstrom somewhere, stuck fast like a fossil in a rock.

He was so angry, and so repelled, and so disgusted, he grasped his swordhilt. His maat was counting up all Roxane's kills, and weighing her clutch of souls against the feather that was maat's measure of justice.

And Roxane was heavier than stone.

His revulsion poured forth and his sword came out of his scabbard. As long as Roxane lived, Nino's soul was trapped. He'd never thought to kill the witch, never even tried.

But the sword from his hip was as ancient as the Riddler himself. Alive in his hand, it slashed at the ectoplasmic thing outstretched to him.

A howl from hell's bowels ripped through his ears. Light exploded from every wisp of the witch called Roxane.

Souls seemed to rush around the room crazily, like frightened kittens.

He struck again, wordless, caught up in maat's need to enforce the judgment rendered here.

Again, a howl buffeted him. A cold, wet thing struck his face. He smelled the stench of ages.

Once again, her face rushed up to his. Black eyes as big as the room nearly engulfed him. Those eyes were full of pain and fury, and fear.

He raised the sword once more, and said, "For my son's sake, die!" He struck.

The room exploded. The sword, red hot in his hand, clattered to his feet.

A concussion threw him back and he hit the door hard. The wind was knocked out of him.

As he gasped for breath, he thought he heard an inarticulate cry, fading. Then a heartrending sob, that seemed to say, "How could you reject me, beloved, after all I've done. . . ?"

He struggled for the first breath he must take, or die there and then. He hadn't managed to kill her. Was she sitting on his chest? His vision grew grainy. He regretted violence, where he'd determined to have none. He tried to find a clear thought, a peaceful thought, a thought to die with. But he couldn't.

And then his lungs filled with air. He rolled his head back.

There was nothing in the room. No sign of witchtaint. No sign that he was dead or possessed. No sign of

Nino's soul, or anything to prove that something had transpired here.

Had he dreamed it?

He rubbed his eyes.

Then he saw the sword, so ancient, on the floor. It was black from hilt to tip, except where the Storm God's bulls and lightnings were engraved.

What had he done?

Now the witch would rage through Sandia, and Nino's soul would be trapped forever.

But he hadn't meant any harm. His maat was a power on its own. And if rejecting the witch had been all it took to banish her, then why had it never worked before?

But maat had never weighed Roxane on the scales of eternity before.

And Niko had never surrendered to his fate before.

If evil could be overcome in the world, his maat could not turn away from it. Like revenge, sacrifice was self-indulgent.

How could he have forgotten?

He levered himself upright, shaking. Never had Roxane hurt him so little, when she'd come to him. Never had he even dreamed he'd lived to see this moment.

He wanted terribly to open a window and look at the sky. But there were no windows here. The sky was denied him by all the sand overhead.

In the bowels of the earth, he'd met Roxane, Queen of Evil, and maat had helped him hold his ground.

If maat thought that the witch must die, and had saved Niko for that result, then he knew what he must do now. He just didn't know how.

But Tempus would know. Niko went over to the sword that the dream lord had given him when Niko was too young to accept such a gift with equanimity or understanding. He'd never wanted to be a pawn of power. He'd only wanted to do maat's work in the world.

If the witch died, Nino's soul would be free. And maat would be satisfied.

Niko picked up the sword. It was still hot. He scratched at the blackened blade. The metal underneath shone brighter than metal should shine. He remembered what Tempus's sword was like in battle.

Maat was pushing Niko toward a fate beyond any he'd ever dreamed, or coveted. But humility, too, can become an arrogance.

Only the soul has no price. Niko sheathed his sword and got up. It was time to find the Riddler. If Niko had to fight this final battle, he knew where he wanted to be: on Tempus's right hand.

Chapter 29:

DREKKA AT THE GATES

Tempus saw Nikodemos coming through the assembled crowd awaiting the Drekkan envoys, and said to Crit: "Watch over things here. Don't let Jihan act prematurely."

Crit squinted at him: "I'll do my best. And . . . Cyrus?"

"Your best will be good enough there, too."

They'd all heard what Randal had to say, between sniffles and tears.

And when Tempus had rufused to let Jihan intercede, saying, "Niko has made his choice. Respect it," Kama had put an arm around Cyrus and taken the changeling youth aside, telling him heaven knew what.

Now the god was counseling caution, because the witch was so fully present to His supernal sight.

Going to meet Niko through the crowd of Sandians, all Tempus could see was the Shepherd, with her cart of god-spawn, and the slight folk of this dustball world, jittery and arguing among themselves.

The Shepherd called out to him, "Tempus, where're you going? Tell the people the truth: any of these fetuses or embryos could be like one of those firebreathing dragons, yes? Isn't it so?"

Puzzled, he said, "Those children of the god will be what the god decrees," and kept going. The Shepherd was pointing at Cyrus, and Tempus looked that way.

His heart grew cautious in his chest. The boy was . . . volatile. But his mother and Kama were with him. Tempus himself could do no better with Cyrus than they.

Jihan had insisted on bearing the boy who'd become a dragon. Whatever happened was as much on her head as his.

Niko met him, dry-lipped and with anxious eyes: "Commander, the witch came to me, and I couldn't . . . I used my sword. I hurt her, but she lives."

"No deal, eh?" Tempus and Enlil both needed to hear what Niko had to say for himself. Of all his fighters, Tempus still loved this one the best.

"I'm myself, and I know the witch couldn't kill me. But she must die. There must be a way. Did Randal tell you—she has my son's soul. It will be free if she dies."

"How do you know this?" Even Jihan didn't know what hold Roxane could have on Cyrus's soul.

"She told me. Commander, if I could have forfended this before, I don't know how. I'm not sure how I did it . . ."

Tempus hugged the bright-eyed fighter for a moment. "Ssh, Niko. I trust you. The god sees you. There's no witchery in this. Just a man who's learned how to use his will."

Tempus pulled back. Niko had fought on Tempus's right, once. He said, "Coming, rightman? We missed you. This may be a battle, yet. I'm not content to let the Drekka have those frozen babies."

Niko nodded, falling in beside him, unquestioning, resolute, and full of the strength a man discovers when fate reprieves him. "Commander, tell the Storm God for me that if my son's soul should go to heaven someday, I am in His eternal debt. And if you could say the rites for Nino—"

"No indebtedness necessary. I'll do it. Now look to yourself, rightman. I don't want to do it for you. Clear?"

Niko looked at him shyly. "I'm sorry, Riddler. I lost my way, for a while. It won't happen again."

"You found your sword, Nikodemos—the one in your heart. Some men never do. Now let's go fight this one to the death, if we must. No regrets."

The god was regretting the begetting of so many Sandian babies, but that was not Niko's problem.

It was his.

Randal and Kama crowded around Niko, asking questions that Cyrus listened to with a thoughtful look on his young face.

The Shepherd and her attendants were separating from the group, wheeling the cart out into the middle of the rotunda where the Drekka would arrive through an open tunnel.

Tempus wished he had his Tros horse under him for this battle. Only the god was truly calm. All his Stepsons were distracted by one thing or another: Niko's brush with the witch was on everyone's mind. The rumors of Cyrus's nature had run through the band like wildfire. Jihan's mere presence portended a debacle. Everyone was uneasy.

Even Crit couldn't bring them to full readiness, not when the battle was so unformed.

But Tempus knew battle would come here. The god was high in him. His body was tingling with Enlil's strength and Enlil's speed. He had to move ever more slowly, not to show his god-given speed.

In his head, a greater battle had been ongoing for hours: Enlil wanted the frozen babies to be born here, to populate this barren heaven and refertilize this tired earth.

Tempus, god-ridden for ages, didn't want that responsibility on his weary soul. He couldn't hide his lust to destroy the frozen babies from Enlil.

So he and the god were somewhat estranged, and tense with each other inside one flesh, which was never meant to hold a full-blown god and the soul of a man.

Pillager, I will make a deal with thee.

Mortal, you importune. What gives you the right to bargain with your god? But say your prayer to Me, that I may consider it in My Mercy.

Enlil's mercy was something to which Tempus considered himself a stranger. But he said to the god, as the first Drekkan wagon lights showed in the dark of the tunnel opposite him, *If Thou wouldst put gods in the heavens here, then stay Thyself, and rule here. These folk cannot survive young gods, testing their strength against one another.*

And what of thee, then, mortal horse? How would you do, without My Eternal Wisdom and Omnipotent Strength in thy ancient limbs?

Am I not still Thy Servant? I will do as You will, as I have always done. Only not so intimately.

And you will not resist me, in the matter of Our children? wheedled the canny god, whose greed for this bargain was so irrepressible that Tempus's own mouth salivated.

I will not, O Lord of Strife. These folk fight a battle for survival against an unfriendly Nature, where Thy mighty hand will be welcome.

Sometimes, the god responded to flattery. Sometimes, He did not. Enlil's ageless ears seemed to prick. His presence rustled against Tempus's skin as if a great cat rubbed against him, marking him a pleasurable possession.

But Enlil said nothing more, and the Drekka convoy was filling the empty space of the rotunda.

Tempus slid among his men, touching an arm here, a shoulder there, saying a word, offering a smile, letting everyone know that this was grave business and he expected their best.

If he knew what he was about to fight, preparing them would have been easier. The god was so high in him, he wasn't sure his feet were touching the floor.

He could barely remember the names of the faces he saw. Even Jihan was a half-recollected creature, possibly a factor in the coming battle, nothing more.

But Cyrus he did recall, and went to stand near the boy. When he said, "Son, this is Nikodemos, the finest fighter you may ever meet," he surprised himself. Part of him had been unaware of Niko on his right.

But of course, Niko was there, with his soft voice and his slow smile and all his maat around him like a resplendent battlecloak that the god could clearly see.

Cyrus said, "I am Cyrus, Tempus's son. Life to you, Niko, and everlasting glory."

With a catch in his throat, Niko said gravely, "Life to you, Stepson, and glory in this battle."

"Battle?" Cyrus drew himself up. "I see no battle. And anyway, my mother and I will save—oh. Thank you, Niko."

The boy was trying, but Cyrus still had a lot to learn.

The god in Tempus's head thought that today Cyrus would learn it. Tempus hoped that the witch wasn't going to teach them all something about Cyrus. He wished she'd manifest.

Kama was sure Roxane was in the Shepherd's body, but it wasn't the witch's way to fight in a guise.

"Niko," Tempus said, "how did Roxane appear to you?"

"As herself. . . . but wispy."

"Not as the Sandian Shepherd?" Tempus's long eyes narrowed as he looked at the Shepherd, in the midst of her functionaries, awaiting the Drekka now climbing down from their bright-eyed wagons.

The wagons stank. The fumes hurt his eyes. He was too conscious of his changling son beside him, and Niko on his right.

The Shepherd put a hand on one of the canisters to lift it, and Enlil roared in fury.

Tempus seemed swept aside in his own body. He felt the god overtake him, enlarge him, wrench him apart and put him together again.

The Drekka started yelling and pointing at him, then running for their wagons. The god who wore his body like a suit of armor stalked toward the Sandian Shepherd, who seemed so small that Tempus knew he must be twice his normal size.

He caught a glimpse of a diminutive Cyrus, openmouthed—and of Jihan, running toward her son. He saw Crit draw his sword and light flash.

Niko yelled, "Take cover."

The Drekka wagons were spitting light, but it didn't matter. The Sandians were milling about, some drawing small weapons, but that didn't matter either.

The Sandian Shepherd was striding to meet Tempus, and she mattered. Roxane was terrible in her fury.

She was nearly as big as he, and the sounds she made drowned out the sounds of honest battle.

Enlil roared with both their voices, *Witch, this is no place for your kind. Get you to your accustomed hells, and leave My people be!*

Enlil raised a hand. In it was a sword of light, brighter than any light that flashed from the Drekka wagons or the Sandians' weapons.

The witch shook the canisters in her giant hands. She laughed through a mouth contorted by jagged teeth and yowled, "Enlil, petty pillager, this is the seed of your heaven, is it not? What if I destroy it? Clench my fists and crush your godlings?"

Enlil hesitated. Tempus beat against the god's control as best he could. He was like a fly buzzing around Enlil's head. The god paid him no mind.

"Harm one and you are dead, witch! Forever dead and lost!"

"Give me Tempus, your useless minion, and you can have the embryos, Storm God. You can have this heaven, too! Cast yourself out from that unworthy servant, and give me him, and all is settled between us!"

Enlil's sword, high above both their heads, swung in a great arc: *"Think you that I, a god of man, would bargain with a thing from Hell?"*

And the god's sword cleaved the head of the witch from the shoulders of the witch, then and there, before the assembled, battling crowd.

Tempus heard screams such as he had never heard before.

The god's arm, which was his, ached and burned. The witch's huge body was not like the Shepherd's body any longer. It was a great hive of stinking honey. In each honeycomb cell was the trapped shape of a tortured soul.

The honeycomb sagged. It began to melt. Souls flew out, their long tails blazing, and darted around the rotunda in a hurricane of anguished cries and cries of joy.

They buzzed around Tempus's head in a swarm. He covered his eyes. Screams and howls and an awful roaring that shook the floor enveloped him.

When Tempus uncovered his face, the witch was a blazing tower, with bits of her falling everywhere.

From that tower, the witch's voice wailed, "Niko, why have you forsaken me? Come to me. Come to . . ."

Then came another blast of light, a flash and a blaze with a hot tongue on concussion that lashed him, though his flesh was deified.

And the battle was once more a battle of men—or almost.

The Drekka were fighting from the cover of their

wagons, and the Sandians from the corners of their stronghold. Crit had the Stepsons fighting prone with crossbows. They lay flat, even Kama and Cyrus—all but Niko, Jihan, and Randal, who were running, crouched and dodged blasts of light, toward the canisters now rolling on the floor.

Amid all this, a pack of dogs from nowhere was raging. Wild dogs. Gargantuan dogs. Dogs that leaped the fire of the light weapons and caught Drekkans by the throats. Dogs that fastened their jaws on Sandian arms and pulled men from their feet.

Striding among the dogs came Cime. The look on her face made Tempus shrink so far and fast that he was nearly cowering when she found him (fighting off the god's quick exit and a dizzying return to normal size), gasping for breath.

"So *this* is what you're doing," Cime shouted at him over the din of yelling men and dogs and Critias, who was hoarsely urging the Stepsons into the fray now that light weapons weren't firing.

"Doing?" he managed to choke out. "Where were you? I couldn't find you in Lemuria."

"Oh, don't give me that! You've been playing gods-and-witches again, that's clear." She put her hands on her hips and surveyed the carnage, then brushed her hair impatiently from her eyes. In her fingers, she held her diamond rods. She began tapping their tips together. Each time she did, a spark jumped from the rods and sped toward a light weapon. When a spark reached a weapon, the weapon would melt like wax.

If a man was holding one, that man yelped and jumped back.

"Stepsons," Cime called, "once you've got this sorted out, bring me what passes for leaders here." Then she turned back to him: "See what you've done, Meddler? *When* will you stop wandering around with no clear purpose, but to get into trouble?"

Her eyes were too bright. Her lips were too swollen. Her chest rose and fell too fast. He said, "It's good to see you. And your dogs."

"Your dogs, if you'd only realized. Can we settle whatever this is, quickly? I need to talk to you."

"Let me gather my men."

He couldn't wait to get away from her.

Jihan and Niko were guarding the canisters in which the god's babies lived. Jihan said, "Riddler, Niko thinks that Cyrus's soul is safe now that the witch is truly dead." She looked at him almost coquettishly. She'd seen him become Enlil, and what the god had done. All his Stepsons had.

So had Cyrus. Tempus had almost forgotten the changeling boy. He looked over his shoulder.

Cyrus was watching him with such adoration that Tempus had to look away to hide his grin.

"We're going to Lemuria, Jihan, now—all the band. Will you bring our son and come with us?"

"Since you have invited us, Riddler, we shall join you. For a time." Jihan's gaze flickered over Cime, and all the dogs.

"Commander," Niko asked, "what about these?" The best of the Stepsons pointed with his ancient sword at the canisters he was guarding. All were there. All seemed unharmed to Tempus's god-given sight.

"I think we can leave them, in Enlil's care, don't you? Since the god is staying on here, none of us need worry."

"But they're you're . . ."

"Don't say it, Niko," Tempus said. "One son with superhuman attributes is plenty to contend with, right now."

He clapped Niko on the shoulder and Niko's slow smile flickered to life. "I'll get Cyrus," said the Stepson.

"Tell Crit we'll want all the horses, and the Stepsons formed up for transit within the hour. He knows how to do it."

Crit would do all that needed to be done to get the band back to Lemuria safe and sound, but Tempus watched critically until he was sure that the Drekka and the Sandians were fully disarmed and talking quietly together, with Randal acting as an intermediary.

Then there was nothing for it but to deal with Cime. Surrounded by her pack of milling hounds, she awaited him imperiously.

He could nearly feel her foot tapping.

"Tempus, before I provide you and your band of cutthroats a neat and effortless exit from this latest scene of your limitless crimes, I want to talk to that god of yours. Now."

"You can't," he said.

"Why not? Of course I can. I demand to, or you'll all stay here to face the consequences of starting this war, whatever it was about. When these folk come to their senses, they'll realize all this mayhem was your doing—you and your marauding god."

"Enlil is not hearing you, Cime." Which was just as well. "He is among these people, now. Let it be." His tone was cautionary.

"What do you mean, 'among these people'?" She craned her neck and looked about her. Then back to him. "You don't mean you've foisted that god off on—"

He didn't want to explain about Enlil's prenatal pantheon. Those progeny were as much his as Enlil's. He really didn't want to tell her how those babies had come to be. It would be hard enough to endure Cime's reaction when she learned that Cyrus, his son by Jihan, was coming back to Lemuria with them.

"Sister," he said, "if the god would leave me—and us—alone, what would you give for it?"

"Anything. And I'm going to have just that—"

"Would you give me some time to explain things,

and would you be patient, and obedient, just awhile—
and ask me no questions until all of mine, and some
guests, are home . . . if the Storm God did not come
with us?"

"If the Storm God of Heaven, Enlil, Lord of the
Armies," she said carefully, "will stay out of Lemuria,
Tempus, I'll even be a good wife to you."

"Done," he said. "Get ready to move the band
home, plus three: Jihan, that boy there beside her,
and Randal."

"We're having a magician to dinner?" she disap-
proved. "Haven't you learned your lesson?" A dog
barked and jumped up, playfully nipping at her elbow. "Get down," she scolded it.

"I thought you and I had a bargain."

"Oh, Riddler." She reached down and petted a big
brindle dog with a scarred flank. "You're impossible."

"But we have a bargain?"

"To be rid of Enlil, there's nothing I won't do."

"Fine. I'll hold you to that." He turned his back
on her: "Niko, Crit, Strat. Let's get those horses
ready to move."

His Stepsons needed him, all the more now that
the Storm God was leaving them, to take up resi-
dence in Sandia.

Chapter 30:

RITES OF HEAVEN

Cyrus hung back as the Stepsons gathered around the bier they'd made on the beach below Pinnacle House. So much had happened to him, so fast. He couldn't blame his father's soldiers for giving him a wide berth. But he did.

Back from Sandia they'd come, under the aegis of Tempus's lover, the Lady Cime, Lemuria's Evening Star.

Cyrus had been afraid that this mighty woman with her pack of dogs would take one look at him, recognize him as the white dragon who'd ravaged her parlor, and set her dogs on him.

One of the dogs, the one with the hairless patch on its flank, recognized him right away: it had come running over to him during the battle in Sandia and growled. Kama, Cyrus's sister, had stepped between him and the slavering jaws of the vengeful hound and said, "Scat. Get out of here."

The dog had slunk away, its tail between its legs.

If not for Kama, and for Mother, Cyrus would not be here to stand in the shadows, sifting sand through his fingers, as Tempus's soldiers lit the bier by the sea in the gathering dark.

The blazing sunset on Lemuria's beach tinted his pale skin ruddy. He turned his hand and looked at it:

a man's hand. He cast long purple shadows on the sand—the shadows of a man.

Back in Sandia, Mother had taken him by that hand when the trouble started and said firmly, "Cyrus, you will not leave my side during this battle. Not for any reason. If you do, you have no mother."

He had been first humiliated, then rebellious, then frightened. His mother was angry with him, this was clear. Public humiliation before his father's people was just the beginning of eons of misery to follow.

Her eyes were full of fire, like Grandfather Stormbringer's eyes. "Mother," Cyrus had said, "you promised you wouldn't be angry with me. Say you're not angry."

But she didn't say that. She stared at him and he could not move. All around him, violence churned the air as if whales approached through stormy waters.

He must escape! Now. No matter what he'd promised Tempus. But Cyrus could not move, locked in the prison of Jihan's stare.

Behind his mother, Roxane, in the Sandian Shepherd's form, had been growing huge. Beloved Roxane. She was calling his soul and calling his heart and the winds of change were whipping about his ears.

His mother had said something he couldn't quite hear through the roaring and the blood pounding in his ears.

Then Kama had stepped up to him and taken his face in her hands: "Live like a man, Cyrus! The way you want to!"

The roaring in his ears had lessened.

Had his mother known he couldn't hear her? Had Kama known the witch was calling him? And stopped it?

The next thing he'd seen was Lord Tempus changing shape. Then he knew everything he'd been told by Mother was true: Tempus was his father, no doubt.

The great Lord Tempus, whom Cyrus had given so much to find, destroyed the witch before Cyrus's eyes.

He had been stricken with a deep and abiding sadness, to see Roxane die—and not known why. The eagle he'd chased through high sky and white cloud was dead. The dragon who'd taught him to breathe fire and taunted him with her twitching tail was dead. But why was he empty and numb inside? Everything died. Nothing could be wasted. In the ocean, on the land, death made way for new life.

Cyrus mourned his first love in guilty silence. All of these humans hated Roxane. Kama thought he'd been shocked by the ferocity of the Stepsons' battle, and by seeing his father become the Storm God. Or so Kama had said comfortingly, when they'd lined up to file through a shimmery space into Lemuria. Kama was worldly, as wise as Mother, and very lovely. When he'd quailed before the shimmery space, she'd held out a hand for him to take. "You have a sister now," she'd reminded him.

On the other side of that space was this place, with its great, never-ending sea. Cyrus could hear his grandfather grumbling in its waves. He could hear Stormbringer's heart beat in its surf.

When they'd first arrived, he had been frightened that Cime would find him out and chastise him. Or make his mother take him away.

Jihan had found him skulking in a corner of Pinnacle House's great hall: "Come, Cyrus, let's go out on the balcony."

There was a whole human town below Pinnacle House. It reminded him of Shaga, seen from the air on dragon's wings. Beyond the town lay the ocean, the horizon of heaven.

Cyrus had almost jumped off the balcony there and then. He could run away from Mother again. Take wing and fly. Jihan would never find him this

time. He could run and run and change and change
and he'd never end up back in his prison under the
sea. No one would punish him. . . .

Jihan had said, "Cyrus, we must talk."

He'd refused to look at her. Eyes on a seagull
diving in the distance, he'd said, "I won't go back to
the prison. I won't go live in the sea again. I want to
live like a man. Tempus—Father—*said* I could!"

"Cyrus, I know," Jihan had said. "Look at me."

When he'd looked at Roxane, she'd taken his soul.
But he looked at his mother. Mother already had his
heart in her hands. "Mother . . . I've been. . . . I've
made mistakes."

"Good that you know it. You want to live like a
man, you say? Tempus said you could? This is true?"

"I do. He did. It is."

"Then what if I say this to you: live like a man for a
year. In this form, only. No changing shape. If you
will agree, I will make it so."

"I . . . I agree."

Jihan had reached out and, with a tear on her
cheek, his mother had touched his lips with a finger.
A shiver had gone through him. His human body
seemed to fit tighter than it had before.

"Now you are a man for a year. When I first came
among humans, I took this shape and vowed to keep
it for a year. You are as a man is, now. You have the
attributes of man."

"You mean . . . I can't fly with the eagles, or the
gulls?" He was chilled to his bones. How could Mother
punish him so cruelly? Didn't she love him anymore?

"Not for this year. Learn to live like a man, but
don't expect to be one. You're more. I can't change
that. When your year is done, come to the shore and
we'll talk."

And his mother kissed him on the cheek once,
saying, "Cyrus, I love you. I will speak with Stormbringer, and he will soften his heart toward you. But

stay off the water for a while, until his temper calms. If you need me, come to the sea and call me, anytime."

Then, before Cyrus could say more than, "Mother, I . . . um . . ." Jihan jumped up on the balustrade, and over it, diving into the dark.

Cyrus listened as hard as he could, to make sure he heard his mother hit the water. The tide was high. The surf crashed against the base of the cliff here. He thought he heard the Froth Daughter splash into the sea, but he couldn't be sure.

A gull flew over, dropping its mussel on the balcony to break the shell, screeching.

Cyrus had never felt so alone, not even when he'd come up out of his prison beneath the sea and first tried to walk among men.

He'd slept on that balcony his whole first night in Lemuria, huddled between the building and the sea wind. Kama had found him there, in the morning, and said to him, "Come on, brother. The day's young and I have much to show you."

"Mother's gone," he said.

"Jihan?" Kama scowled at him: "You're too old to need your mother. Anyway, we can find her if we need to. Aunt Cime knows all about the Lemurian windows, now. Don't worry." And Kama, laughing, had dragged him by the hand down into the city, to see how men lived.

Now dusk had fallen, and all the Stepsons were somber and sober, on the shore in the last light of day. The wind blowing off the sea was full of salt spray.

Kama had come over to him once, saying, "Join us. We do the rites for Nino, Niko's son."

But he couldn't. He just couldn't. They knew he wasn't one of them. He *wasn't* one of them. He wasn't a Stepson, not really. He'd tried to kill his father the day they'd met. Tempus surely couldn't love him. This was all just a horrid punishment for his mistakes. The Sacred Band was made up of partners. He had none. He wasn't even a man. Just because his mother had trapped him in a man's body for a year, didn't make him one. Yet he must be a man for a year. Men died. He might die as one.

And death was different to men than to Cyrus. He didn't understand men. Or women. Or death, really.

When Roxane had called him to fight his father with her, for her, he'd almost done it. She was his love. Now she was dead.

His father had killed Roxane with a mighty arm and a bright sword and the aspect of a god.

He watched the fire grow brighter, growling and crackling, hissing toward the sky. Flaming red and gold and white, its heat dried the tears on his face. No one would understand why he cried for a witch: not Kama, not Aunt Cime, not Critias or Straton or Gayle, or Randal or Niko. Especially not Tempus.

He knew now that Roxane had lied to him and tried to use him to harm his father. She'd wanted him to attack Tempus and the Sacred Band of Stepsons. And he might have tried it, despite his mother, if not for his new-found sister, Kama.

But even so, Cyrus wept for Roxane, not understanding why or how he did. No one else would weep for Roxane here tonight. No one would weep for Cyrus, either, who'd been punished by his mother and left in the care of a father he hardly knew, in a new prison by the sea, for a year.

But Tempus himself came to him then, striding over the firelit sand like the god Cyrus had seen him become.

"Cyrus, come join in. The rites of heaven are part of man's heritage." Tempus's face was grave. "We must see the soul of Nino, Niko's son, to the heaven of the Storm God. And the Sandian Shepherd's soul, as well."

"Do I have a soul, Father?" Cyrus wanted to know.

Tempus's long eyes narrowed. "You do. The witch is dead. Guard your soul, Cyrus. It's heaven's gift, the one thing you can't afford to lose. Now, come."

He couldn't disobey. Cyrus fell in beside the man who'd sired him, looking close, seeking anger in that face, or love or hate, or hidden purpose.

He saw only a mask of ageless power, hooded eyes, tight lips, and the firelight playing over a face that pushed through time like the sun in the sky or the prow of some god's boat.

"How can I join these men, when I'm not one?" he nearly wailed, breaking a silence he couldn't bear.

"How can you not? Your mother left you in my care for a year. You yourself have agreed, soldier. Your word is your bond, here." Tempus turned his face from Cyrus and bawled, "Kama!"

The Riddler's daughter appeared from the shadows around the fire. "Commander?" Cyrus's sister said.

"How's a partner suit you, Sacred Bander?"

"I . . . would be honored."

"And you, Cyrus? Will you take Kama as your partner, shoulder to shoulder, to the death, with honor, in my service?"

"Um—to the death?" That was longer than a year—wasn't it? Cyrus, shocked, stopped in the sand. He looked from his father's face, to his sister's face. His fingers played in the soldier's belt that his father had given him. And he remembered what Tempus had said to him about community. "Yes, Father," he said in a quavery voice. Unaccountably, his eyes filled with tears.

"Then it is done. Kama, walk him through the rites."

"Father—"

But Tempus was gone, across the sand, a larger-than-life silhouette before the fire, among his Sacred Band.

And Cyrus's sister was explaining to him how, during the rite for Nino's soul, Niko's son would go to heaven with many gifts and the great love of the Stepsons to keep him company.

Niko saw the ghost of the Slaughter Priest come down to take Nino's soul, and a great weight left Niko with the coming of the ghost who took the soul of his son in his arms.

The ghost of Abarsis, the Stepsons' warrior-priest, met Niko's eyes, and the ghost's eyes were like clearest water.

Not until then had Niko caught a glimpse of his son's face, or Nino's form, or any sign to show that the boy's soul was truly freed. Then, as the priest held out his arms in the midst of the fiery bier, the boy materialized in them. Nino's arms were around the priest's neck, and the boy was smiling.

Niko cast his gift upon the fire, and stepped back.

Randal was underfoot there. "I saw it too," Randal whispered. "Leftside leader," Randal said then, more formally, "my blessings go with your dead to heaven."

Niko couldn't give the formulaic answer. He clasped Randal to him and just breathed the mage's salty sweat.

When he pulled back, Niko said, "Life is for the living, Randal. All's forgiven. Another night. A new start."

Asking and offering absolution at a funerary bier was more than ritual: it was the heart of the Sacred Band oath.

"A new start," said Randal, and grinned from ear to floppy ear. Niko's maat saw the healing of old wounds begin between them, there by the bier.

When your partner is a sorcerer, and your son was murdered by magic, only maat's blessing could put truth in words of forgiveness.

But the truth was there. Niko said softly, "I have
to see the Riddler," and left Randal. The fire at his
back burned up all their sins, so it was said. The heat
of it warmed him against eternity's long night.

Men had known what a prize fire was, from the
first. And known what price mankind would pay for
it. The Riddler had told him once that "the world
was, is, and ever shall be an everliving fire, with
portions of it kindling, and portions going out."

Men seemed like that fire tonight, to Niko. Even
his son's soul, in heaven, was in its rightful place.

He found the Riddler with Crit and Straton. The
pair seemed laved by the fire. Tempus hung back as
his Stepsons approached Niko.

Strat's aura was as bright as Nino's smile in the
flames. "Critias; Straton: life to you, brothers," Niko
said.

Both fighters shook his hand. Crit said, "It's a
good farewell, Niko, we gave tonight. And a fine
party, your son gave us."

Straton said, "Life to you, Niko. All the Storm
God's blessings are in you this night." The big man
quirked his lips. "Now that we're reunited, if you'll
wish me luck, I'm going to go get as drunk as possible in Nino's honor."

"Do that, Straton. For all of us," Niko told the
battle-weary veteran.

Reunited they were, if Strat could say so.

Tempus came away with him: "So, Niko—are you
content?"

"With you presiding, Riddler, how not? I'm honored. I . . . saw the Slaughter Priest take Nino. My
son looked happy. He had his arms around Abarsis'
neck."

"I saw too. A good omen, that the priest is still
with us, now that the god is gone."

"Truly gone?" Niko's maat saw Tempus, in the
firelight, with swathes of colors around him, all the

shades of man, extending up toward heaven like flame.

"The Storm God," Tempus said with a gruff voice and a wry smile, "has left us to tend things here. I wouldn't want to be those Sandians when they find out that they got what they wished for—more than living seas. A living heaven. Living gods."

The Riddler trudged through the sand beside Nikodemos and for a moment, Niko couldn't think of a thing to say. Then he did: "Riddler, I'm proud to be here. It's a greater honor even than this ceremony—Lemuria. What it promises."

"Promise of glory, is it, Niko? Endless sorties, herding the flocks of man?"

"A home. For all these who've fought so long and well. And, yes . . . my maat is content, Riddler, in your service."

"Not mine, any more," Tempus chuckled. "I think we're all in Cime's army, now. But never mind, the Storm God hasn't forgotten us. Heaven is no farther away than it ever was. Tonight proved that."

"It's life I'm trying to thank you for, Tempus," Niko said softly. And stopped.

Tempus stopped too, and faced him. "Niko, the worst is over. For you. For the band. For all of us. From Lemuria, Cime thinks, even your maat will find what it seeks in the world. This is a night for celebration. Celebrate."

"I know. I . . . love you so, Riddler. Nino would have loved you, too. If there's anything I can do to help with Cyrus, just let me know."

"Whatever maat thinks, Niko," said Tempus, and left him there, calling back: "We're going to have our hands full, teaching that one what it means to be a man."

Niko found himself alone, away from the funerary bier and the Stepsons before it, who were beginning to sing songs and feast in his son's honor.

He smelled the aromatic, sacred fire. He heard Kama's clear voice, and Gayle's croak. He heard the barking of dogs and the sea pounding against the shore. And he heard, in the distance, his mare whinny in her stable. Her voice was unmistakable.

Niko crouched down there, picking up the sands of home and running them through his fingers. From here, the whole world was open to him. For the first time in his adult life, the witch wasn't beating about his head like a curse.

He had so much to thank the gods for, he didn't know where to begin. He saw again the soul of his son, and he pulled his maat around him. He could feel the balance reestablishing itself in him. No wonder he couldn't find a way to truly thank the Riddler.

For the gift of life, the only true thanks was in living fully, and facing death with honor.

The fire on the beach and the men around him should have told Niko that.

He got up and walked away from the bier, toward the town and the horsebarns. Jihan hadn't taken the sable mare when she left. He'd feared she would. He was just beginning to trust in the wondrous gift that was Lemuria, the home of the Sacred Band.

From here, everything was possible. Here, all the gods smiled on men, and the glory of the sun and the sea and the stars shone clearly.

Here were all his brothers and sisters, and nature in perfect balance with the maat in his heart. To take care of the world seemed, finally, a privilege rather than a burden. The Riddler had led them to life's greatest victory. They had found a home.

"You can't be serious," Cime scoffed, in their bedchamber filled with white pillows and the hair of too many dogs. "The god had *how* many babies out of that Sandian whore—using your body, by-the-by?"

"Never mind." He swept pillows from the bed and

stretched out on it, fully clothed. His feet were muddy; his jerkin was sandy; he still had half his armor on.

"Get up, you philandering warrior-midget! You're filthy."

"Clean this place of dog hair, then talk to me of dirt," he said, throwing a final pillow at her.

Face flushed, she came at him, vaulting onto the bed and straddling him: "Don't you talk to me about dogs, either. If you'd listened to Chiara, and paid attention to the dogs, and what she was trying to teach you, you wouldn't have been in Sandia long enough to get into so much trouble that I had to rescue you!"

"You think the god's will had nothing to do with where I was, and for how long?" The hand-held oblong that could bring him back to Lemuria from anywhere was unaccountably working again.

"Don't blame everything on that god of yours. He's gone, so you say. Good riddance. At least you can't hide behind His Will anymore. You're responsible for your own actions, now."

"Get off me," he said, and tumbled her as he sought to rise. "I've never shirked responsibility—"

She righted herself. They sat on their bed, glaring at one another, she with her legs under her, he with his spread. "Oh, no? And what of this Cyrus creature, this . . . thing . . ."

"Cime. If you want a child of your own, we can arrange it, now that Enlil has no part in such choices. Otherwise, you'll be—" He reached out and took her head in his hands. "—as good as any mother to my son, who needs your wisdom. Promise me."

"Tempus, you can't be serious. . . ." Then the rage went out of her. She came against him, and he held her. "We have too many brats to tend, thank you. But I'll see to Cyrus, as I did to Kama. As I suppose we must to all of yours, whenever they come straggling in here."

Then she pulled back. "But you *must* let me instruct you in the ways of Lemuria."

"In time," he growled. "What I need to know, you'll tell me when I need to know it."

"As the god did? Without your deific coach, you'll need some knowledge of your own, now."

"I have you. What more wisdom do I need?"

He got up. This was no good. The funeral had upset her. There was no comforting her, or comfort in her. She was always like this after she'd been frightened that they might lose each other.

"I'm going out."

"I suspected as much."

"Tell me one thing."

"Only one? Well, what is it you need to know today?" Her fine face was in shadow, but he could see her nostrils flare and the hint of a smile quirk her lips.

That smile and those lips had driven so much of his striving. Just seeing breath in those nostrils was a sign from heaven that he'd done something right.

"About reproductive rights and reproductive rites. Which takes precedence, do you think: the need to procreate, on the man's part, and to call the child his; or the need to nurture, on the woman's part, and to have control over what her body does?"

She looked up at him then and stared with those eyes that had seen so much he wished she hadn't suffered. But she was strong because of it. A fit partner for him, at the end of it. Her life was dedicated to all life, as the Evening Star of Lemuria.

She said in a measured way, "I think, brother, that a life being lived takes precedence over a potential life. Free will belongs to all human beings, yet the universe favors the strong. If what you are asking is, 'does a woman have dominion over her flesh,' the answer is yes. Otherwise, a man would be required to provide sperm to any woman on demand, to make the division of responsibility equitable."

"So you agree with me? The god was wrong, to risk everything to preserve the Sandian embryos over my objections?"

"I do not. How did those babies *get* into Sandia, Riddler? There's a riddle worth your time. First you say they're the god's, not yours; then you say the god had no right to preserve them against your will. If the Sandian Shepherd was given the tools to reproduce in good faith, then neither you nor the god had anything to say about it. But in the end, I think, she had what she wanted."

"Her funeral on the Lemurian beach? More than she bargained for. And it killed her," he said thickly, and strode out of there. Cime threw a pillow after him, but the missile did him no permanent harm.

If life was the gods' to give and take, then the gods made a mistake giving the same power to humans—unless that was what the gods had in mind.

Tempus, free of the Storm God, knew for certain now that what the gods gave humans was a chance at divinity. The closer humanity came to godhead, the greater its responsibility. From Pinnacle House, he could change the fates of whole civilizations, if he wished. The fate of a single life was no less—or more—to have in your hands than the fate of millions, of yourself, or your friends, or your enemies, or the animals you ate to survive, or those you bred to endure.

What was needed, was to admit how much god was in one's self, and stop foisting responsibility unto heaven.

He'd known it well before Enlil had left him. But he'd needed to hear Cime say it. Man was but half of the riddle; woman was the knowledge man sought.

Together, he and Cime might do a decent job here,
after all.

But no paradise was complete without its temptation, and Cyrus was Tempus's greatest test.

He knew it. He never should have begotten the
changeling on Jihan. He'd known it then.

But the future was his to mold. Jihan had left him
the boy who'd been a dragon: "It's only fair," she'd
told him, as if anything about Cyrus could be weighed
on normal scales.

He found the boy down by the horsebarns, as
dawn was breaking, asleep in a haystack.

Out in the wind, near the sea, where his grandfather's voice could lull him.

Not a good sign.

"Wake up, Cyrus."

"What . . . ? Fath—Tempus, what is it?"

"I'm going riding. Get your horse."

"I don't . . . have one," said the changeling, knuck-
ling his eyes. The boy was full of fear, resentment,
and uncertainty. Jihan had trapped him in a human
body for a year. Tempus had trapped him into pair-
ing with Kama.

The power that was Cyrus had much to learn. And
Tempus must begin to teach it.

"Of course you have a horse. All Stepsons have
horses. Can you ride a horse?"

Tempus went into the barn, hoping the boy would
follow.

Cyrus ran after him: "Ride? I . . . of course I can.
Anyone can."

Much to learn. Tempus stopped by a stall, and
opened the top half of the door. "Here's your horse,
the one Jihan left for you. A parting gift, she said."

"Mother's horse . . ."

Cyrus looked in upon the great and magical seahorse
floating there in ineffable water, and it became a
land-horse, complete with frothy mane and tail, stomp-

ing its straw. It snorted softly, and stuck its wise-eyed head over the stall door.

"Now, Cyrus," Tempus said, who'd known all about what kind of horse Jihan had left her son, "let's see you tack up your pony."

The seahorse was Jihan's way of hedging her bets. Leaving the boy locked in a human skin had been Tempus's idea, not hers. But it would go well enough, he was sure of it.

When the seahorse, who wasn't all that happy to play land-horse for a year, was saddled and bridled, Tempus got out his Tros and swung up, bareback, with only a halter. "Race me to the shore," he told the boy.

There's only one way to face life, and that's straight on. Tempus's Tros leaped with a whinny of pleasure into a gallop and, from somewhere, Lemurian dogs joined in the race.

When he reached the shore, he looked back. The froth-maned seahorse was galloping on four legs, looking for all the world like a purebred Tros horse. Dogs barked around its legs, but the seahorse paid no attention. It was too concerned with the rider it bore, who was holding on to the saddlehorn and bent low in an uncertain balance of legs and arms.

When Cyrus caught up to him, Tempus was cantering his Tros in the surf.

Cyrus's face was pale with concentration. His chest heaved. His knuckles were tight on his reins. But he was still astride.

And the dogs of Lemuria, cavorting around their horses' legs, were barking joyously.

Tempus said, "See, the horse loves the ocean."

The seahorse was headed toward the horizon, splashing deeper and deeper into the water. The boy was nearly floating from its back.

Tempus stopped his Tros, knee-deep in the surf, and watched.

He thought he saw the seahorse shake its chitinous head, and the boy, swimming beside it, raise an arm and wave.

Then they came back, toward the shore, and the seahorse was a land-horse once again, drenched and blowing, plunging in the surf with a dog on either side.

The sun sparkled off the horse's flanks and the boy's wet hair, but it was nothing to the shine in Cyrus's eyes.

"I can do it! I can do it! See? I can ride as well as any man."

Tempus's Tros snorted softly in the surf and pawed the waves with a forefoot. A passing dog on shore shook water on them. A cloud scudded across the sun, then moved on. The changeling boy had braved the sea and his grandfather's clutches, and survived.

Tempus had needed to see it.

"Good," he said, to the boy and the horse and the dog and the pounding of the surf. "A good start."

Cyrus grinned like the dawn behind him.

And in Tempus's head, from very far away, he thought he heard the god Enlil, saying, *A good start, mortal. For Me, and thee.*

But perhaps he'd just imagined it.

So he called the god's name.

This time Tempus got no answer. But then, he needed none.

A good start, indeed.